"I know *nothing* about buffalo."

Pony's words were clipped and brusque.

"You know all you need to know," Pete told her. "You worked a whole summer with the tribal buffalo herd."

Pony snatched up the stack of papers she'd been marking. Her heart was hammering and her mouth was dry.

Pete continued. "I told Caleb McCutcheon I'd ask around for someone who could help him. You'll live right there on the ranch. McCutcheon's a good man and the Bow and Arrow is beautiful...."

"I appreciate your coming, Pete," she said. "But I'm not interested."

"Take the job, Pony. It pays more than you make here as a teacher or what you'd make over the summer working for some farmer." Pete turned and walked out without another word.

Pony returned to her desk. She wanted to ignore what Pete had said, but he was right. She needed the money.

But Caleb McCutcheon would look her up and down and try not to laugh. He would probably make an effort to be polite—Pete had said he was a good, kind man. But he'd think that a woman applying for the job of managing a herd of buffalo was ridiculous.

And he would be right!

Dear Reader,

Even in this age of routine space travel, the American West has the power to evoke images of a time when buffalo roamed in herds beyond number, a time when the wind blew across plains so vast and over mountains so tall that all of eternity could not measure the boundaries of it. No animal was more closely associated with the West, or was more powerful, both physically and spiritually, than the buffalo.

For the most part, the West we romanticize is gone, paved over and plowed under by the relentless tide of humanity seeking to settle and civilize everything that is wild. The great herds of buffalo are also gone, hunted to near extinction in the nineteenth century, and the sound of their thundering hoofbeats is only a memory…or is it?

Buffalo Summer explores the possibility of returning the buffalo to their native range and restoring these venerable denizens of the wild to the American West. It also explores the conflicts and courageous hearts of two people from two vastly different cultures struggling to find common ground in the midst of a sometimes very hostile and chaotic world. Caleb McCutcheon and his herd manager, Pony Young Bear, take up the story where *Montana Dreaming* leaves off, and together they bring the history of the legendary Bow and Arrow full circle.

Enjoy the journey.

Nadia Nichols

Buffalo Summer
Nadia
Nichols

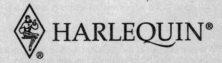

HARLEQUIN®

TORONTO • NEW YORK • LONDON
AMSTERDAM • PARIS • SYDNEY • HAMBURG
STOCKHOLM • ATHENS • TOKYO • MILAN • MADRID
PRAGUE • WARSAW • BUDAPEST • AUCKLAND

ISBN 0-373-71138-7

BUFFALO SUMMER

Visit us at www.eHarlequin.com

Printed in U.S.A.

Thank you, Grandmother, for teaching me the old ways.

CHAPTER ONE

Oh give me a home where the buffalo roam...
                              —Brewster Higley, 1873

PONY YOUNG BEAR'S TRUCK was old. It had belonged
to her older brother, Steven, who had gotten it from
one of the elders, who had gotten it from some gov-
ernment program that found used trucks for needy
people on the reservation. It was an '83 Ford, standard
shift, four-wheel drive. At one time it had been red.
Now it was rust-colored, but it could still squeak out
an inspection sticker if taken to the right place, and
Pony always made sure she took it to the right place.
It was cheap and reasonably reliable transportation,
but this morning she wished that it didn't look so
battered, that the paint wasn't peeling away to reveal
big brown boils, that it didn't rattle so loudly, that the
tires weren't bald.

Above all, she wished that she didn't have to be
driving to a ranch called the Bow and Arrow outside
of someplace called Katy Junction, Montana, to beg
for a job she wasn't qualified for. But she needed the
money to buy school supplies for the children. Without them the kids would be at a disadvantage, and
that was just one more disadvantage they didn't need.

Pete Two Shirts had understood this. Which was
why he had come to the school yesterday afternoon

to tell her about this job. She'd been sitting at her desk in the sudden quiet that always descended on the heels of the departing third-grade students when a man's voice spoke her name from the doorway.

She glanced up, startled, and laid down a stack of papers, giving no reply to his greeting. Pete walked into the room in his lean, catlike way, long hair tied back with a red strip of cloth, dressed in his typical cowboy attire of blue jeans, boots, denim jacket and red plaid shirt. He kept his thumbs hooked in the broad leather belt at his waist sporting the big fancy silver rodeo buckle and stopped just short of her desk, gazing at her beneath his black, flat-crowned hat brim. "I came by to tell you about a good-paying summer job."

She dropped her eyes, picking up the stack of papers and tapping them on the desk to straighten them. Anything at all to avoid looking at him. Pete reminded her of a time in her life that she would much rather forget. "So tell me," she said, suddenly short of breath.

"I got a call this morning from Guthrie Sloane, the foreman of a rancher who's looking for someone to help with their buffalo herd. It's the ranch I worked at this past fall, when Sloane got crippled in a horse wreck and they needed temporary help. Over near Katy Junction."

"I know the place." She laid the papers down again and smoothed them with her hands, avoiding his eyes. "The Bow and Arrow. Steven told me about it." Her heart beat painfully, and her body tensed with shame and guilt even after all these years. One summer, one night, and her life had never been the same. Would never, ever be the same...

"I thought of you," Pete said.

"I know nothing of buffalo." Her words were clipped and brusque.

"You worked for me one whole summer with the tribal buffalo herd. You know all you need to know. You can ride a horse pretty good, too. You need that money to buy school things for the kids."

She snatched the stack of papers yet again and rose from her chair, walking to the window and staring out. Her heart was hammering and her mouth was dry.

"I told him I'd ask around for someone who could help out," Pete continued. "It would be an easy job. You'd live right there, on the ranch. Room and board included. Caleb McCutcheon's a good man and the buffalo herd is tiny, nothing like the size of ours."

"I appreciate your coming," she said. "But I am not interested."

"Take the job, Pony. It pays more than what you make here as a teacher, or what you'd make hoeing weeds in some farmer's field." Pete Two Shirts turned and walked out without another word. She stayed where she was until the sound of his boot heels and the faint ring of his spurs faded from her burning ears.

One summer. One buffalo summer…

When she finally returned to her desk, the children's papers she held in her trembling hands were hopelessly crumpled, and no amount of smoothing could flatten them. She wanted to ignore what Pete had said, but he was right. She needed the money. And if the job paid well, did she have the right to deny her students such a windfall?

Unlike many of the children she taught, Pony had been handed the best of everything, the best that any

Indian born on the rez could ever hope to have. Her brother Steven had pushed her hard, pushed her to do well in school, pushed her to apply for colleges, and when the pushing had opened doors for her, he had made sure those doors stayed open by footing the bill for her education with the money he earned as an environmental lawyer. She'd graduated from one of the best schools in the country, had gone on to get her master's degree in early childhood education.

Steven had sacrificed so much for her since the death of their parents, and she loved him fiercely. She'd loved him ever since she'd been a little girl and he'd tolerated her pesky company, defended her against his taunting friends, lifted her onto his broad shoulder and carried her when her legs grew tired. Later, as she grew older, he'd driven off unwanted suitors. He'd never asked for anything in return for being the best brother a girl could ever have. That was Steven's way. Yet when he changed his name to a white man's name and chose to live in the white man's world, she couldn't understand that his needs might not be the same as hers.

Her resentment toward the lifestyle he had chosen had limited her visits to his pretty little house in Gallatin Gateway with the name Brown stenciled in big block letters on his mailbox. It had taken her a long time to realize that her brother had the right to walk his own path.

Last night when she had had gone to see him to ask him about Caleb McCutcheon and the job at the Bow and Arrow, the neatly stenciled letters on his mailbox had read Young Bear. Unbeknownst to her, he had taken back his own name. His hair had grown long again and was drawn back the way he used to wear it. He had looked so good, so handsome, standing there in the doorway of his cozy little house, that she had been momentarily unable to speak, overwhelmed by a sudden and poignant surge of remorse that brought her to the verge of tears.

"Pony," he said. "It's good to see you. It's been a while. Christmas, wasn't it?"

She blinked the sting from her eyes. "It's good to see you, too."

He nodded. "Come in. It's not a teepee but it's comfortable." He stood to one side for several moments, and when she didn't move he reached out and drew her firmly inside, closing the door behind her. "I'm cooking supper. You can watch me and tell me all the things I'm doing wrong." He turned and walked back into the kitchen, picked up the spatula he'd left on the counter and added strips of cooked chicken into the stir-fry mix that was sizzling in the wok. He shook in a generous splash of soy sauce, added a little more water and a small mound of freshly grated gingerroot. He stirred for a few minutes before turning off the gas burners beneath both the wok and a pot of steamed brown rice. "There's plenty here for both of us," he said, taking two plates from the cupboard.

"I'm not hungry," Pony said, standing uneasily on the other side of the counter. Steven paused for a moment to look at her and then divided the rice between the two plates and spooned the stir-fry over the mounds. He carried the plates and silverware to the table, returning to the kitchen to strip two paper towels off the roll, grab two glasses from the counter and a quart of milk from the refrigerator. "Unless you'd rather have wine or a beer?'' he said, pausing at the refrigerator.

"Milk's fine."

"Sit then, and eat. You're too thin." He dropped into a chair and Pony did the same.

"I came here to ask you about Caleb McCutcheon."

"I know," Steven said, pouring the milk. "Pete called me. He told me that he'd gone to see you at the school to tell you about the job."

Pony wasn't surprised that Steven already knew. Pete Two Shirts was his boyhood friend, and they still kept in close touch. "I know nothing about buffalo. The job would be a farce."

Steven ate for a while then picked up his glass of milk and drank half of it. Finally he lowered the glass and studied her across the table. "You know enough," he said. "McCutcheon would be lucky to get you. Now eat. This stuff is good for you. It's not sage hen or buffalo tongue, but it's healthy."

She picked up her fork and stabbed it fiercely into a piece of broccoli. "Why do we always argue?"

"You're mad because I don't live on the rez like you do, because I don't champion the Indian's fights the way you do."

"The way you should," she said vehemently.

"The way you think I should," he amended.

"Steven, you paid my way through college," she said, leaning toward him. "You made it possible for me to do the things I'm doing now. Working with the children, teaching school and lobbying the Bureau of Indian Affairs, trying to make things better. If you and I don't do these things, who will? The changes have to come from us."

Steven finished his meal and glass of milk while she sat and watched him, the same piece of broccoli still speared on her fork. He wiped his mouth on the paper towel. "McCutcheon's a good man. Go talk to him about the job."

"Is he one of those rich movie stars?"

Steven laughed at her disapproving glare. "Caleb was a star, but not in the movies. He was a professional baseball player with the White Sox. He grew up as a poor kid in the slums of Chicago and pitched his way to the top of the world. People still sing his praises, and he hasn't played for years. He had to retire when a baseball shattered his ankle during the World Series.

"Is he married?"

"Until recently. He was divorced last fall, shortly after he bought the Bow and Arrow. Seems his wife didn't share his dream of living on a remote ranch."

"Any children?"

"Nope." Steven looked at his sister and grinned. "He definitely ranks up there as one of the most eligible bachelors in the State. If I were you, I'd hurry right over there."

"I'm not looking for a man. I'm applying for a job."

"Just filling you in on the particulars. No need to get testy."

"Even if I go to talk to him and he offers me the job, what will I do about the kids?"

"How many are there now?"

"Five. Nana's watching them tonight," she said, referring to her aunt.

"Five." Steven poured himself another glass of

milk. He fixed her with a solemn gaze. "Pony, you can't save the world."

"I know that, but I can help make their lives a little better."

"I'll send you more money. I didn't know there were that many kids. The last time we talked, you just had the two boys."

Pony set her fork down abruptly and raised the folded paper towel to her eyes, holding it there for a long moment, hiding from him until he reached out and squeezed her arm gently. She lowered her hand and blinked rapidly. "I can't turn them away," she said in a voice tight with pain.

"I know."

Her eyes stung. "And I can't walk away and leave them for the summer. Nana can't take care of all of them. There's no point in even thinking about taking that job, even if it were offered to me."

"I'm almost afraid to ask this, but these other three kids you've taken on...are they juvenile delinquents like the first two?"

"They're not delinquents, Steven. They're school dropouts that I'm tutoring. They're just confused. They're living in a mixed-up world and they don't know where they belong."

"Teenagers?"

Pony nodded.

"All boys?"

She nodded again. "The girls tend to stay with their families. The boys rebel against everything, especially their parents."

Steven pushed his glass with one finger, back and forth. "Can any of them ride a horse?"

"They're teenage boys. They can do anything."

"Then go talk to McCutcheon," Steven said. "Sell him a package deal. He gets you, and for the same price he gets five more hard workers who would be really good at pulling down miles and miles of rusty barbed-wire fence. Tell him the truth about the boys, about how you've taken them in. Talk to him, Pony. He's a good man. Go tomorrow morning, first thing. Now clean your plate, or I'll send you to bed right after supper with no dessert."

She had spent the night at Steven's little house and had risen before dawn to drive to Caleb McCutcheon's ranch. The sun was just shy of peeking over the Beartooth Mountains when Pony turned onto the five-mile gravel road that headed into the foothills and ended at the Bow and Arrow. She downshifted and swerved to avoid a large pothole. She was nervous, and her driving reflected it. Caleb McCutcheon would look her up and down and try not to laugh. He would try to be polite, because Steven had said he was a good, kindhearted man. But he would think to himself, What's this? A woman applying for a job managing a herd of buffalo? Ridiculous!

And he would be right.

CALEB MCCUTCHEON AWOKE in the early morning and lay in bed, hands laced behind his head, listening to the song of a white-crowned sparrow lifting sweetly over the rush of the creek. He thought about how much his life had changed. One year ago he hadn't set eyes upon this place. He hadn't yet met the full-blooded Crow Indian Steven Young Bear, the young conservation attorney who had introduced him to Jessie Weaver and had been instrumental in helping Caleb purchase her failing cattle ranch.

One year ago he'd still been married to a woman who'd held his heart from the first time he'd set eyes on her, when he was full of fire and his career as a professional baseball player for the Chicago White Sox still sizzled. He had pledged his allegiance to this sophisticated woman who had shepherded his rise to fame and guided him along the complicated paths of stardom. She'd stood beside him when fate had dealt its untimely blow to his career, and he'd undergone multiple surgeries on his ankle, and then drifted off when his name faded into history to find a more interesting life for herself.

Divorce was an ugly word, but he had never realized just how ugly until his wife had asked him for one. Their divorce this past November had been a staggering blow, although in retrospect he should have seen it coming. Rachael craved the bright lights and the big cities. Her life was lively and political and she traveled in the highest social circles, whereas he had followed his childhood dream into the backwater wilderness of Montana. It was here that they had parted company.

The winter that followed had been long and dark, and Caleb had spent countless hours in this cabin on the edge of the Beartooth Wilderness reexamining his life. He had no regrets about being in this place. In spite of the loneliness that at times overwhelmed him, he never tired of this land and its many moods, the vast and palpable silence that dwarfed the imagination, the thundering wind that blew tirelessly, the crashing roar or the gentle murmur of the creek. He loved this old cabin, hewn of big-mountain cedar over a hundred years earlier. Caleb had never felt so much at home as he did here. In time, he supposed, he'd learn to live with the loneliness. He'd made some good friends. He counted Guthrie Sloane, his twenty-nine-year-old ranch manager and Jessie Weaver's fiancé, as one, and of course Jessie herself. Steven Young Bear, café owner Bernie Portis, the old ranch hands Badger and Charlie…all good friends. A man could do much worse.

Caleb's lifelong dream of owning a ranch in the Rocky Mountain West had come true, but unfortunately the ranch hadn't come with an operations manual, and his attempts to persuade Jessie Weaver to remain as manager were thwarted when she returned to veterinary school to finish her degree. It was Caleb's great good luck that Guthrie Sloane, who had worked for the ranch and had loved Jessie Weaver since he was thirteen years old, had taken the job and was patiently teaching Caleb the ropes.

Jessie and Guthrie's long-awaited wedding would take place this coming September, and for months already it had been *the* topic of conversation in Katy Junction. Caleb could certainly understand all the buzz. It was reassuring to know that true love still existed.

He rolled out of bed and walked barefoot into the kitchen, which was nothing more than a little nook off the living room. The cabin boasted three rooms: bedroom, bathroom and kitchen/living room. There was a sleeping loft above and a root cellar below. Though the place was simple and spartan, Caleb was very comfortable in these quarters and preferred living here than in the main ranch house. He put on a pot of coffee, threw a few sticks of firewood into the woodstove and opened the door to the porch. It was a few moments before sunrise, yet already he could feel the burgeoning energy of the season. The sounds and smells of springtime warmed his blood and charged his spirit.

There was so much to do, and it was a solid, satisfying feeling to fill the days with activities that meant something. Just splitting firewood was a joy to him. He devoted an hour a day to the task, keeping his woodpile tidy and arranging the split wood by size so that he could easily grab what he needed when he needed it.

But tending to his firewood was nothing compared to the daunting task of ripping down the cross fences that partitioned the land into separate pastures. The plan was to leave the pole corrals around the barns, the penning corrals and the boundary fences that would need to be strengthened to contain the small herd of buffalo that Pete Two Shirts had talked Caleb into buying last fall. All the rest of the barbed wire would be removed. The men would coil the wire as they took it down and reuse the newest of it to bolster boundary fences. Then they'd pull out the metal posts and cut the wooden fence posts off at ground level, so as to leave no holes for the animals to step in. It sounded simple, but there were over sixty miles of barbed-wire fence to deal with.

The sharp fragrant smell of coffee tantalized him, and he returned to the snug warmth of the cabin, closing the door on the cool mid-May morning. He poured himself a cup and carried it with him to the chair beside the window. He opened his notebook and stared at the scrawl of figures on the page. Took a sip from his cup and felt himself frown as he studied his jottings. Lord, what a huge job he'd undertaken when he'd accepted Pete Two Shirts's suggestion that they bring the buffalo back to their home range.

Pete had assured him that the venture would be both environmentally beneficial and financially sound. But now that Pete had returned to his full-time job on the reservation managing the Crow buffalo herd, the project had suddenly become unwieldy. Huge. Almost terrifying. After all, Caleb was just a city boy— born and bred in the Chicago slums. What the hell did he know about two-thousand-pound animals that stood six feet high at the shoulder?

Caleb lifted his mug of coffee for another appreciative sip. Maybe Guthrie would scare up someone who would be interested in teaching them how to manage the herd. After readily admitting his own ignorance in buffalo husbandry, Caleb's ranch manager had put the word out, but so far there had been no applicants. Not a single one. Guthrie had cautioned him against impatience, but Caleb was beginning to wonder if this buffalo venture might not have been too ambitious for a greenhorn wanna-be rancher.

Yet, as intimidating as the buffalo were, they had to remain. Somehow he had to make this plan work. There was bound to be some big, burly, ham-fisted, tobacco-chewing, burly buffalo-loving expert out there looking for a job in one of the prettiest spots in all of Montana.

Bound to be…

Caleb pushed out of his chair with a sigh and carried both the notebook and his cup of coffee as he left the warmth of his cabin and headed up to the main house.

His cook and housekeeper, Ramalda, didn't like it when he was late for breakfast.

PONY CAUGHT her breath and hit the brake as the truck crested a rise. For a moment all she could do was stare as the sun's first rays spilled over the rim of rugged mountains and laid their golden fingers across the valley floor. She'd learned about the history of the Bow and Arrow from Steven. The ranch had been around since the mid-1800s and was one of the longest surviving in Montana, an enduring testament to a Texan by the name of Weaver who had come here with a solid dream, a dream that had been good for the Crow. Weaver had been generous and had fed them in hard winters when the buffalo were gone. During the winter of starvation he had saved an entire village with his gift of cattle, and in return was given a young woman from that village to be his wife.

So the Bow and Arrow had been founded by a white man from Texas who had taken a full-blooded Crow as his wife, and his son from this union had married a Blackfoot, the sworn enemy of the Crow. And so Jessie Weaver, who had sold the ranch to Caleb McCutcheon, was of three worlds. Crow, Blackfoot and white. Pony had never met her but had wondered at such a legacy, for to carry the blood of three such disparate worlds could surely only create confusion. Yet Pony had heard only good things of this strong young woman.

Steven had told her how Jessie Weaver had lost the ranch to falling cattle prices and her father's skyrocketing medical bills as cancer had slowly robbed him of life. How she had quit veterinary school in her third year to take care of her ailing father. And how, after her father's death, Jessie could have sold the ranch to developers and made a tidy profit even after the debts had been paid, but instead chose to write conservation restrictions into the deed and sell the ranch to Caleb McCutcheon at a huge loss in land value. She'd sacrificed a great deal—including her long-term relationship with Guthrie Sloane—to protect the place she loved, and Pony could understand and sympathize. In the end, Guthrie Sloane had, too; he and Jessie Weaver had reunited and were getting married in the fall.

Sitting here in her rusty old truck, looking down the valley at this historic place, Pony felt a sense of wonder. To live surrounded by such beauty would surely give grace to the spirit. The Crow had first cast their shadows in this valley long ago, in the good years when the sun still shone upon them, in the years before the buffalo were gone. Her great-great-grandfather might have set his horse in this very spot and looked upon this same valley and felt the same way she did now.

She put the truck in gear and drove slowly, not wanting to miss anything. She parked briefly at the place where the road first paralleled the creek and stood on the banks, listening to the rush of cold mountain water—happy music rippling over the smooth rocks lining the shallows. The air was cool and sharp with the tang of the tall evergreens that grew here. When she climbed back into the truck she felt relaxed. The tension that had been building in her at the prospect of speaking to Caleb McCutcheon had mysteriously vanished, and as she drove past the old cabin and headed toward the main ranch buildings, a curious calm settled over her.

Maybe she would get the job. Maybe she wouldn't. Whatever the outcome, she had made the journey, followed the path. She parked beside two other trucks, both Fords, both much newer than hers and she drew a steadying breath before climbing the porch steps of the weather-beaten ranch house. Hopefully Caleb McCutcheon himself would be available to speak with her. Pony knocked on the door.

Which was opened almost immediately by a very fat old Mexican woman wearing a large and shapeless housedress and apron. A red bandanna covered most of her white hair.

"Yes?" Her voice was gruff and her black eyes were not the least bit friendly.

"I've come to speak with Mr. McCutcheon about the buffalo," Pony said.

The woman abruptly closed the door in her face. Pony waited, patient in the way she had learned to be. She looked down toward the pole barn and corrals. Horses grazed on piles of hay while curlews hopped amongst them on the ground, looking for something to eat. Below the barn, near the bend in the creek, she could see the roofline of the old cabin. Smoke curled lazily from the massive fieldstone chimney. Steven had told her that McCutcheon preferred to live in the original homestead but took his meals at the ranch house with the rest of them. She thought it was odd that he wouldn't choose to live in the big house.

The door opened, and Pony swung around. A man stood in the doorway, one hand on the doorknob, the other holding a notebook, eyebrows raised in a mute question. He was tall, lean and athletically built, with sandy-colored close-cropped hair, a neatly trimmed mustache and clear eyes the color of prairie flax with deep crow's-feet etching the corners. His face was wind-burned, rugged and purely masculine. He was unexpectedly handsome, and she felt her heartbeat skip as she looked up at him and tried to remember why she was standing on his porch.

"You'll have to excuse Ramalda's behavior," he said, studying her with those keen blue eyes. "She doesn't trust strangers, even small female ones."

"Mr. McCutcheon," she said, her voice sounding tense because all of a sudden it mattered very much that she get this job. "I am sorry to bother you, but I had heard that you were looking for someone to help manage your buffalo."

"My buffalo?" If anything, her words seemed to confound him more than her presence on his porch.

"Yes. Pete Two Shirts told me this. I worked for Pete on the reservation with the tribal herd."

His expression cleared somewhat at the mention of Pete's name and he nodded. "Pete helped get me started with the buffalo," he explained, "but when he returned to the reservation…" He paused for an awkward moment. "Well, to be honest, I guess I wasn't expecting a woman. I mean, it's just that…" He took stock of her again, his eyes narrowing in a critical squint. "Please," he said, stepping aside and gesturing with the sheaf of papers. "Come inside."

Pony felt a flash of anger and shook her head. "If it's a man you're looking for, Mr. McCutcheon, I will not waste your time or mine."

She was surprised to see the color of McCutcheon's face deepen. "I meant no offense," he said.

"It's all right. I understand completely," she said. "Of course you would prefer a man to manage your buffalo herd. A man is so much stronger than a woman, and strength is very important when dealing with the buffalo, especially when you wrestle them to the ground to brand them."

His forehead creased skeptically. "Brand them?"

"And a man rides a horse so much better than a woman," Pony continued, "because a man is so much stronger, and a horse truly appreciates brute strength."

"Now look…"

"Mr. McCutcheon, if you talked to Pete Two Shirts, he would tell you that I know my stuff. And I would tell you this. I have five strong boys who would do your bidding for the summer. They would cost you nothing more than room and board. I was told you have a lot of work. If you have buffalo, you will need good boundary fences. Six strands of wire at least six feet high. Panels seven feet high would be even better, with wooden corner posts sunk into four feet of concrete. Putting up sturdy boundaries takes a lot of time and work, but without them, your herd might run clear to Saskatchewan."

"Look, why don't you—"

"And you're right about the branding, Mr. McCutcheon. You don't brand buffalo. But you do need a good set of corrals with an eight-foot-high fence and an indestructible chute of welded pipe, because even though they don't get branded, they do need to be tested for brucellosis, tuberculosis and pregnancy. They need to be wormed and vaccinated. I know how to design such a set of corrals and a good chute. I know how big and how strong the buffalo are, Mr. McCutcheon, and how wild."

McCutcheon eyed her appraisingly. He ran the fingers of his free hand through his hair. "Please, come in and have a cup of coffee. We can talk—"

"I don't drink coffee," she said. "Why don't you call Pete and ask him about me?"

He nodded. "Okay." He hesitated. "Won't you at least come inside while I call?"

"I'll wait out here, thank you," she said, not wanting to run into the unfriendly old Mexican woman.

He nodded again, clearly perplexed. "Who should I tell Pete I'm checking on?"

"Steven Young Bear's sister," Pony said.

McCutcheon's blue gaze intensified. "*That's* why you look so familiar. I'll be damned! Why didn't Steven tell me you were coming?"

"I asked him not to. I'll wait here while you call Pete."

McCutcheon shook his head with a faint grin. "I don't need to call anybody. If you're Steven's sister, that's good enough for me."

Pony's heart leaped. "Does that mean you will consider me for the job?"

"That means you're hired, you and your five boys. There's plenty of room for all of you here in the main house. When can you start?"

"In three weeks."

"That long?" His face fell.

"I'm a teacher and school lets out in three weeks." Pony held her breath, her heart hammering. *Please, oh please...*

McCutcheon nodded reluctantly. "All right. We've survived this long. I guess we can wait until mid-June. The job pays three-fifty a week, plus room and board."

She could hardly have hoped for as much, and struggled to maintain a neutral expression. "I can only work the summer."

"I'm hoping you can teach me and my ranch manager all we need to know in that time."

"I am sure that I can."

"Good. Then I guess I'll see you in three weeks." He put out his hand and took hers in a warm, firm handshake; a single up-and-down motion that made her fingers tingle curiously. She turned to descend the porch steps and was almost at her truck when his voice stopped her. "Ah...miss?" She turned and glanced up at him questioningly. "What's your name?"

"Oo-je-en-a-he-ha," she said. She stood for a few moments, watching him mentally grapple with the impossibility of it, and then, with a barely suppressed smile, she said, "But you can call me Pony, if you'd rather."

CHAPTER TWO

"SHE HAS FIVE BOYS," McCutcheon said, pulling the mug of coffee that Bernie Portis had just topped off closer to him and studying the whorls of steam rising from the strong black brew. It was midmorning of the following day and the Longhorn Cafe, the only eating establishment in Katy Junction, was enjoying a brief lull between breakfast and lunch.

"Five?" Bernie paused, coffeepot in hand. Her friendly face split into a smile. "She's been a busy gal. How old is she?"

"Not old enough. At least, she didn't look like the mother of five kids." *Too young and too beautiful,* he thought.

"How old?"

McCutcheon lifted his shoulders. "Hard to say. Late twenties. Early thirties, maybe."

"Okay, so she started young. Say, eighteen years old. First baby. Second baby at twenty. Third at twenty-two. But how much work are you expecting to get out of a bunch of little kids? And who's going to wipe their noses and change their diapers while their mother is out herding buffalo? Ramalda?" Bernie gave him a teasing smile before making a run through the tiny restaurant, refilling customers' coffee cups and pausing to chat briefly here and there. She was Guthrie Sloane's big sister, and a sweeter, more generous soul did not exist west of the Rockies nor east of them, either.

McCutcheon took a sip of his coffee and frowned. He hadn't thought to ask Pony how old her children were. He had a sudden vision of a three-year-old boy in the saddle, reins in his teeth, horse running flat out, twirling a lariat better than a washed-up baseball player by the name of Caleb McCutcheon could. It wasn't Caleb's fault that Badger and Charlie hadn't taught him how to throw a rope yet. They kept promising, and then one day slid into the next, one week followed another, and he was no closer to being a cowboy than he'd been the day he'd bought the ranch.

Ramalda had already threatened to quit. "Indians!" she had muttered when he told her, as if the word itself were a bitter poison in her mouth. Her venom had surprised Caleb, but not Badger, who'd been sharing the table the way he and Charlie almost always did nowadays, at suppertime. Or any other time for that matter. The two old cowboys had sort of come with the ranch. "Now, Ramalda," Badger said, smoothing his white mustache. "When I first laid eyes on you, I thought to myself, that there's an Apache woman, sure as shootin'. How do you know you ain't part Injun yourself? And what gave you such a sour take on things, anyhow? I thought you liked little 'uns."

Ramalda had turned her broad back to them with a string of heated Spanish that neither he nor Badger could make heads or tails of, banging pots and pans about and letting her feelings be known in no uncertain terms. "Six Indians *here*?" she exploded, brandishing a frying pan in one fat fist. "I queeet!"

"Whoa!" Caleb said, alarmed at the thought of

losing such a phenomenal cook and housekeeper. "They're Steven Young Bear's nephews. They're his sister's children. You *like* Steven."

Ramalda turned and slammed the frying pan down on the woodstove, cut a big chunk of lean salt pork into it and turned again, wielding the knife as if she intended to use it on Caleb. "Six Indians here, I queeet," she repeated emphatically.

"Well, it's too late. I've already hired them," Caleb said. "But I'd sure hate to lose you, Ramalda. I can't imagine coming into this kitchen and not having you cussing me out in Spanish or feeding me those delicious meals. Look at me. I'm getting fat." He glanced down and felt a twinge of alarm at the truth of his words. "I guess maybe it would be better for my waist if you left, but I'd sure hate it. I hope you stay. You're important to this place. We need you here, and Jessie's coming home soon. It would be awful if you weren't here for her wedding to Guthrie."

Jessie. That name had been enough to melt Ramalda's stern visage. She turned back to the stove to stir the sizzling pork with the point of her knife and never said another word about quitting. Maybe she remembered that Jessie was part Indian, too; that Jessie's father had been a half-breed, and that the history of the Bow and Arrow had been linked with Native Americans since the very beginning.

Or maybe she'd really quit when Pony and her five boys came in three weeks. "You're looking mighty pensive," Bernie said, sliding a piece of apple pie in front of him. "Thinking about what having five kids stampeding around the place will be like?"

Caleb picked up his fork and grinned. "I'm think-

ing about all the work we'll get done this summer,"
he said, feeling another twinge at this half-truth and
recalling Badger's troubling prophecy. "One good
boy can do the work of half a man," the old cowboy
had said when Caleb told him about the new hires.
"But two boys? Put two boys together and they're
worthless. Five, you say? Hell, boss, I don't even
want to think about it."

Five boys. Caleb forked a piece of apple pie into
his mouth and savored the blend of tart apples and
spices and tender crust. Five boys…and one very intimidating young woman, Oo-je-ne… He shook his
head and gave up. Pony. Strange name, but a whole
lot easier to say. Put all of them together with a herd
of buffalo rampaging across the ranch… Caleb laid
his fork down and pushed the plate away, overwhelmed with a sudden surge of anxiety.

In three weeks the summer would begin, and quite
suddenly he was dreading it.

PONY WASN'T SURE how the boys would take the
news that she had hired out their services for the summer. She was especially leery of Roon, the latest of
the five to have taken refuge in her little shack on the
edge of the Big Horn foothills. Roon was an introvert
with so much anger and confusion bottled up that
Pony sometimes feared he would explode. She had
taught him in her third-grade class. He had been like
the others then, a normal nine-year-old on the brink
of discovering the universe. Now he was thirteen and
the world was his enemy. Four years had passed.
What had happened? She had not pried. When he'd
shown up one cold snowy night on her doorstep,
she'd stood aside and let him in. He had been there

since December, a quiet brooding presence who listened to the lessons she gave the others but did not participate.

One of the rules of her household was that any child she took in had to learn the lessons she taught and eventually take the GED. It was a fair trade. Since she had been living on the reservation in the capacity of teacher and unofficial foster parent, she had launched four young people into far more promising futures than they might have had the opportunity to explore otherwise. Two of them had gone on to college, a major triumph for her. The other two had taken mining jobs off the reservation, and she still had contact with all of them on a regular basis.

So what of Roon? How would she ever reach him, turn him around, make him obey the rules she laid down? She had threatened repeatedly to throw him out, but in the end she never did. Where would he go? His own parents had left the reservation. They had leased their land allotment to a white farmer and gone to Canada, to live on a Cree reservation where the wife had blood relatives. They had taken the younger children with them. Roon had stayed with Pony, and she did not have the heart to displace him.

But would he work willingly for Caleb McCutcheon? That, and so much more, remained to be seen. She would tell the boys about the job, and if they didn't want to go to the ranch, they could return to their own families for the summer. That was fair.

But the boys were not at Nana's place. "They took your uncle's old truck," Nana said, sitting in her rocker and smoking one of her acrid-smelling hand-rolled cigarettes. "Went back home."

"But none of them can drive. None of them even have licenses!"

Nana shook her head, her deeply wrinkled face impassive. "They went home."

Pony drove the five miles to her little house much too fast, but the tribal police were not on patrol. She spied no wrecked vehicles along the way, and was relieved to see Ernie's truck parked safely in her yard. She ran up the steps and burst into the kitchen. The boys, four of them, were crowded around the table, eating peanut butter sandwiches and drinking cans of soda.

"Where's Roon?" she said.

"In the back room," Jimmy replied, mouth full of sandwich. "Nana gave him a book to read."

"Who took Ernie's truck? Who drove here?"

"Dan did," Jimmy said. "Nana said we had to leave."

Pony looked at Dan. "Why?"

Dan's dark eyes dropped and he lifted his shoulders. Pony looked at Joe. "Why did she tell you to leave?"

"We took her tobacco," he said. "We told her we'd replace it."

"Yes, you will," Pony said grimly. "Right now. Let's go."

"We already smoked what we took," Martin said, staring at her ruefully through his thick glasses. "It's gone. But we'll get her more. Don't worry."

"How? By stealing it from someone else? You promised me you wouldn't smoke, but I never thought I would have to make you promise not to steal." Pony sat down and dropped her head in her hands. There was a long moment of quiet around the table. She raised her head and studied each boy in turn. "Right now I think I should open the door and ask you all to leave. Right now I feel as if all of you have betrayed me." She drew a deep steadying breath. "Right now I am very angry, so I am going to take Ernie's truck back to Nana's and then walk home. That will give me some time to think about things."

She stood up from the table and left her little house and the silence of the four boys that filled it.

THE SECOND WEEK in June came faster than it should have, and Caleb glanced at the calendar on his way out the kitchen door. He paused, coffee cup in hand, to look at the scrawl that was written on this date. "Five boys/Pony" was a memo that he had made, but in another hand was written, "Day I quit!!!" The word *quit* was underlined strongly three times. He glanced to where Ramalda stood at the kitchen sink, washing the breakfast dishes. The brightly colored bandanna she always wore covered most of her white hair, but a few strands lay on her shoulders. A wave of affection warmed him, and he shook his head with a faint grin and pushed through the door, stepping onto the porch where his ranch manager waited patiently. He looked for the little cow dog who was never very far from Guthrie Sloane.

"Where's Blue?"

"Left her to home. Figured you'd be wantin' to ride after the buffalo."

"You figured right. There are ten old cows and one huge bull out there, and we have no idea where they are. It would be nice to be able to tell my buffalo expert that they're still on the home range, but for all

I know they're halfway to Canada." The sun wasn't up quite yet but the horses were saddled and tied to the hitch rail. "If the last you saw of them was over on Silver Creek, maybe we should start there."

"I saw signs of them this past week near the headwaters of the Piney."

"That high up?"

"Yessir."

Caleb drained the last of his cup and set it on the porch rail. "Let's ride."

Guthrie's halting footsteps followed Caleb's down the porch steps. Caleb unwrapped Billy Budd's rein from the rail and stepped into the saddle, wishing the old gelding's legs were a little shorter or that his own legs were more flexible. It was a hard thing to look graceful while hauling his six-foot frame into the saddle. Still, he couldn't complain. Guthrie was still so crippled up that he had to use the porch steps to mount his horse. That had to burn deep down inside, because Guthrie Sloane had been one of the best horsemen in Park County before that mare had fallen on him last October.

The ranch manager was a hard man to read. He didn't say much, didn't reveal himself in long-winded conversations the way some people did. He was quiet and competent and he worked damn hard. Caleb liked him very much and counted himself very fortunate to have the skilled cowboy in his employ.

"Steven's sister is coming today," he said, nudging Billy into a walk and giving him a loose rein.

"The boys, too?" Guthrie said, falling in beside him.

"As far as I know. I didn't dare broach the subject at breakfast. Didn't want to get Ramalda too upset."

"She cleaned the bedrooms yesterday."

Caleb's eyebrows shot up. "Oh?"

"I saw her bring out the rugs and hang 'em over the porch rail to air. Then she disappeared down the back hall carrying a whole bunch of clean bed linens, muttering away to herself."

"I'll be damned. Maybe she isn't going to quit after all."

"If Ramalda leaves, she knows Jessie'd never forgive her."

"No, I guess she wouldn't," Caleb agreed. "Speaking of Jessie, when's she coming home? Classes must be over for her."

"Yessir, they are. She's way ahead of where she thought she'd be, and the school has advanced her into senior-year studies."

"Does that mean she's going to be graduating sooner than you thought?"

"Yessir. She's apprenticing with that horse doctor down in Arizona again to finish her credits."

"She's down there now?"

"Yessir. She's there for the summer."

"Huh. Too bad she couldn't come home for a little visit, but at least you got to see her at spring break. And she'll be back in September. I assume she's planning to be here for her own wedding."

"Oh, probably," Guthrie said with a faint grin, smoothing his horse's mane with one gloved hand. "She said she might."

They rode up along the creek to the place where a smaller tributary fed into it, then threaded through groves of Engelmann spruce and across high meadows of greening grass spangled with wildflowers. They caught sight of some cattle but no buffalo. After an hour they stopped to rest their horses on a high knoll from which they could survey the valley. The wind pushed tall, bunched-up clouds across the vast expanse of blue sky. "I'm buying the leases back," Caleb said, leaning his forearm on the saddle horn. "The ones Jessie's father had to sell. Ten thousand acres of leased land, most of it belonging to the Bureau of Land Management. That gives the whole ranch a footprint of fifteen thousand acres. Enough room to run us some buffalo."

"Damn," Guthrie said. "That's good news."

"I didn't want to tell Jessie until it was a done deal."

"She'll be real glad to hear about it."

"I paid too much for them, but the ranchers who sold them needed the money."

"Ranchers always need money," Guthrie said, smoothing his horses mane with one gloved hand.

Caleb nodded. "I guess. I know they think what I'm trying to do here is nuts, but how much crazier is it than what they're doing—fighting a losing battle trying to raise enough cattle to make land payments when cattle prices keep falling?"

"It's the only way of life they know."

"How many buffalo do you figure we can run on fifteen thousand acres?"

Guthrie's gaze swept over the valley. He shook his head. "That's a question for your buffalo girl," he said. "In the meantime, we have ten cows and a bull to find, and five thousand acres to search. We'd best get at it."

PONY TURNED her old truck down the ranch road with a premonition of impending doom. Her hands gripped the steering wheel far more tightly than necessary. Jimmy and Roon shared the bench seat beside her. Roon sat pressed against the passenger door, staring broodily out the side window. Jimmy squeezed against him, trying to avoid the stick shift. Jimmy was the youngest at eleven. The other three boys rode in the back of the truck. Dan was fifteen, Martin and Joe were both fourteen. None of them was smiling, but all of them were clean and presentable, and all had agreed—albeit grudgingly—to be on their best behavior.

Pony knew from past experience that their perception of what constituted best behavior was the reason why she was gripping the steering wheel so tightly. By the time she pulled up in front of the ranch house, her hands were so badly cramped that she had to sit for a moment rubbing them together. "Okay," she said to Jimmy and Roon. "Now remember. Best behavior!"

They both stared at her. Nodded. Roon wrenched his door open and dropped to the ground. Jimmy followed. The boys in back jumped out. Pony was the last to climb from the truck. She stood in the yard, looking up at the ranch house and then down toward the barn and corrals. The place was quiet. Peaceful. She could hear the flutelike song of a meadowlark and the distant bawl of a cow. The wind was moderate, warm and out of the south. The sky was a wide blue dome overhead, providing a vivid backdrop to the snowcapped peaks of the Beartooth Mountains. She drew in a lungful of sweet air and exhaled slowly, willing the tension from her body.

The house door opened and an enormous figure emerged, carrying a broom. It was Ramalda, the Mexican woman who had shut the door in Pony's face, and she looked as grim as ever. "Good morning," Pony said. "I've come to see Mr. McCutcheon. We're reporting for work."

Ramalda held the broom as if she wished it were a rifle. She scowled fiercely at the boys, who stood in a group, seeking safety in each other's short mid-day shadow. "Work?" she said as if she had never heard the word before. She threw her head back and laughed. It was neither a long laugh nor a friendly one. She lowered her head and scowled at them again. "Come. *Entra.*" She turned and squeezed her body through the kitchen door, letting the screen bang shut behind her.

"Get your things," Pony said to the boys. She lifted her own small satchel out of the truck bed and climbed the porch steps. The last place in the world she wanted to be was inside that ranch house with that woman, but she squared her shoulders, lifted her chin, pulled open the screen door and stepped inside.

The room she found herself in transported her into another time. There was almost no hint of modern life among the simple furnishings and wall cupboards, the huge wood-fired cookstove, the hand pump at the big slate sink, the oil lamps—some in their wall gimbals, others set on the table. Even the gas stove was an antique, a cream enamel with green and gold piping and the words *White Star* scrolled ornately across the oven door. It was a beautiful kitchen, and in spite of her initial trepidation, Pony felt instantly at home.

Ramalda was standing by the sink with her hands on her hips, watching them with great suspicion. "You're hungry," she accused.

Pony shook her head. "If you could just show us where to put our things, we can get right to work."

She was afraid Ramalda would laugh at them again, but instead she turned and walked out of the kitchen and into a back hallway that ran the length of the rambling ranch house and exited at the far end of the porch. Pony and the boys followed. Off the hallway were several doors. She pushed the first one open. "This is my room," she said, and before they could glimpse inside, she pulled the door shut again with a sharp bang. "*My* room," she repeated. She led them to the next door and opened it, turning to Pony. "*Your* room." Pony stepped inside, followed closely by all five boys. It was a small room, perhaps ten by sixteen feet, papered in an antique rose print of pinks and greens, with a double bed, a bureau, a chair and a mirror hung above the dresser. A braided rug fit neatly between the bed and the bureau, and a narrow door opened onto a little closet. Pony set her satchel on the chair and smiled.

"It's very nice," she said, and the boys all nodded in solemn agreement.

Ramalda led them down the hall and opened yet another door. This room was a third again the size of Pony's and had two sets of bunk beds on opposite walls and a twin bed set beneath the single window. The boys looked around at the plain whitewashed walls hung with old cowboy prints, the well-worn desk and chair, the one tall bureau, the small closet. A braided rug similar to the one in Pony's room graced the floor between the sets of bunk beds. The boys laid their duffels down on the bunks, each choosing by order of rank. Roon, Pony noticed, though not the oldest, chose first, and he picked the bed beneath the window. Dan and Martin took the top bunks, Jimmy and Joe got the bottom.

The next room they were shown was the bathroom. It was small, basic, no bathtub, just a shower. Clean, Pony noticed. The entire place was spanking clean. The Mexican woman might not care to host a passel of Crow Indians, but she was a good housekeeper.

Ramalda led them back to the kitchen. "You eat now," she said gruffly, motioning for them to sit. Pony stood for a moment in indecision, wondering if their hunger was that obvious, and then nodded to the boys, who immediately dropped into five chairs. Pony slowly followed suit. Ramalda then served them a meal that could have fed Pony and the boys for a week. It began with a thick spicy stew of lamb, onions, beans and chili peppers ladled into deep colorful Mexican bowls and set before them with big bone-handled soupspoons on the side. A platter of fresh soft tortillas, still warm, was plunked down in the middle of the table, along with a brimming pitcher of cold milk and six tall glasses. The savory aroma of the stew overcame the awkwardness of the moment. They glanced respectfully at the strange old woman who stood by the stove and watched them eat with a fixed scowl on her face.

Breathless with the joy of having full stomachs, they pushed back from the table with dazed expressions. Every bit of the delicious stew was gone, every tender tortilla devoured, the pitcher of milk empty. Ramalda nodded grimly, went to the oven and drew forth a pan of beef ribs done to a tender turn and dripping with sauce. She used a spatula to push them all onto a serving platter and slid the dish into the center of the table, refilled the pitcher with more cold milk, then stood back and waited.

They stared around the table at each other, and then at the ribs. Even Roon was smiling as they dug into them with rapturous abandon, wearing the sauce shamelessly on their chins and laughing, finally, when there was nothing left but a stack of gnawed bones.

"WE'VE MISSED the noon meal, I guess," Caleb said as they let their horses pick a careful descent down the steep draw. "Ramalda was going to make barbecued ribs."

Guthrie was ahead of him. "Don't worry. She'll save some for you." He glanced back, grinning beneath his hat brim. "She likes watching you get fat."

Caleb didn't presume to tell Billy how to get down the steep slope. He gave the gelding free rein and shamelessly clutched the saddle horn to keep from tumbling over the horse's shoulders. "That's no lie," he said. "I was in a whole lot better shape when I first came here than I am now."

"Winter," Guthrie called back. "All those long dark days with nothing to do but eat what Ramalda cooks, and she's a damn fine cook. Thinks if a person ain't always hungry they must be sick. But don't worry, you'll burn it off. From now till the snow flies you can eat whatever you want and you'll still lose weight."

The slope bottomed out, and Guthrie drew rein, leaning over his horse's shoulder and studying something on the ground. "That's fresh," he said. "Them buff are here somewhere close by." He straightened and sat for a moment, contemplating. "Wind's out of the south. We ought to be able to work up this draw and maybe catch sight of them, but if they catch a whiff of us, they'll be on the far side of tomorrow in the blink of an eye. Ride quiet and follow me.''

Caleb did just that, and in less than an hour they had ridden up onto a knoll that overlooked a high, pretty meadow shaped like a basin lying amongst the lower flanks of three rugged snow-clad mountains. ''That's Piney Creek,'' Guthrie said, raising his arm and pointing toward a dark ribbon that snaked through the meadow. ''The old line camp is in that big clump of fir.''

Caleb had seen the camp once. ''Joe Nash flew me in here last fall,'' he said. ''He said it was the prettiest place in all of Montana, but it wasn't quite so pretty on that particular afternoon.'' He looked at Guthrie. ''That was the day we brought you down off the mountain more dead than alive.''

Guthrie glanced sidelong at him and then faced forward again. A muscle in his jaw corded. He pulled his hat brim down a little lower. ''Well, that's all in the past, and right now we're hunting for your buffalo.'' He shifted in his saddle. ''As a matter of fact, I think I'm lookin' right at one.''

Caleb leaned forward. ''Where?''

''See that little black dot way down there, followed by a dash? Down near the creek? That black dot is a buff, sure as I'm sitting here. That dash is three or four others, following along behind. I bet the entire bunch is hiding in that brush along the creek.''

''How close do you think we can get?''

''If the wind holds, pretty close. Close enough to count 'em, anyhow. You game?''

''Hell yes, I'm game. What are we waiting for?''

They heeled their horses and set off at a slow jog.

The distance to be covered was over a mile. Guthrie reined his horse to a walk when they got within a quarter mile, and Caleb did the same. The afternoon was a fine one, with a steady breeze and the warm June sun to gentle it. Caleb wished he'd brought his field book along because he was seeing birds and flowers he'd never seen before. The vitality and diversity of the land continually astounded and humbled him. He wondered if he would ever truly be connected to it the way he really wanted to be.

Sometimes he felt he was so close…

"Whoa," Guthrie said, his voice low, and they stopped side by side, stirrup to stirrup. "That big old cow there. See her?"

Caleb tried to follow Guthrie's point but he could see nothing yet. No buffalo. He shook his head.

"She's watching us, standing in that bunch of chokecherry down in that brushy draw. Hold now. Hold…"

They sat very still and the horses were motionless as if they knew that any small movement would betray them. There was a sudden explosion in the thicket and before Caleb's dazzled eyes a huge buffalo cow burst from the draw, tail held high, and made off at a dead run. She climbed a knoll at a speed that seemed impossible for such an ungainly-looking beast and yet she was pure grace and incredible power as she fled their presence and sought the safety of the rest of the herd.

"What's that?" Caleb said, his breath catching in his throat. "Look, beside her. What *is* that!" He watched the little blond ball that bounced at the cow's flank as she raced up the knoll.

Guthrie's reply was an affirmation of something

Caleb already knew. "That's a baby buff, boss," he said. "That cute little critter is one of your first baby buffs."

THE EUPHORIA of the afternoon stayed with Caleb on the long ride home. The buffalo were all there. Not only were they all there, but the ten cows had made seven calves. Not bad at all, considering he'd bought all ten without having them certified pregnant. Seven out of ten wasn't bad, and maybe they weren't done calving, either. Caleb was feeling pretty good about things.

"Lord, they were something, weren't they?" he said for the umpteenth time as they jogged home.

"Yessir," Guthrie said.

Hard to tell what Guthrie really thought about it all. Did he really think the buffalo were a good thing? Or was he too much of a cattleman to ever change his ways? "They scare me a little, I won't lie," Caleb said. "But they're the true natives of this land. They belong here."

"Yessir."

"I think this ranch will be a better place for having them."

"Me, too," Guthrie said.

Caleb drew rein so abruptly that Billy snorted in protest. Guthrie was slower to follow suit, easing his horse to a walk and pivoting it around to face him. He gave Caleb a questioning look.

"Do you mean that?" Caleb said.

"You forget that I grew up here with Jessie," Guthrie replied. "I've been working on this ranch since I was thirteen years old, and she's been wanting this to happen for a long time. Ripping down the cross fences and bringing back the buffalo. Giving the land back to itself and letting it heal the wounds we've made in it over the years.''

''But what about you? How do *you* feel about it?''

Guthrie studied him for a moment then shifted his gaze to the distant mountains. ''All my life has been about beef cows and alfalfa hay,'' he admitted. ''Worrying about the weather and the cows. Worrying about the graze and the cows. Worrying about makin' hay and makin' money and losin' all of it when the cattle prices just dropped and dropped. I'm just like all them other ranchers. I think in beef cow. But when I look at them buffalo I feel like someone's taken me by the scruff of the neck and given me a good shake, and I catch myself thinkin', what the hell took us so long to get smart?''

The two men regarded each other for a long silent moment. Caleb nodded. ''I want to make this work.''

''So do I,'' Guthrie said.

''Good.'' He nudged Billy with his heels and walked him up beside Guthrie's horse. ''You really think Ramalda saved any of those ribs?''

Guthrie grinned. ''Dunno. How much do you suppose five hungry boys can eat?''

''I think they could eat a whole buffalo.''

''Let's just hope they don't, or we might be out of business by summer's end.''

CHAPTER THREE

CALEB WAS RENDERED speechless at the size of the boys. He'd been expecting a spread of five- to twelve-year-olds. He'd been expecting to have to smooth Ramalda's feathers when she realized she'd be baby-sitting in addition to her other duties at the ranch, but he'd been way off base. These weren't little kids. He sat in the saddle, gazing at the five young men who stared silently back at him, lined up along the corral fence just outside the pole barn. They'd been sitting on the top rail when he and Guthrie had ridden in, studying the horses inside the corral, and had jumped down at their arrival, lining up as if for inspection. Pony was nowhere to be seen.

"Well," he finally managed to say. "I see you made it here all right. Did Ramalda feed you?"

All five nodded.

"Good. Did she show you where you'd be bunking?"

Another somber nod of five heads.

"You picking out your horses, are you?"

The smallest boy said, "I like the dun."

"That's a good horse. His name's Gunner."

"I'm Jimmy," the boy said, standing taller. "This is Roon, Dan, Martin and Joe."

"I'm Caleb McCutcheon," he said, shaking each boy's hand in turn, "and this is my ranch manager,

Guthrie Sloane. You boys will answer to him as long as you're riding for the Bow and Arrow." He hesitated. "Is your mother around?"

"Mother?" Five blank expressions met his gaze.

"Pony."

"She's down near the creek," Jimmy said. "She wanted to see what grew along the banks."

Caleb glanced at Guthrie. "Why don't you introduce the boys to the horses? We've got a couple hours to kill before supper. I'll find Pony and then give everyone a brief tour of the ranch."

He touched his heels to Billy's flanks and headed toward the creek, half dreading the encounter with the dark-eyed young woman. Ever since the moment they'd first met he'd been more than a little intimidated by her.

"She's a lot like Jessie," he told Billy Budd, and the gelding flicked his ears at the sound of his voice. "And I have to tell you, old boy, she kind of scares me."

He almost hoped he wouldn't find her, but he came to the bank of the creek and spotted her almost immediately. She was standing in the shade of a gnarly old cottonwood, holding a bunch of wildflowers she'd picked, dressed in jeans and a red-and-black plaid flannel shirt with the sleeves rolled back. Her thick, shiny black hair was plaited in a braid that hung over her shoulder.

"We would have gone to work right away," she said when he approached, regarding him with those dark, direct eyes. "But there was no one here to tell us what to do."

Caleb reined Billy in and swung out of the saddle

to stand beside her. "Those five boys can't all be yours," he said.

"Mine?" For a moment her eyes were puzzled, and then she shook her head. "No. At least, not in the way you mean. I am not their biological mother." Her slender shoulders rose and fell around a helpless shrug. "It's more like they've adopted me. I'm sorry. I should have explained that beforehand. You must have been expecting—"

"Babes in swaddling clothes," he admitted. "But those boys are big enough to do a man's work, and I'll be glad to pay them a working wage."

"They are big enough to work," Pony agreed, "but they will work for room and board, as we agreed, and if you can get that out of them you'll be doing well."

He recalled Badger's prophecy with a twinge of unease. "What does that mean?"

"That means they are teenage boys."

"I don't have any kids of my own," Caleb admitted. "The closest I ever came to parenting was playing uncle to a bunch of my ex-wife's nieces and nephews for an hour or two at time, once or twice a year."

Pony smiled. "Mr. McCutcheon, you are about to get a whole lot closer than that. But if the day comes when you think you've had enough of us, you must tell me. They are good boys, but they can try the patience of a saint."

"Can they ride?"

She nodded. "They have been on horseback and I've been teaching them all I know about buffalo."

"We'll be doing a lot of fence work. That's hard going."

She nodded again. "It will be good for them." She

gazed out across the creek to where the rolling grass-land reached out toward the timbered mountain slopes. "They need a place like this to show them what life can be like. They're disillusioned and discouraged. They dropped out of school, got into trouble. Not big stuff, or serious, but their parents couldn't or wouldn't deal with them anymore." She shook her head. "They don't know where they belong, or what the future holds for them."

Caleb gripped the reins in his hands as anxiety tightened his stomach muscles. He was sailing onto an uncharted ocean and he wondered how deep and dangerous the waters were. "What *does* the future hold for them?"

She shook her head again, staring straight at him with a frankness that was disarming. "I don't know. When they come to me for help I tell them that I will feed them and give them a place to live, but in turn they have to study for and pass the GED. And then I tutor them so they can do this."

"You do that on your own time and at your own expense?"

She shrugged. "It seems the least I can do after what my brother did for me. Steven put me through school, through college. He gave me a life I never would have had otherwise. What I do for these boys is not nearly as much as what he did for me."

"But he's your brother."

"Those boys are my tribal kin. There is a bond there, Mr. McCutcheon. We are family. We take care of each other."

He saw the fierce pride shining in her dark eyes and felt a surge of admiration. She was so slender, so small, and yet her spirit encompassed an entire tribe. "Five boys must eat a lot."

"Steven sends me money every month. I don't make very much teaching and he knows that. I never asked him for the money. He just sends it."

Caleb nodded. Steven Young Bear was as big-hearted as his sister. Their sacrifices made him feel small. He dropped his eyes and studied the ground at his feet. The creek rushed past and a surge of wind rustled through the cottonwood. Her nearness was strangely unsettling. He was acutely aware that she was watching him, and he felt as tongue-tied as a teenage boy. He glanced up. "Have you eaten?"

"Yes, thank you." Her expression spoke volumes. "Your housekeeper fed us."

"Ribs?"

"Very delicious beef ribs, and an excellent lamb stew."

He nodded again. "Well, I guess I'll grab a peanut butter-and-jelly sandwich then, before giving you a tour of the ranch."

Pony's smile was shy. "Ramalda saved some ribs for you. She said that you had a big hunger all the time, like a—" She stopped abruptly and glanced down at the wildflowers she held, her expression softening. "This is a place that my grandmother would have liked. Already I have found seven of the sacred healing plants she made her medicines with."

"Seven? How many did she use?"

"As many as she needed."

Caleb paused, running the strip of rein through his hands. "What did Ramalda tell you my hunger was like?" he asked, curious.

"Like a cow in a feedlot," Pony replied, the smile reaching her eyes before she lowered them.

They walked back up the hill toward the ranch house side by side, in awkward silence.

PONY DID NOT GO on the tour of the ranch with Caleb McCutcheon. She watched the boys pile into the back of the pickup truck, Jimmy sharing the front seat with the rancher, and felt a pang of regret that she had offered to help Ramalda with supper. The woman had readily accepted her offer, which was why Pony was standing on the porch and watching the others drive off in a billow of dust, thinking that if she had gone she would have ridden in the cab with him. She would have been sitting where Jimmy was, and they would have had a chance to talk more.

She could have asked McCutcheon about the job. About his buffalo herd. About the land.

But what she really wanted to ask him was why he had no wife. A man like Caleb McCutcheon should not be traveling through his days all alone. He had once been married and had spoken of his ex-wife's nieces and nephews.

She felt a flush of embarrassment at wondering about something that was none of her business. She was here to do a job, and that was all. Her interest must therefore stay with the buffalo herd. She was here for one brief summer to earn money to buy school supplies in the fall. She was not here to speculate on Caleb McCutcheon's past.

And she most definitely would not want him speculating about hers.

FACED WITH THE TASK of entertaining five boys for two hours, Caleb was beginning to count his blessings

that his life had been so uncomplicated. He gripped
the steering wheel and glanced sidelong at the youngest boy, Jimmy, with a curt nod. "You heard what
I said. You open a gate, you shut it behind you. Those
are the rules out here in cattle country. Now go on
and shut the gate."

"If we're going to be ripping all these fences out
and running buffalo through here anyway," the one
called Martin said from the truck's open bed, "why
bother closing the gates?"

"Because I said so." Caleb turned to look through
the open rear slider and lasered the boy with a steely
glance. "And my word is the law around here."

There was a soft snicker at his words. Roon? Dan?
But Jimmy was already moving, jumping out of the
passenger seat to close the gate behind them. Caleb
was taking them up to the holding pens where the
annual branding was done. He'd had no idea what to
do when Ramalda had accepted Pony's offer to help
with supper preparations, leaving Caleb to the task of
supervising the boys. Guthrie was nowhere to be
found.

Caleb carefully guided the pickup around the worst
of the ruts and rocks that made the road a challenge
at the best of times and pretty near impossible in mud
season. He pulled to a stop at the series of corrals and
chutes that stood on one side of a big wide-open
meadow high above the ranch. Caleb climbed out of
the cab and followed the boys to the nearest corral,
where he hooked one arm over the top rail. He gazed
at the weathered wood posts and rails, and in spite of
his ranching ignorance knew that this arrangement

would never hold a two-thousand-pound bull buffalo that went by the name of Goliath.

"This is where they used to work on the cattle in the spring. The branding, castrating, vaccinating, deworming, ear notching," he said. "We'll probably use this area for the buffalo, too, once we strengthen the fences. This high valley is a natural place to do the work, because once we're done we can turn them out and they'll already be at summer pasture. You can see how the land lies, and where the good graze is. That pass between those mountains to the east of us leads to more high meadows just like this. Good grass and water. Once in a while a few head will stray over Dead Woman Pass, way up on the shoulder of Montana Mountain, but for the most part they stick around on this side of the range. They have all they need right here."

He glanced around at the circle of faces, looking for some response, some flicker of interest. Nothing. "You boys won't be working with cattle because there aren't many left. All the Herefords and shorthorns were sold off a year ago. There aren't many longhorns, maybe twenty head, all told. Sometimes a whole summer'll go by and you won't catch sight of a single one, or so my ranch manager says. They're as wild as deer, and just as wily."

"Why keep them?" Jimmy said. "Why not eat them or sell them off?"

Caleb plucked a stem of grass and chewed on it for a moment. "Well, I'm told that their meat is tougher than hell. But they're here because Jessie Weaver wanted them to stay on the land, and I agreed to that."

"Who's Jessie?"

"You'll meet her in a few months, maybe. She's away for the summer, finishing up her veterinary degree, but she grew up here. The Bow and Arrow was in her family for generations, up until this past October when she sold it to me. She's marrying Guthrie Sloane, my ranch manager, this September—"

"You call it the Bow and Arrow," the one called Roon interrupted, "but it says Weaver on the ranch sign."

Caleb threw the grass stem to the ground. "The name Weaver was carved into that cedar plank over a hundred years ago because a hundred years ago you wouldn't hang a sign that said Bow and Arrow, not when you were a half-breed ranch owner and your neighbors were all old Indian fighters."

"What about now?"

"Things are a little different now, and before the summer's over there'll be a new sign that tells it like it is."

The sun was setting, the shadows were long and blue, and a golden wash of color swept over the meadow. The sky to the east was a deepening violet and to the west the mountain peaks snagged at salmon-pink clouds. Already there was a chill in the air as the cold sank back down into the valleys from the higher climbs. "Well, boys," Caleb said. "It's getting late and it's a slow crawl back to the ranch. Get back aboard and we'll haul on home and see what Ramalda and Pony are cooking up for supper."

"Supper?" Jimmy said, brightening. "You mean we get to eat again?"

"Three square meals a day. That's the deal. You work, you eat."

Jimmy climbed into the cab beside him while the

others piled into the open bed. "Well then, I'm for working," he said as Caleb put the truck in gear. "I'm for working real hard. Hold on up there, Mr. McCutcheon, and let me get that gate for you."

BADGER SAT on the porch bench, his shoulders slouched against the wall, his worn, scuffed boots stretched out in front of him, legs crossed at the ankles. His hat was pulled down almost over his eyes and he was sleeping, or he thought he was. In his dreams he was young again, riding a pale horse called Moon across the lower pasture down near the creek and the old homestead cabin. He caught a whiff of wood smoke from the cabin's big stone chimney and he could see Jessie's father standing on the porch, pulling on his pipe and studying something across the creek. Badger drew old Moon in and shaded his eyes against the westering sun, following his boss's gaze.

By God, it was a buffalo silhouetted against the fiery Rocky Mountain sunset. A big honest-to-God bull buffalo! "Well, what do you know about that?" he said to Moon. "There ain't been a buff on this land for a century or better."

The smoke smelled of cedar. Badger filled his lungs with the sweet fragrance and watched the buffalo. He folded his hands across his stomach, adjusted his rump on the bench, eased his shoulders against the rounded logs of the cabin's west wall, and then opened his eyes a little wider, wondering with a little jolt what had happened to Moon and Jessie's father. Badger realized he was napping on Caleb McCutcheon's cabin porch. The dream had left him, but the buffalo was still there, standing across the creek from the log cabin, watching with an almost haughty and proprietary grandeur. Badger sat up. He swallowed and rubbed his hand over his eyes, removed his battered hat and ran his fingers through his thin white hair.

"Damn," he said, clearing his throat. He reached into his vest pocket for a foil packet of tobacco and stuffed a big wad of it in his mouth, working it around to his left cheek. "I may be gettin' old and senile," he muttered to himself, "but that there's a buffalo I'm lookin' at, sure as shootin'. What's the old bull doing way down here?"

He heard the approach of a pickup truck behind the cabin and the slam of the cab's door. Caleb McCutcheon rounded the corner of the cabin and headed for the porch steps carrying a paper bag. He grinned when he spotted Badger sitting there. "You hiding out?" he said, climbing the steps.

"Yep," Badger said. "That ranch house up yonder is way too crowded for an old coot like me. But look'it over there and feast your eyes on that!" He nodded toward the big buffalo. McCutcheon swung on heel and froze, staring in disbelief.

"By God, a hundred more yards and that bastard'll be on my porch!"

"He won't cross that creek."

"Oh? Well, I'd like to believe that, but he's crossed the Silver and east branch of the Snowy all in less than a week, and just this morning he was way the hell up on the mountain hanging with the rest of them. He's covered a good five miles since then. This little ribbon of water isn't going to slow him down. What do you suppose he wants?"

Badger levered himself off the bench and walked over to the corner of the porch railing, leaned his hip into it, and spat over the edge. "Maybe he's tired of hangin' around all them sexy buffalo cows," he said, wiping his chin.

"Well, if that's the case, I bought myself a bum bull. He's supposed to be romancing those cows in another month or so." Caleb McCutcheon shook his head with a disgusted sigh. "To hell with him. After spending the past few hours trying to entertain five boys, right now I'm more interested in having a drink. I just drove all the way to town to pick this bottle up and hide out here on my porch for a little while before going up for supper. Care to join me?"

"Be my pleasure," Badger said.

A few moments later they were ensconced side to shoulder on the wall bench, watching the buffalo. The daylight waned as they sipped smooth scotch whiskey and enjoyed the silence of the early-summer evening. McCutcheon was halfway through his drink and relaxing more by the moment. "Were they all up there at the ranch house?" he said.

"Well, I counted five boys and one little woman. Guthrie was there, too, lookin' mighty peaked, but just before I snuck off I seen that Ramalda was pouring a big slug of her medicinal brandy into his coffee. Now, boss, I got to warn you, just in case you don't know," Badger said, his gravelly voice ominous. "She speaks Spanish."

"Pony?"

Badger nodded, taking another sip. "Yep. She and Ramalda were chattering away like two jaybirds in that kitchen. Laughin' and everything!"

"Ramalda was laughing?"

"Yep." Badger looked grim. He took another sip. "Laughin'."

"What about the boys?"

"Them boys is downright determined not to show anything of themselves."

"Mmm." Caleb raised his glass, gazing at the darkening bulk of the big bull standing broadside to them across the creek. "I've been thinking about those kids. There isn't really anything for them to do here, once the working day is done. I mean, when supper is over, what then? It seems to me they're going to need something."

"Like what?"

"Like maybe a television."

Badger snorted. "That jabber box was the ruination of this nation's youth, and if them boys put in a hard day's work like you seem to think they will, all they'll be needin' after supper is a mattress to flop onto and about eight hours of solid shut-eye."

"But they could watch things if we had a television."

"What kind of things? The news? You ever seen anything good on the news?"

"Movies, then."

"Them movies they show are pure violence! Trust me. Those kids don't need to be learnin' that stuff."

Caleb took another sip of whiskey. "There are a lot of good movies out there that aren't mindless or violent. I could buy a few and they could watch them once in a while, for a special treat."

"Just what the hell would you power that useless thing with?"

"The same setup we use for the water pump in the bathroom and the computer we enter all the ranch data into," McCutcheon said. "Guthrie rigged it up. Same as he did in his own cabin. Two seventy-five-

watt solar panels, four six-volt batteries, a cheap in-
verter. It works great and it would easily power one
of those TV/VCR combos for a couple hours a
week.''

Badger shook his head. ''Maybe, but a movie ain't
gonna make 'em happy if they don't want to be
here.''

The buffalo shook his head suddenly, and Caleb
leaned forward, his keen eyes narrowing. ''True. But
I want this thing to work. I want them to like it here.''
He watched as the bull took two steps and then lowered his massive head to graze. ''I want them to
stay,'' he said with conviction.

Badger drained the last of his glass and felt the
whiskey burn deep. ''Well, boss, you keep tellin'
yourself that and you might just come to believe it.
Meantime, you best finish off your drink. It'll give
you the courage to face that silent tribe at supper. I
don't know about you, but I ain't lookin' forward to
it one little bit, much as I admire Ramalda's cookin'.''

''Maybe we have time for another,'' Caleb said,
lifting the bottle from the floor beside him with the
expression of a condemned man.

Badger examined his glass. ''That ain't the worst
offer I ever had,'' he said, holding it out for a refill.
''No point rushin' into things.''

CHAPTER FOUR

PONY WAS STANDING at the kitchen counter when he came into the room, just as Ramalda was running through yet another string of heated rants about Caleb McCutcheon always being late, always late! And then quite suddenly the tall lean broad-shouldered rancher was there, and just as suddenly Pony felt all confused inside, turning quickly back to the task she had set herself—sliding the hot biscuits out of the pan and into a deep basket lined with a clean kitchen towel.

The boys were already seated at the table, washed and silent, watching this next culinary performance with a kind of suspicious anticipation. McCutcheon stopped just inside the kitchen door and glanced around the room, nodding almost imperceptibly when his eyes met hers, and then again at Guthrie Sloane, who stood in the back hallway as if hiding from the moment. "Sorry we're late," Caleb said to Ramalda, removing his hat as if he were in the presence of royalty. "It's my fault. I hope you aren't too angry."

Ramalda paused in mid-waddle from stove to sink, holding a pot with something delicious-smelling in it. *"Lavate las manos!"* she said, nodding her head curtly toward the sink and glaring at them. She wrinkled her nose as if smelling something bad. *"Hueles a vaca.* You wash!"

"Yes, ma'am." McCutcheon nodded humbly. He

and Badger hung their hats on pegs beside the door and made for the sink, standing politely to one side until Ramalda had finished with it.

Pony had discovered that beneath that gruff and scowling exterior, Ramalda had an exceptionally soft heart. From speaking with her during supper preparations, Pony had also learned that the Mexican woman had worked for Jessie Weaver's family back in the ranch's glory days, before the fall of cattle prices, before Jessie's father had gotten cancer. Ramalda had been like a mother to Jessie, whose own mother had died when she was just a child. When hard times had come to the ranch, both Ramalda and her cowboy husband, Drew Long, had been laid off, and Ramalda had confided that it had been a kind of miracle when Caleb McCutcheon had bought the ranch and hired her back—at Jessie's prompting—shortly after Drew's death.

Having washed up, both McCutcheon and Badger approached the table, where they stood awkwardly for a few moments before claiming chairs together at one end of the table. Guthrie joined them, and the three sat down and rested their elbows on the table, glancing around the room. McCutcheon's eyes touched hers again briefly and Pony felt her cheeks warm. He cleared his throat.

"That bull buffalo is standing right across the creek from my cabin," he said, reaching for the coffeepot that Ramalda had plunked in the center of the table and filling his cup. He did the same for Guthrie and Badger.

"I'll be damned. Guess he traveled some today, didn't he?" Guthrie said, raising his cup for a swallow. "Maybe in the morning he'll be standing on your porch, lookin' in the window."

"That big buff's like a mountain on hooves," Badger said. "I've never seen any bigger. Kind of spooky, if you ask me. I'll take beef cattle any day."

"That's because you don't know what from wherefore," Guthrie said. "Buffalo are the wave of the future. The meat is healthier, tastier, and since when could you sell a beef cow's skull and hide for nearly a thousand dollars?"

"Since when could you throw a rope around a buffalo and slap your brand on it?" Badger challenged, adding three heaping spoonfuls of sugar to his coffee.

"Speaking of which," McCutcheon interrupted, "Badger, weren't you and Charlie supposed to give me a roping lesson yesterday? Charlie mentioned something about it when I ran into him at the Longhorn Cafe."

Badger's eyebrows raised and he rubbed his whiskery chin. "That's the first I heard of it." He shook his head in disgust. "Charlie's a senile old coot."

Pony helped Ramalda with the final preparations while listening to the conversation, and the boys' heads turned solemnly from one speaker to another as if watching a tennis match.

Guthrie reached for the coffeepot. "Charlie and Badger can't throw a rope anyhow," he said, topping off his mug. "Between the two of them, I doubt they could rope a stump and tie it to a tree. Why'd you want to take lessons from them?"

"I was throwin' a rope long before you hit the ground, son," Badger said, adding another spoonful of sugar to his cup. "And I expect I can still throw one better'n you."

"Maybe we should have us a rope-throwing contest after supper," Guthrie said. "I could use a little extra pocket money betting on a sure thing like that."

Badger laid down his spoon, straightened his spine and smoothed his mustache. "Son, there's no such thing as a sure thing, but if you want to run on the rope, go right ahead. To my way of thinkin', you'd be better off keeping your money in your pocket. You're going to need all the cash you can get to pay for this big wedding of yours that your sister Bernie's plannin'."

Guthrie sipped his coffee. "Why, Badger, I thought you was plannin' to foot the bill. You're always talkin' about how Jessie's been just like a grand-daughter to you."

"That she is," Badger said, his voice gruff but his expression softening. "Maybe we'd both best be saving our money."

McCutcheon leaned back in his chair. "I guess this means I'm never going to get my roping lesson."

Pony set the basket of golden biscuits on the table, but when Jimmy immediately reached for one she said, "Wait." She helped Ramalda bring the rest of the food, and then took a chair between Jimmy and Roon. Ramalda went back to the sink and began fussing with the dirty pots and pans. Badger reached for a biscuit. "Wait," Pony said again, and Badger drew his hand back as if he'd been slapped. Pony folded her hands in front of her. "We must wait."

The boys sat silently. McCutcheon and Guthrie exchanged a questioning glance while Ramalda scrubbed noisily away at the pots in the kitchen sink. The wait stretched out for several long minutes and finally Badger cleared his throat. "Now, maybe I'm practicing rude behavior here, ma'am, but just what the devil are we waiting for?" he said, giving her a reproachful look. "Are you about to say grace?"

Pony's clasped hands tightened. "It is impolite to begin eating before everyone is seated."

Badger snorted. "Hell's bells, Ramalda never sits with us. We'll all starve if we wait for her. She eats in her own place, at her own time."

Pony looked at McCutcheon with a surge of indignation. "You mean that she is not allowed to eat with you?"

His face flushed. "She's more than welcome, but she won't. Maybe you can convince her to, but I can't. Believe me, I've tried."

She looked behind her to where the woman worked at the sink. *"Ramalda, sientate, y come con nosotros."* Ramalda swung her bulk about and scowled, raised a dripping hand holding a scouring pad and shook her head.

"No. Comaselos ustedes ahora que están caliente."

Pony faced front again, her cheeks flushing with embarrassment. "She says for us to eat while the food is hot."

"There now, you see?" Badger said. "She's an old-time camp cookie, Ramalda is. She knows full well that us cowboys is nothin' more than a big appetite ridin' a horse." He reached for the basket of biscuits and helped himself, handing the basket to his left, and did the same with the platter of two plump roasting chickens. A spicy dish made of cornmeal with peppers and onions followed, and finally, the big pitcher of milk. For a while there was only the noise of cutlery scraping against plates as the boys dug in and the men followed suit. Pony glanced up as Ramalda plunked a big cast-iron pot of spiced beef and beans onto the table and replenished the biscuits and the milk. She tried to eat but couldn't, her nerves were that rattled. But it didn't matter. The noon meal had been sufficient to last her several days.

"So tell me why that big bull buffalo roams," Caleb McCutcheon said, startling her. She caught his gaze for a moment and then dropped her eyes to her plate and pretended to concentrate on her food.

"The bulls will generally remain near the herd, but they hang together in their own group. The cows stay with the cows, the bulls with the bulls," she said to her plate. "The only time the bulls run with the cows is during the mating time. Your bull is lonely, but not for the cows. Not right now. Right now he needs other bulls, the same way you men seem to need each other's company."

"But won't they fight amongst themselves?"

Pony nodded, glancing up briefly. "In the mating time they'll test each other. They'll fight sometimes, and sometimes there'll be injuries. But the rest of the year the bulls like each other's company."

"Yepper," Badger said, deadpan. "Maybe you'll find him on your porch in the morning. Maybe he just wants to hang out with you, boss."

"How many bulls do you think I should have here?" McCutcheon asked.

"That depends. How many cows do you want to run?"

"How many cows could this ranch support?" he said, fork poised halfway to his mouth.

"How big is your range?"

"It'll be fifteen thousand acres in another month,

but right now we're working with five thousand,''
McCutcheon said.

"And you have ten cows and one bull." Pony
broke a biscuit in half and laid it on her plate. She
buttered both halves carefully, concentrating on the
task. "You'll need five bulls to start, and at least
thirty cows. Three times that would be better. Anything less, and you won't make any money at all."

She laid down the knife and raised her eyes.

He regarded her steadily. "The money part doesn't
matter," he said.

She paused, carefully considering his statement.
"Maybe it should, Mr. McCutcheon." She felt her
heart rate accelerate. "Maybe it isn't enough for this
little herd of buffalo to be the token toys of a rich
man. Maybe it would mean more if you could prove
that what you are doing here is a good thing, that it
is good for the land, good for the buffalo, and good
for the people, too. And if you can make money doing
a good thing, and make the ranch work again and hold
itself up without your support, maybe *that* would be
the very best thing of all."

Dead silence.

McCutcheon pushed his plate away and set back in
his chair. All eyes at the table were on him, awaiting
his response. He picked up his coffee and took a swallow. Set the mug down gently. "Okay," he said, nodding slowly, his blue eyes calmly speculative. "So
where do we get these buffalo?"

"There are auctions," she said. "Usually these are
held late in the year. You can also buy directly from
other ranches. You could talk to Pete and see if he
will sell you some more. But first you need to get

your fences fixed, or the buffalo will just push them down and wander off.''

McCutcheon nodded again and glanced at Guthrie. ''We'll make an early start in the morning. Everyone had better get a good night's sleep,'' he said, standing abruptly. ''That was a good meal, Ramalda. *Muchas gracias.*'' He lifted his hat off the wall peg and walked out of the kitchen without looking back, the screen door slamming behind him.

Pony watched him go and felt a sudden twist of anxiety at her brashness. The words she had spoken were true, but they had hurt the way the truth sometimes did. He was no doubt standing on the porch thinking about how he could politely ask her and the boys to leave, because this much she already knew about Caleb McCutcheon; he might be a rich man, but he had a good and honest heart.

CALEB WALKED OUT into the twilight, grateful for the chill air that cooled his flaming face. The words she'd spoken had stung, but she was absolutely correct. If he wanted to make a real difference, it had to be in a real way. He couldn't rely on his inexhaustible bank account, because that wouldn't help this land or the people who lived upon it.

He walked to the porch rail and leaned over, elbows braced, gazing at the last shreds of color in the sky. The cow dog, Blue, rose from her nap and crossed the porch to sit beside him companionably. He let one hand drop to stroke the top of her head and shortly afterward heard two sets of boots come onto the porch behind him. Guthrie and Badger walked up to the porch rail and stood—one on each side of him—staring out at the June evening.

For a while they were quiet, and then Guthrie made a strange choking noise and turned away, limping a few steps to put some distance between them. His head was ducked and his shoulders rounded over. Caleb stared at his back for a moment, wondering if Guthrie was all right or if the pain he had lived with for the past eight months had suddenly overwhelmed him. Just as he was about to voice his concern, the young man straightened, drew a deep breath, wiped his forearm across his eyes and turned to face him.

"You're laughing," Caleb accused. He shot a suspicious glance at Badger, but the old man was stuffing a wad of chewing tobacco into his mouth. "Damn!" he said, beginning to get angry. "The both of you think I'm a fool, don't you? A rich fool, just like she does."

Guthrie shook his head but he was still fighting down the laughter. "Nossir," he said. "God's truth, we don't. Nobody in this whole valley feels that way about you. But the look on your face while she was talkin' to you…" He ducked away again in another paroxysm of laughter, and Caleb watched him. He couldn't remember ever seeing Guthrie Sloane laugh before. He swung around to face Badger, but the cowboy's expression was neutral.

"Yepper." Badger nodded, working the tobacco into position with his tongue. "It took millions of years for man to evolve from monkeys, but a woman can make a monkey out of a man in seconds." He pondered for moment before adding, "Now I ask you, is that the least little bit fair?"

The anger drained out of Caleb as quickly as it had come, and he slumped in defeat, resting his forearms on the porch railing. "All right, then, have your laugh. But just remember, we're in this buffalo fiasco together.'' He gazed toward the pole barn, watched the horses walking about in the corral, and felt his tension slowly ebb. ''Tomorrow the work begins, but tomorrow's still half a day away. I'm heading to the cabin for a nightcap, and you're welcome to join me.'' He started down the porch steps, and the two men fell in behind, trailed by the cow dog. Halfway to the cabin he paused and looked back up at the ranch house. ''Did any of those boys say one word during supper?'' he said.

''Nossir,'' Guthrie said. ''Nary a one.'' He stood beside him, wearing a puzzled frown. ''It's like they were just sitting there, waiting for something to happen.''

''Yeah,'' Caleb said. ''But what?''

WHEN THE KITCHEN was tidied and the dishes washed, dried and put away, Pony walked into the living room looking for the boys, but they were nowhere to be found. Ramalda had retreated to her bedroom after banking the cookstove and lighting the oil lamps, and Pony allowed herself the luxury of enjoying the peaceful room in silence. It was a comfortable space, not too big, with the fireplace as its focal point. Above the mantel hung an old gilt-framed oil painting of a herd of longhorn cattle being driven across an arid plain, with a wall of mountains shimmering in the heat-baked distance. She knew little of art but recognized and admired the quality of the work.

A couch and two overstuffed chairs flanked the fireplace, and there were bookshelves on either side, filled with hardcover books. She withdrew a few to thumb through the pages. A book by Einstein about the theory of relativity. A very old copy of Stewart Edward White's *The Forest*. Her eye caught another title and she drew the book from its spot. *Hanta Yo,* by Ruth Beebe Hill. This volume was well-worn and her hands caressed it as if she had found an old friend after a long absence. She had read this book as a young girl, read it again as an adolescent, read it one more time in college. It had taken her on a mystical journey down the red road, and she had absorbed more each time she'd traveled it.

The room had a pleasing smell, a mingling of cedar, saddle leather and winter apples, though she could find no evidence of any such things. The floor was sheathed in wide boards and covered over with a large handwoven rug of Navajo design. There were several periodicals scattered on a scuffed plank coffee table in front of the sofa—cattlemen's journals and such. And over on the wall, beneath a window, was a desk with a large computer workstation. The computer seemed glaringly out of place in this room. Pony replaced the book and walked down the hallway that led to the bedrooms, tapping lightly on the boys' door.

Nothing.

She peeked into her own room. Empty. She walked through the kitchen and out onto the porch, standing in the darkness and wondering where they were. Her eyes came to rest on the dark bulk of the pole barn, and she descended the porch steps and walked toward it. She could hear the horses moving about in the corral as she drew near and the murmur of low voices from inside the barn. She opened one half of the big door just wide enough to peek inside, and stared, unnoticed, at the sight of five boys and one flashlight crowded around a big western stock saddle draped over a stall partition.

"No, stupid," she heard Jimmy say as the flashlight beam shifted. "That's called the *horn*. This part back *here* is the cantle."

"Then what's *this* thing called?" Martin said, and Jimmy's head bent over the little paperback guidebook he carried—the one Pony had given him a week ago.

"That's the cinch. It goes around the horse's belly and holds the saddle on."

Pony quietly closed the barn door and stood for a moment beneath the bright spangle of stars. She smiled with relief at what she had just witnessed. It was going to be okay. If Caleb McCutcheon didn't send them packing tomorrow, everything would be all right. And in the event that he allowed them to stay, she had some studying of her own to do before blowing out the lamp. In her little bag she had packed the notebook that Pete Two Shirts had given her, filled with his unruly, nearly illegible scrawl. It contained all his notes about the buffalo—everything he had come to know from his years of working with the tribal bison herd.

Pete had given her the notebook shortly after finding out she'd gotten the job. He'd come to the school again—it was a safe place to see her, a neutral place—and he'd waited until the children had gone home before walking into the classroom and laying the book on her desk. "Thought you might need this," he said. "In case you've forgotten what you learned that summer."

The blood had left her head with a rush, and for a

moment, looking up at him from the relative security of her chair, she felt as if she might faint. "I will *never* forget," she said. "I only wish I could."

His eyes had held hers in a steely grip that she couldn't break. "Don't let the past haunt you, Pony. Don't let it destroy your life."

He was right. She knew he was right. But she couldn't change what had happened by pretending that it hadn't. She would have to live with the guilt for the rest of her life.

Now Pony climbed the ranch-house steps, arms wrapped tightly around her waist, and stood for a moment in the vast, almost-palpable silence of the night. She suddenly felt alone and lonely, overwhelmed and scared. Sometimes those dark memories became too powerful to push back and she felt as if she were drowning in all the mistakes she'd made.

Sometimes, she wished she'd died that summer.

CALEB MCCUTCHEON WAS NOT a night owl, but at one o'clock in the morning he was still reading by lamplight, studying the history of the Crow Indian tribe. He was reading a book called *Parading Through History* by Frederick E. Hoxie, because he felt compelled to learn more about Pony and her boys. He found the book fascinating enough to make a pot of coffee at midnight, turn up the lamp wick and draw an old wool blanket over his lap to thwart the night chill. At 1:00 a.m. he paused to listen to the wild and eerie song of a group of coyotes yipping in the foothills and wondered where the old bull buffalo was, glancing at the window and hoping he wouldn't see the reflection of the great beast looking back at him.

He didn't. He got up, poured himself another cup

of coffee and returned to the comfortable chair, the warm blanket and the book. It was 2:00 a.m. before he finally blew out the lamp and went to bed, and a short three hours later he was rolling out from under the warm blankets with a reluctant moan, boiling up a fresh pot of coffee, drinking his first cup on the porch, bare toes curled over the edge of the weathered porch boards, and shivering in the quiet, mist-shrouded dawn.

He watched the graceful, ghostlike mule deer coming down to the creek for one final drink before heading back to the safety of the high country. He didn't see the buffalo and was relieved that he didn't have to chase the shaggy monster off his porch. He heard a horse whinny up at the corrals. Billy? Might be. Kind of sounded like that old bay gelding. Maybe he was telling Caleb to get a move on, to get on up there and fork down some hay, scoop out some grain, get on about the business of the day. Daylight was burning, after all.

And what might the business be today? Caleb raised his cup for a mouthful of hot strong brew. Saw Pony's face in the wraith of steam that rose. Felt his heart rate accelerate. Fear? Anticipation? Or something else altogether? She had reprimanded him well last night. Put him in his place. He felt no resentment toward her for pointing out the truth, but nonetheless there was this need to prove himself in some way. To somehow change the image she had of him as a rich fool playing with a bunch of toys.

Thirty minutes later he was washed, dressed and walking up to the barn to feed the horses, more than halfway wishing that he'd never heard the word *buffalo* before. Never set eyes on one of the impressive monsters, never listened to Pete Two Shirts's advice, and most of all, he found himself thinking he might've been better off if he'd never met the slender young woman called Oo-je-en-whatever-the-hell the rest of her name was.

She threw him completely off balance. He didn't know what to make of her, how to treat her or how to relate to her. And for some reason, he wanted desperately to be able to relate to her.

Most of all, he wanted her to see that he was more than just an ex–baseball player who had hit the big time and retired rich. He wanted her to see that he could measure up in her world, but a sudden thought drew him up short, just shy of the corrals.

Could he?

PONY WASN'T USED to hot running water in any form. Not since college days had she known such bliss. She stood in the steamy heat of the shower and let the water needle the spot between her shoulder blades that was always tight, always tense. She closed her eyes, tipped her head back and sighed deeply. The boys, once they discovered it, would be hard to get out of the bathroom. Or maybe they had all grown up with showers at their homes. Most did, nowadays. But Pony had stayed in the place where her grandmother had lived and raised her, and the old shack had never known the luxury of indoor plumbing. Their baths had been laborious events that involved heating quantities of water and standing in a zinc washtub, scrubbing up and pouring dippers of hot water over themselves.

Or jumping into the river and washing quickly in the icy water. Neither way could compare to this. A person could get addicted to this sort of thing quite easily. A hot shower cleansed not only the body but the mind as well, banishing tension and dark thoughts with a healing balm of steam.

A sudden bang on the door startled her. "I'm almost done!" she called. "One more minute!"

She shut off the water, grabbed a towel from a wall peg and exited the shower stall, dripping on the floor until she spied a short coarse towel and flung it down to stand upon. She dried herself briskly and efficiently, wrapped her hair in the thick towel and began dressing. Her thoughts raced as she pulled on her jeans and buttoned her shirt. Would McCutcheon show up at breakfast and tell them that he had no further use for her and the boys? Would they be piling back into her rusted old truck and driving back to the rez to look for jobs as farm laborers for the summer?

It might happen. After her poor performance at supper last night, Caleb McCutcheon would be well within his rights to fire her. And she would not, could not blame him. But she hoped that he would give her and the boys a chance to prove themselves.

There was another forceful bang on the door.

"Okay, okay!" she said, grabbing her toiletry kit. She opened the door and a cloud of steam escaped past her, unnoticed, as she stared speechlessly up at Caleb McCutcheon, who looked rugged and handsome and very, very stern. "I'm fired, aren't I?" she said as the towel unraveled from her head and tumbled down with a cascade of damp black hair as she reached to grab it. "It's all right. I understand completely."

He stared for a moment as if she had spoken in a

foreign language. "One of your boys is missing," he said.

"Who?" she said, snatching for the loose towel with a sharp clench of panic.

"Roon. When I came up for breakfast Jimmy told me that he never slept in his bed last night."

"Oh, no." She edged past him and raced down the hallway to her room, where she threw down the towel and the kit and grabbed her jacket.

"Where do you think he might be?" McCutcheon asked from the doorway.

"I don't know," she replied, breathless with anxiety. "But I have to find him. He's so alone." She whirled to face him. "He was on suicide watch at the reservation." She shrugged into her jacket, her hair long, tangled and dripping wet, and would have rushed out the doorway but his hand closed on her upper arm, gently halting her.

"I'll help you look," he said, "but dry your hair first. You'll catch a cold, going out into the dawn like that."

BY THE TIME Guthrie and Blue arrived at the ranch, the bedlam surrounding Roon's disappearance had been somewhat calmed by a domineering Ramalda, who had the other four boys under her scrutiny at the kitchen table. She set a fresh pot of coffee atop the table as he came into the kitchen, and said, in her very broken English, "You sit," nodding to his chair, and then, "They went to look for missing boy. You eat. You too thin. You sick, maybe?"

Guthrie hung his hat on a wall peg and glanced at the four boys who sat at the table. Jimmy, Martin, Joe and Dan. "Roon's gone?" he said.

Jimmy nodded. "Never slept in his bed last night. Must've run off." The boy's thin shoulders lifted and fell on a shrug. "Maybe he didn't want to work here."

Guthrie sat down and poured himself a cup of coffee. "So they're searching for him?"

Jimmy nodded again. "They left about half an hour ago. They took the truck."

"You think he went back to the reservation?"

"Maybe. Roon doesn't say much."

Guthrie tasted his coffee and glanced at Ramalda, who was stirring something on the stove. He got to his feet, taking his cup with him. "Maybe I'll go down to the barn and check on the horses while she finishes up breakfast. You boys stay put."

Blue followed closely as Guthrie descended the porch steps. His hip pained him badly, and no amount of willpower could negate the depth of that pain. He took the steps one by one, carefully balancing the cup of strong brew and rewarding himself with another sip when he reached the bottom. He limped down to the barn, where the horses were milling about in the corrals, having already finished their hay and grain. Billy Budd watched his approach, ears pricked and dark eyes calm and intelligent. "Hey, Billy," Guthrie said, leaning against the fence and reaching to brush the long tangled forelock out of the gelding's eyes. "Hey, old man."

He pushed the inquisitive muzzle gently away and was turning toward the barn when he froze and looked back into the corral. He counted heads once, then twice. The little grulla mare named Mouse was missing. He finished his coffee, set the cup on a post and grabbed a rope hanging inside the barn. The horses immediately crowded to the opposite side of the corral with much snorting and head tossing when he opened the gate. It was a game to them, this duck-and-shy business. Any one of them would gladly spend the day under saddle out on the range, but that didn't mean they'd rush over and open their mouths for the bit. Nossir. They liked this little game and they played it well, but they knew when Guthrie shook out his rope that it wouldn't last long.

He dabbed the loop over Gunner, the dun gelding that Jimmy had favored, and twenty minutes later he was in the saddle and he and Blue were heading up the trail that edged the creek, following the tracks of a little mouse-colored mare and hoping that they would lead him to Roon.

"SO TELL ME," Caleb said as he pointed his pickup toward Katy Junction. "What did you mean when you said that Roon was on suicide watch?"

Pony was looking out the windows, scanning the sides of the road, the ditches, the gullies. "He tried to kill himself after he was caught stealing a bottle of whiskey from a liquor store. He thought they were going to put him in jail, so he took a rope and tried to hang himself."

Caleb glanced at her, appalled. "He failed, obviously."

"The rope he used was rotten and it broke. His mother found him unconscious in the shed. Adolescents who are at risk for suicide are given special counseling and are monitored closely at school, but when Roon dropped out of school he lost that support. Then his parents and younger siblings left the reservation, and shortly after that he came to me."

"Has he tried suicide again?"

Pony shook her head. "That doesn't mean he won't. I try to talk to him, but he is so full of anger. He keeps it all inside and shares nothing. I hoped that a summer on your ranch, being outdoors and doing hard physical work, would help him work through this bad time."

Caleb drove in silence for a while, and when he passed through Katy Junction he slowed and, on a hunch, pulled up beside a forest-green pickup with official insignia on its side, parked in front of the Longhorn Cafe. "Ben Comstock, the warden, is inside," he explained. "I'll just go in and tell him to keep his eyes peeled, then we'll head wherever you think Roon might have gone."

"The only world he knows is the reservation," she said. "But his family is gone. I don't know why he would want to return there."

She waited in the truck while he went inside and stepped up to the counter beside Ben Comstock, nodding to Badger and Charlie, who were sharing their usual table and quarreling about something. Bernie slid a cup of coffee in front of him, and Comstock gave him a questioning glance over the rim of his own cup.

"What's wrong?" Bernie asked. "You've got trouble written all over your face."

"I've lost one of my hired hands," Caleb explained. "A thirteen-year-old named Roon."

Badger abandoned his quarrel with Charlie, pushed out of his chair and carried his coffee to the counter. "Well, I guess it's begun," he said with a shake of his head. "The work was too much for them and they're sneakin' off."

"The work hasn't even started yet," Caleb reminded him. "He never slept in his bed last night."

"That right?" Badger cocked an eyebrow. "Hell, when I cowboyed full-time at that ranch, I use to throw my bedroll up in the hayloft. It sure beat listening to Charlie and Drew snoring their brains out in the bunkhouse, and a bed of sweet-smelling hay is pretty tough to beat."

"Did you check the barn?" Comstock asked.

Caleb felt a flush of embarrassment. "Well, actually, no. Never thought to. I fed the horses, but I didn't check up in the loft."

Bernie handed him the portable phone. "Call the ranch and have someone go look," she said. "He's probably sound asleep. Boys his age need lots of it."

Caleb dialed. Ramalda answered. He tried several times to get her to put one of the boys on but she didn't understand. *"No comprendo, no comprendo!"* she kept repeating. "Hold on!" he ordered, laid the phone on the counter and went back out to the truck. "I need you to tell Ramalda to put one of the boys on the phone," he told Pony. "Badger and Comstock seem to think Roon might be sleeping up in the barn loft and I need them to go check for me."

Pony followed him into the restaurant, eliciting admiring glances from the male patrons and a warm, welcoming smile from Bernie. She picked up the phone and spoke a stream of rapid-fire Spanish into it, listening for a long moment afterward before ending the conversation with words that even Caleb understood. *"Sí, sí, muchas gracias, Ramalda. Hasta luego."* She handed the phone to Bernie and looked at him. "Roon took one of the horses and Guthrie has gone after him,'' she said, then abruptly turned on her heel and departed the little restaurant.

''Yepper.'' Badger nodded sagely as soon as the door closed behind her, smoothing his mustache with the knuckle of his forefinger. ''Horse stealing is one of an Injun's favorite old-time occupations. That and killing buffalo.''

CHAPTER FIVE

GUTHRIE HAD NO IDEA if Roon knew much about horses, but the boy was headed for the high country on a mare that could take him there and then some. Guthrie also didn't know how much of a head start Roon had. He gave Gunner free rein and let him lope when he could in order to close the distance between himself and the boy more rapidly, but soon the only gait possible was a walk or jog as the trail climbed the steepening flank of Montana Mountain, heading toward Dead Woman Pass.

"Damn-fool kid," he muttered, reining Gunner in to let the gelding blow after a particularly steep stretch. He would have swung out of the saddle and led the horse for a while but he wasn't sure he'd be able to get back aboard. "Sooner or later he'll run into snow. The pass is still full of it." Gunner's ears flickered at the sound of Guthrie's voice, and he rubbed the horse's shoulder with a gloved hand. "Where does he think he's going to, and what's he running from?"

It was easy enough to track the mare. She was freshly shod, and her hoofprints were clearly defined by her iron shoes. By noon those hoofprints had left the main trail and skirted along the south flank of the mountain, as if heading toward the high meadow and the line camp at Piney Creek. When he finally spotted the mare, he did a double take before reining in the dun gelding. Mouse was standing beside a big out-cropping of rock, grazing on the tender shoots of young grass at its base. The boy was sitting on the rock, arms folded and resting on his knees, which were drawn to his chest. In one hand he held the mare's halter rope. Roon sat motionlessly while Guth-rie approached. Only the mare showed any response, raising her head and whickering softly when she rec-ognized Gunner, then lowering it to sniff at the little cow dog.

The sun was strong here, and it felt good. Guthrie eased himself in the saddle and let the warmth soak into him. The boy didn't speak. Guthrie gazed out at the distance that reached beyond the rugged peaks of the Beartooth Mountains, beyond the plains, beyond the boundaries of his imagination. He filled his lungs with the wild Montana wind and said, "It's real pretty up here, isn't it? You can see just about forever."

Still the boy said nothing. His hair was long and loose and blown back from his face, and his expres-sion was devoid of emotion. He kept his eyes fixed on the distance, never looking in Guthrie's direction or acknowledging his presence. Guthrie reached back and unbuckled a saddlebag. He took out a couple of Snickers bars and several long twisted pieces of dried beef wrapped in a piece of muslin cloth. "You must be hungry after that ride." He reached over and laid the snacks on the rock beside the boy. "It ain't much, but it'll hold you till Ramalda can fill you up proper." He bit into a piece of jerky and commenced to chew. "Jessie made this stuff," he commented after he'd worked on it for a while. "I guess she figures most of the enjoyment is in the chewin', because it takes about half an hour of solid work before you can swallow the stuff. Not that I'm complaining. It's mighty tasty.''

He finished the stick of jerky and decided against a second, tossing it to Blue instead and uncapping his water bottle for a long drink. The dog devoured the tough beef strip with no problem at all. ''Well, I guess if we're gonna make it back before dark, we'd best get started. Drink?'' he offered, extending the water bottle.

Roon looked at him for the first time. His eyes were black and turbulent with some emotion Guthrie couldn't read. ''I came here looking for the buffalo,'' he said.

Guthrie capped the bottle. ''They're up here somewheres, I don't doubt.'' He dangled the bottle's strap around the saddle horn. ''Maybe we'll spot 'em on the way down. We'll head over to Piney Creek and start down from there. That's where we spotted 'em last, over on the Piney.''

The black eyes studied him intently. ''I took one of your horses.''

Guthrie nodded. ''A good horse, too. Mouse is about as tough as they come. You did well to ride her that way. She's an independent-minded lady.'' He smoothed the dun's mane, wishing the pain in his hip would ebb and dreading the ride back down the mountain. He drew a steadying breath and tugged his hat down a bit tighter against the pull of the wind. ''Well, Blue, let's see if we can't scare us up some buff,'' he said to the dog as he headed Gunner into a downhill walk, angling the slope toward the cutoff that led to Piney Creek. He didn't look behind to see if Roon was following. There was nothing he could do to make the boy obey. There was only the certainty that the sun was westering, that the ride ahead of them was long, and that darkness would eventually come.

By the time the dun entered a grove of wind-stunted spruce less than a quarter mile from the rock outcropping, Guthrie heard the swift, light hoofbeats of the grulla mare playing catch-up, and his stomach muscles unclenched.

It would have been a sorry thing to have returned to the ranch without Roon.

PONY SHADED HER EYES against the powerful rays of the setting sun and looked for the hundredth time to where the trail to Dead Woman Pass began. Nothing. She whirled about, digging her hands into her jeans pockets and rounding her shoulders. What had Roon been thinking, riding off with one of McCutcheon's horses like that? A whole day wasted—watching and waiting for Guthrie Sloane to return from his ride into the high country. And hoping that Roon would be with him.

McCutcheon had been understandably grim on the drive back to the ranch after learning that Roon had taken one of the horses. "You told me that he once stole a bottle of whiskey from a liquor store," he said. "Has he stolen anything else that you know of?"

"Yes," she said quietly. "When he first came to my house, he stole five dollars from my purse to buy a pack of cigarettes."

"Just once?"

"Just once. I told him not to come back, that I would not live with such disrespect. But he came back anyway a week later and repaid me the five dollars. He said he'd earned it digging a garden plot for one of the elders. I didn't believe him, so I asked and it was true."

"And you let him stay."

"Yes. Roon's a good boy. He's trying."

"He took one of my horses."

"He borrowed your horse, perhaps to see if that horse has any worth."

"And what will he do if he discovers that the horse has worth?"

"He might just steal it." She turned to stare directly at him. "And then he might paint its shoulders and flanks with his handprints, and ride it into battle against enemy warriors."

McCutcheon let his foot off the accelerator. The truck coasted, slowing. "So how does a boy like Roon become a man in the twenty-first century?"

"I don't know," she said, her voice gentling, surprised that he understood. "I wish I did, but I don't."

The truck rolled to a stop. "I sense that Roon isn't the only one who has a lot of anger inside him."

Pony dropped her eyes from his intense gaze and felt a strange shortness of breath. "I have learned to live with the way things are."

"Have you?"

A surge of rage heated her blood, and she raised her eyes. "Who are you, to ask such a question?"

"I'm your boss," he said. "But I'm beginning to wonder if being your boss is a particularly safe occupation."

Pony had remained silent for the rest of the journey back to the ranch, and once there, McCutcheon had left her at the main house and gone to his own cabin as if relieved to be rid of her company. And why shouldn't he be? Had she brought him anything thus far in her short employ but trouble? She turned and looked toward his cabin. Rich man that he was, it made perfect sense that he would be sitting on his porch, reading a book and lazing the long summer afternoon away. She shoved her hands deeper into her pockets and drew a deep breath, shoring up her resolve.

Tomorrow she would take the boys and leave here. Go back to the reservation. They could get field jobs for the summer, working for any number of farmers in the area who would be delighted to hire a bunch of Indians for minimum wage or less. Maybe she could get a job up in Billings, working at one of the bigger hotels cleaning rooms. She had heard that the money was pretty good, and sometimes there were tips, too. Either way, field hand or housekeeper, it would be better than staying here and living under Caleb McCutcheon's stern and disapproving rule.

CALEB FOLDED the top corner of the page of the book on Crow Indian history and raised his head, listening. The noise of the creek rushing past was a constant undercurrent of sound, but he'd heard something else. The solid footfalls of a horse—no, two horses—coming down the trail. He laid the book aside and stood, leaning over the porch rail and looking upstream to where the trail emerged from the timber. Guthrie came into view first, riding Gunner. Behind him came Roon, riding bareback with nothing more than a halter and a rope to guide the grulla. Caleb stared. Leaned out farther and caught a glimpse of Pony. She must have been waiting at the trailhead for them. She took the halter and stopped the mare, and he could hear her say, quite clearly, "Roon! What were you think-ing?"

Caleb descended the porch steps, listening, watch-ing as Guthrie halted his mount. "Don't be too hard on him, ma'am," Guthrie said as Caleb approached. "I guess you could say this was his first day on the job, being as he spent most of it chasing after this runaway mare."

Pony swung on him. *"Runaway?"*

"Yes, ma'am. She's a real escape artist, a wild mustang through and through. Come spring, the urge to wander gets real strong. She must've jumped the corral fence and taken off for the high country."

She looked back at Roon. "Is that true?"

"'Course it is," Guthrie replied before Roon could answer. "Why, if it weren't for Roon, here, that mare might've made for the Dakotas. She was heading straight up Dead Woman Pass and going like a bat out of hell."

"And Roon caught her?" Pony said.

"Yes, ma'am. When she hit the snow in the pass she turned around and went right to him. All the spit and vinegar went out of her when she saw that deep snow and she started thinkin' about how nice a scoop of grain would taste." Guthrie looked at Roon. "Mat-ter of fact, why don't you take her to the corral, rub her down, give her a big feed of oats and a couple flakes of hay. She must be gettin' hungry about now. Then go to the house and wash up. Ramalda hates it when we're late for supper."

The boy nodded somberly and kneed the mare up-hill toward the barn. Pony watched after him for a long moment then turned back to Guthrie, catching sight of Caleb at the same time. She shoved her hands into her rear pockets. "That was quite a story," she said to Guthrie.

"The boy's a good horseman," Guthrie said.

"He took the horse, didn't he?"

"Ma'am, I remember what it was like to be his age," Guthrie said. "I came to this ranch when I was thirteen. Me'n my daddy were hired on, and it was like a miracle, being able to live and work here. It changed my life." Guthrie glanced at Caleb. "Maybe it can change his, too," he said. "Hell, all the boy wanted was to see the buffalo." He straightened in the saddle and reined his horse down the trail that paralleled the creek.

"Ramalda's probably waiting supper," Caleb said as Gunner stepped past.

"Me'n Blue are headin' for home. It's been a long day. I'll see you first thing in the morning."

Watching Guthrie ride off toward his own place, Caleb's shoulders slumped around a weary sigh. He glanced at Pony. "Well, Roon's safe and no harm was done. We'd better head on up to the house. Guthrie's right. Ramalda hates it when we're late."

"I'm sorry," she said, staring right at him with those dark eyes that stirred all kinds of turbulent feelings within him.

"Sorry?" he said, gently touching her elbow to turn her toward the ranch and falling into step beside her. "Whatever for? I should be thanking you. The way Guthrie tells it, one of your boys just saved one of my best mares."

BADGER WAS WAITING on the porch, thumbs hooked in his belt, hat pushed back, and a big chaw of tobacco bulging in his cheek. He spat over the railing as Caleb and Pony climbed the steps, wiped his mouth on his shirtsleeve and nodded his head toward the kitchen door. "They're inside, all five of 'em," he said, as if accounting for a road crew of convicted felons. "Washed up and waiting for their chow. Only thing holdin' things up is the two of you."

Caleb paused beside him while Pony went inside. "Did you look the mare over?"

Badger nodded. "She's fine. A little tuckered, but that was a good day's ride for her and she sure enough needed it. Where's Guthrie?"

"He headed home. Took the dun gelding and left his truck here." Caleb removed his hat and ran his fingers through his hair. "He looked pretty wrung out."

"Probably couldn't get out of the saddle after that long ride, or didn't want to try in front of an audience."

"That's what I figured. I'm going to head over there in a little bit and make sure he got home okay."

"He won't like that," Badger cautioned.

"I know, but he was in rough shape." Caleb pushed through the kitchen door followed by the old cowboy, hung his hat on a wall peg, nodded to Ramalda and washed up at the kitchen sink. The boys were sitting quietly around the table. He sat down next to Badger, poured himself a cup of coffee, picked up a fresh biscuit and broke it in half.

"Boys," he said, buttering the biscuit, "I'd advise you to hit the sack early tonight because tomorrow I want you down at the corrals at dawn. We're going for a little ride. I think it's time we found the buffalo, and they're high on the mountain right now, hiding out in some rough country." He filled his plate with

Ramalda's savory stew and pushed the deep kettle toward Badger. "There's no way to get there except by horseback, and it'll be tough going." He shifted his gaze to Pony. "I was told that you boys all know how to ride, so I won't worry about it."

He spooned up a mouthful of stew, still watching Pony, and she dropped her eyes, color staining her smooth cheeks. "We'll be there," she said. "At dawn."

"Good. Ramalda, Guthrie's gone home to check Jessie's mares. I'll bring him some of your delicious supper, if you'll pack it up for me."

Ramalda may not have spoken much English but she understood what he asked and set about the task immediately.

"Badger, can you be here by 5:00 a.m.?"

"Sure thing, boss," Badger nodded.

Caleb finished his bowl and got up. He ate the last of his biscuit, took the wire-bailed pot and muslin sack of biscuits from Ramalda and left the table. He grabbed his hat on the way out and pulled it on as he descended the steps, feeling ornery and out of sorts. He was pretty sure some of those boys had never set foot in a stirrup before. Roon could ride, that much was certain, and Pony, too. But it was time to throw down the gauntlet. He wouldn't allow himself to be trampled by a bunch of delinquent boys. If Roon was any indication of what they were capable of, this could prove to be a difficult summer.

He drove to Guthrie's place pondering his strategy. Should he turn his head the other way when he saw errant behavior, or rule with an iron fist on all issues? He had no idea which method would be more effective. No idea how to make them behave. Could anyone control a teenager, or did they simply rule the earth? How much leeway did Pony give them? The whole issue baffled him.

It was nearly dark by the time he parked below Guthrie's cabin. He was relieved to see that his foreman had made it home okay and that Gunner was browsing on a pile of good timothy hay in the corral. Guthrie was sitting on the bottom porch step, his bad leg outstretched and the other raised. Blue sat beside him, apparently too weary to do much more than wag her tail in greeting as Caleb approached.

Guthrie removed his hat and dangled it on his fingers. "I don't recall ordering out," he said.

"Ramalda sent me over with some supper. She was kind of put out that you didn't eat with us, but I told her you had to check on Jessie's mares...." Caleb's voice trailed off into silence beneath Guthrie's sardonic stare.

"I'm fine. I made it here just fine, and I'll make it to work in the morning just fine. It was a long day, that's all, and I was too tired to feel sociable."

Caleb nodded. "I told the boys we were going to find the buffalo tomorrow."

"Good. Get it out of their system."

"I don't want you riding for a while. There's a lot to do on the computer. We're way behind entering data, and—"

"I can ride," Guthrie said, his voice carrying an edge. "I'll take the boys to find them buffalo."

"Back up in the high country?"

"Yessir."

"No."

Caleb walked past him, climbed the steps and entered the cabin. Blue skirted past him, anxious for her own supper. He found a lamp and lit it, glancing around for the bottle of prescription pain pills. He gave up the search and focused on Blue's supper instead, opening a can of meat, mixing it with kibble and a little water, and putting it down for her. "There you go, old girl. Eat up." He watched her for a moment as she dived enthusiastically into the bowl. "Okay," he called from the cabin door. "Where are you keeping your pills these days?"

"I threw 'em out," Guthrie said. "They addled my head."

"They cut the pain, and you need some relief from it, especially right now."

"I'm fine."

"If you're so damn fine, then why are you sitting there?" He stood for a few moments then pushed through the screen door and descended the steps. "Come on," he said, extending a hand.

Guthrie started out toward the creek. "Goddammit."

Caleb kept his hand out. "Food's getting cold." For a long moment he thought that Guthrie was going to ignore him, but then the younger man reached up and gripped the offered hand. Caleb pulled him to his feet, helped him climb one painful step at a time, guided him inside and over to the only comfortable chair the cabin boasted, and brought his supper to him. He went out to his truck and returned holding the bottle of whiskey taken from his own cabin. "This is genuine cowboy medicine, or so Badger says," he said, pouring a generous amount into a water glass. "I'm hoping you don't throw it out. It's pretty good stuff."

"Well, I just might do that," Guthrie warned as he took the glass, "if you don't share a glass with me."

"Well, I just might do that, if you let me take those boys up onto the mountain."

"Alone?"

"Badger said he'd come along." Caleb poured himself a shot and dropped into a chair. "Look, somehow I have to come to terms with those kids. I can't do that with you running interference."

"That's a hard ride."

"I've done it before. And you have to admit, my riding has improved."

Guthrie nodded. "True enough, but you don't know anything about how those boys fit in a saddle, except for Roon."

"I'm hoping they're terrible," Caleb said. "I'm hoping that they don't know which end of the horse the bridle goes on, because there has to be one thing I can do better than them."

"You've already lost that edge with Roon. He's a natural."

"I'll think of something else to impress him."

Guthrie raised his glass for a swallow. "You don't have to be better than the kids at anything," he said, blinking his eyes against the burn of the whiskey. "Bottom line, you're the boss. They work for you. If they don't like that, show 'em the door."

"You're forgetting one thing," Caleb said. "Or perhaps I should say, one woman. I want this to work for her sake."

Guthrie eased himself in his chair. "I don't blame you. She seems real nice. Worth keeping around. Okay, so you find the buffalo. What then?"

Caleb shrugged. "The boys get an eyeful. We

watch them for a while and keep our distance. Then we come home. Day after that, we start on the fences.'' He took a sip of whiskey. ''You work on the computer tomorrow and get some of that data in. Let me ramrod those kids for a day. And get that worried look off your face. I know what I'm doing. It'll be okay.''

PONY SAT UPON her bed, knees drawn up and notebook propped against them, reading by lamplight. Tomorrow at dawn they were riding out to find the buffalo. Tomorrow would prove to Caleb McCutcheon whether or not she was worth keeping on as an adviser after Roon's poor behavior today and her own poor behavior at supper the night before. She read the scrawled words laboriously, wishing she'd had the foresight to buy a good book on bison management. But then, how did one ''manage'' an animal who was already perfectly adapted to its environment? What could they do to regulate this creature who had, in fact, survived quite nicely and in enormous numbers on its own until humans nearly exterminated it?

She sighed and sat up higher. Management was all about the buffalo surviving in a world where everything was reduced to a monetary value. There was no place for spirituality in such a capitalistic, cold world. It was difficult to see the buffalo in that way.

And yet she had been hired by Caleb McCutcheon to manage the herd, and it had been her own suggestion that the buffalo help make the ranch a financial success. What did that make *her*?

A glance at the bedside clock roused her from her brooding. She glanced down at the notebook and frowned: ''...when faced with mean bulls, it is sometimes necessary to use the pistol and fire at close range…'' She read the passage several times and then closed the notebook. Definitely a worst-case scenario—a mean bull charging. The chances of it happening were practically nil.

Pete had given her a pistol along with the notebook, and several boxes of bullets. She laid the book down and climbed off the bed, reaching for her small bag on the chair. She drew forth the Smith & Wesson .357, and stared at it for a moment. Carrying a weapon seemed like overkill, but perhaps not. If somebody's life was threatened, she would have to take action. She rummaged in the bag for the box of bullets, sat down on the edge of the bed and loaded the gun.

By 5:00 A.M. it was plenty light enough to saddle the horses, and Badger did so with practiced ease. He loved these long days of summer, loved the long days in the saddle, loved life as much now, at seventy-five, as he had as a boy when his ma use to call him down from the loft at dawn and kiss the top of his head to start each day. He saddled the horses and when he was done, he leaned against the corral fence and watched the dawn paint the mountain peaks a pale yellow. He felt a pang at the beauty of the sight, the same lonesome pang he felt at the clear, pure ring of a church bell tolling for some unknown soul.

''Badger?'' The voice at his elbow startled him and he stared down at the boy, Jimmy, standing flat-footed with his small hands shoved into his jeans pockets. ''Can we pick out our own horses?''

He scowled, rubbing the back of his neck. ''No, you can't!'' He glared at the boy, and Jimmy stared back in an innocent sort of way that made Badger draw his horns in. "But if you could," he said, his gruff voice gentling a bit, "who'd you choose?"

The boy didn't hesitate. "This one," he said, pointing to Billy.

"Well now, that's a fine choice. Only trouble is, that there's the boss's horse. He always rides Billy."

"Oh." Jimmy's face revealed nothing. He studied the others. "That one, then." He pointed.

"Huh." Badger pulled at his whiskery chin. "Well, that's not a bad horse for a greenhorn. Can you ride?"

Jimmy's eyes fixed on his. "No," he said.

Badger gave the boy a curt nod of approval. "Then you done all right, pickin' old Sparky. He used to put up a big fuss back when he was a youngster, but he's a long ways from that now. Hell, if Sparky can even hold a lope for more'n a minute, I'll eat my hat. He'll do for you, son, and he'll bring you home safe."

Jimmy frowned at Sparky. "You think he'll be too slow? I don't want to miss seeing the buffalo."

"Sparky? Hell, no. He'll get you there and back, with some stories to tell." Badger looked around. Joe, Martin, Dan and Roon had all arrived and were eyeing the horses with varying degrees of interest. "You boys are gettin' off easy today," he said to them, spitting and wiping his chin. "You'll be saddling your own hay burners after this."

Roon looked at him and puffed out a bit, the way a young man will. "I don't need a saddle," he said.

"Suit yourself, but what you'll tie your rope off to is anyone's guess."

"I don't need a rope," the boy challenged.

"No?" Badger pushed his hat back and regarded

the youth with a puzzled expression. "The way I heard it, yesterday you rode Mouse using nothing more than a rope and a halter. I thought that was mighty impressive, given that she's an ornery bitch and just as likely to pitch you off as pack you around. But if you can ride her with just a halter, I'd sure as hell like to see that."

The two regarded each other with mutual dislike and then Roon's eyes dropped. "It's the white man's way," he muttered. "Saddles and ropes."

"You show me a better way and I'll pay the strictest attention," Badger said. "Meantime, you boys pick out your horses. Here comes the boss, and he don't like to waste much time on foolishness."

PONY COULDN'T EAT the breakfast fajita that Ramalda offered, nor could she drink the milk. She stood on the porch staring down at the corrals and felt a churning in her stomach. It had been several years since she'd ridden a horse, and at least that long since she'd fired a gun.

She spotted McCutcheon walking toward the corrals and drew a deep breath. She watched him for a few moments, admiring the graceful, athletic way he moved and wondering again why there wasn't a woman in his life. A man like McCutcheon needed a woman to care for him, not just the way Ramalda did, cooking and keeping his house. He needed a woman to tend his heart. Caleb McCutcheon's heart was lonely and no amount of good food would fill the emptiness. Pony was startled when he paused, glanced at the ranch house, spotted her on the porch and raised his arm in a beckoning wave.

"Come on!" he called in his deep, pleasing voice.

"Daylight's burning, and we've got a lot of miles to cover."

Her heart leaped. Moments later she reached the corral, where Badger was fitting the boys to their stirrup leathers. Jimmy was already aboard, walking his horse slowly around the corral. Roon stood apart from the rest, as if disdaining the entire procedure. Caleb was feeding something to his chosen mount, a handsome bay gelding that stood taller than all the others. He caught her eye and grinned. "One of Ramalda's corn tortillas," he explained, stroking the gelding's silken neck. "Billy has a fondness for them."

Pony took the reins of a gray gelding from Badger's outstretched hand. "His name's Dobey," he said, cheek bulging with tobacco. "He's a smooth ride, won't give you no trouble."

Dobey was small and fine-boned, with the distinctively dished forehead and convex nose of a Spanish mustang. His eyes were wide set and dark, and he extended his velvety muzzle to delicately waft her scent. "Hello, Dobey," she murmured, smoothing the long thick forelock down the center of his face.

"Okay, let's burn some trail!" Badger said. "Boss'll ride point and I'll ride drag. How you boys sort yourself out in the middle is up to you. Ma'am," he said to her, "you'd best ride up behind Caleb. That way, if he has any buffalo questions, you'll be right there with all the answers."

Pony nodded and climbed aboard Dobey, who stood quietly while she adjusted her stirrup leathers to the proper length. Badger opened the corral gate and held it while they filed out. "I feel like a wrangler at a dude ranch," he groused, spitting at a fence post and watching them ride past. "Boys, you're about to find out that there's a whole lot more to ridin' a horse than just sittin' in the saddle and lettin' your feet dangle. It'll be some kind of miracle if you don't all fall off on the first rough stretch.''

"We won't fall off, old man," Roon said, kneeing his horse past. "It'll be you who holds us up on the rough stretches!"

Pony opened her mouth to deliver a rebuke but never had the chance because Badger instantly did something that catapulted Roon out of the saddle and landed him in a heap on the far side of his horse. She heard the muffled "Oof!" of expelled breath as the boy hit the ground and lay in stunned silence, staring up at the cowboy.

"Let that be your first ridin' lesson, son," Badger said smoothly as Roon's horse sidled away. "A smart-ass just don't stay in the saddle. Now dust yours off and let's ride."

CHAPTER SIX

IT WAS A FINE MORNING to be following the old Indian trace that climbed up the shoulder of Montana Mountain and led them into the clear yellow light of dawn. Caleb wished that the trail was wide enough to accommodate two horses abreast, because it would have made conversation with Pony so much easier, and he had a hundred questions for her about the buffalo. He was also anxious about the boys, especially when the trail steepened and the horses lowered their heads and lunged over certain spots. Yet every time he swiveled in his saddle to check, they were still seated. His face must have mirrored his concern because after several such backward glances Pony said calmly, "They'll be fine. Don't worry."

But he was worried. How would Roon react after his dressing-down by Badger in front of all the other boys? What had gotten into the old cowboy? It was important that everything went well, and starting the ride on such a discordant note had thwarted Caleb's plan to show the boys just how much fun a day in the saddle could be. What had prompted Badger's irritation with Roon? All Badger had said when he climbed onto a quick and sometimes mean-tempered paint called Rocket was, "Hell, boss, let's show these boys what a real mountain looks like from the back of a real horse."

Caleb didn't want this to turn into some kind of punitive marathon. He swiveled in his saddle again and caught Pony's eye. "I'm sorry about what happened to Roon," he murmured in a voice just loud enough for her to hear.

She shook her head. "He deserved it," she said. "He said something mouthy."

Pony rode with a kind of grace that gave itself to the horse. It was as if the two had become one sympathetic entity, and Caleb watched her admiringly for a few moments before turning to the front. He didn't doubt that any horse she chose to ride would carry her willingly to the ends of the earth. She had that way about her. He patted Billy's neck and after a few moments glanced behind again.

"Tell me about the buffalo."

"What do you want to know?" she said.

"Everything. I want to know their history, and how it relates to your own."

She nodded. "The buffalo held an important place in our life, our culture," she said. "They were the food we ate, the clothes we wore, the shelter that kept us from the storms. On the Medicine Wheel, the buffalo represents the north direction. The color of north is white, the same as the winter snows. The direction of north is a place of wisdom and renewal, a place of personal power based on knowledge. The buffalo is a strong spirit animal. A white buffalo is a messenger from the spirit world. White Buffalo Calf Woman is the oldest messenger, and tells of our spiritual origins."

Damn, he wanted to watch her while she spoke. Her words made a gentle cadence in the chill morning air, but the trail was steep and demanded all of his attention, so his glimpses of her were stolen between Billy's uphill lunges. "Tell me about White Buffalo Calf Woman."

The silence that followed his request was long enough that he glanced back, questioningly, and she nodded. "Long ago, before we had horses, the People were hungry and were trying to find the herds. A woman came walking upon the land, dressed in a buffalo robe that was the purest white. When she came to the village, the People welcomed her and took her into the medicine lodge and gave her the seat of honor. She gave them some sage to smudge the lodge and clear their minds, and from her bundle she drew forth a pipe with a red stone bowl and stem made of wood. She said that the red bowl represented the life-blood of all the animal people, including humans, and the stem represented all green and growing things."

A raven flew overhead, the swishing of its wings loud in the early stillness. Pony glanced up, following its flight, and then continued. "The smoke from the pipe represented the spirit of the wind, which binds all things together. The woman offered the tobacco to the four directions. She showed how this must be done starting with the east, which is the direction of birth, and then to the south, the direction of growth, then to the west, the direction of the elder years, and finally to the north, the direction of death and rebirth. The pipe should be passed always in the same direction, and in this way the People would remember the sacred circle of life and death, the moons, the seasons, the rains and the migrations, and all the moods of the earth. She told them to smoke the pipe in silence so they would remember her teachings. And then she

walked away and became a white buffalo, disappearing over the horizon.''

"So she was the old messenger," Caleb said.

"Yes. But the white people did not listen to her
message. And when the great herds were slaughtered,
the People gave up hope and thought that White Buffalo Calf Woman was dead, too. But now the buffalo
are coming back, and some think that her message
will be heard again.''

Caleb swiveled. "What do you think?''

"I think that the buffalo have gone into the mountain and will not come out again until we understand
ourselves. I think we are still a very long way from
that. We may never come to that place again.''

Caleb faced front and tried to concentrate on the
ride but all he could see was her face, the solemn
beauty of it, and hear the smooth resonance of her
words. She was like no one else that he had ever
known, and the world that she moved within was so
different from his own that he wondered if they could
ever find a common ground, a comfortable place
where they could be easy in each other's company.
As long as he was a white man and she was a Native
American, he doubted they ever could.

And suddenly there was nothing he wanted more.

ROON STARED between his horse's ears and imagined
what it would be like to make that old cowboy beg
for mercy, get down on his bended old knees and
plead for his worthless used-up life. His bitter anger
intensified as the morning drew on. He could hear the
faint murmuring of conversation between McCutcheon and Pony up ahead, but he was far more aware
of the rider directly behind him. Badger. The codger

with the bowed legs and the quick hand that had dumped him out of his saddle. No one could treat him like that and get away with it.

He hated it here. One day, two days, the summer just beginning and it felt like a prison sentence stretching out before him. He should have taken that mare yesterday and just kept riding. He could've ridden her into forever, she was that good of a horse, but when that other cowboy caught up to him, somehow he'd lost the reason for running away. Guthrie Sloane was all right. Roon thought that he could come to like that one, even though he was white. Most white men would have dressed him down for taking that mare, but Guthrie had acted as if what Roon had done had been perfectly normal. He'd also covered for Roon, making up that story about Mouse escaping from the corral when he knew that Roon had taken her in the middle of the night and ridden up on the mountain to find the buffalo.

They never saw a single one, but by that time the anger that had driven Roon into the high country had been replaced by fatigue and growing hunger, and Roon had been ready to ride back to the ranch, and to the meal that was waiting there. That Mexican woman could cook. The food was good. But good food wasn't enough to make this place a good place. This was a white man's ranch, and it was like Pony said. The rich man, McCutcheon, was keeping the buffalo like toys, and Pony and the rest of them were the token Indians in his make-believe western world.

Roon's scowl deepened. He thought about his family, how they had moved away and left him behind. Only his younger brother, Ralph, had said goodbye. He'd ridden that old bike with the bent frame clear to Pony's place and straddled it in the mud of the yard, his secondhand jacket patched with duct tape at both wrists, wearing his favorite Detroit Tigers baseball cap. "I wish you were coming, too," he'd said. "I'll send you our new address. Maybe you could write." And Roon had said, "Sure, I'll write you, Ralph," knowing he probably never would.

There was nothing left for him back at the rez and nothing for him here. There was really no reason on earth for him to be.

GUTHRIE SAT at the computer and stared at the blue screen. He had been sitting in front of it for nearly an hour now, gazing out at the morning, listening to Ramalda in the kitchen, reaching down to stroke Blue's ears and doing anything to avoid looking at the blue screen. He didn't like computers. He didn't enjoy being indoors when the day was wide open and beautiful. He didn't like typing with two fingers, searching for each letter before tapping the key. The stack of papers propped against the wooden book stand was full of ranch information and data that needed to be entered, but so far the only thing he had typed were the words *Dear Jessie* because he had thought that maybe starting out with a letter, printed on a clean white piece of paper and sent off to Arizona in the afternoon mail, would be a good start to the day.

Dear Jessie.

He sighed and arranged his leg to ease the cramping pain in his hip. "Well, Blue, at this rate we'll be here a month or better."

He heard the sound of a vehicle approaching and glanced out the window. An old truck rattled into the yard, and Pete Two Shirts climbed out, stretching his lean frame after the long drive. Guthrie pushed out of his chair, relieved to have a legitimate excuse to abandon the computer. He limped out onto the porch with Blue at his heels and shook hands with the man who climbed the steps.

"I thought I'd come by and see how Pony and the boys were making out," Pete said.

"They're up on the mountain today, looking for the buffalo. McCutcheon thought they ought to see them before starting the fence work. He thought maybe it might inspire them. C'mon inside and have a cup of coffee," Guthrie invited. "Lunch'll be ready in a little bit."

"I still dream about Ramalda's cooking," Pete said, following him into the kitchen. He took his hat off and nodded to the Mexican woman, who waved a wooden spoon in his direction, a gesture that could have been threatening or friendly. "She still likes me, that's good," Pete said with a grin, dropping into a chair. "So, the boys are behaving?"

"So far," Guthrie said, carrying the coffeepot to the table and filling two mugs.

"Roon, too?"

"Sure." Guthrie nodded, taking his seat.

"That kid has some problems. I warned Pony about that one, but she'd take in any stray. Never turns them away."

"What kind of problems?"

Pete sipped his coffee, raised his shoulders and let them fall. "He's kind of messed up in the head. My guess he'll wind up in prison if he doesn't straighten himself out. Too bad, because he's a bright kid."

"What about the other boys?"

"They're okay. Dropouts, dead-ended until Pony took them in. She'll drill enough into their heads to get them through the high-school test. I don't know how she does it, but she does it."

"She must like kids."

"She loves kids." Pete took another swallow of hot coffee and glanced around the kitchen. "I bet she likes being here."

Guthrie cupped his hands around his mug, wondering what had really brought Pete out to the ranch just three days into the summer. Did he and Pony have some kind of relationship? Was he missing her? If so, Guthrie could certainly sympathize. If it were at all possible for him to travel to Arizona to visit Jessie, he surely would.

"I brought some things for Pony," Pete said, as if reading Guthrie's mind. "A letter from Nana, her old aunt. The schedule for the Crow Fair in August. And some news about Roon's family. Bad news. His youngest brother, Ralph, was killed in a car crash. I guess it happened over a week ago on the Cree reservation up in Canada. We only just got word."

Guthrie felt his heart drop. The last thing Roon needed was to hear something like that. "What about the funeral?"

"Over and done with. I called his mother and asked her if she wanted us to bring Roon. She said no, she had troubles enough."

"Roon doesn't need to know she said that," Guthrie said.

"But he needs to know about his brother."

"Yes." Guthrie sighed. It was a bad way to start the summer. He glanced out the screen door, wondering where McCutcheon and the others were, and if they'd found the buffalo yet. Wondering about Roon, and how he would take the awful news.

WITH BADGER RIDING DRAG, they made pretty good time climbing into the high country. Caleb enjoyed sporadic conversations with Pony, the boys managed to stay in the saddle, and it looked as though they'd reach the line camp at Piney Creek by noon. Caleb was pretty sure that the herd would be somewhere in the vicinity.

At least he hoped so. "They were there less than a week ago," he said to Pony. "The grass is really good in that meadow. I don't see why they'd stray too far." He was facing backward, one hand holding the reins and the other resting on Billy's rump. Suddenly Billy gave a mighty forward lunge to scale a particularly steep section of trail, and Caleb was toppling out of the saddle, rolling over the gelding's hindquarters. He had the disorienting sensation of spinning through air and then his feet came down with a resounding thump and he was standing upright behind Billy, grasping the horse's tail with one hand to keep his balance.

For a moment he remained still and so did Billy. Then the gelding turned his head to look behind him, ears pricked in a silent question mark. "Whoa, Billy, good boy," Caleb said, slightly dazed. He glanced back at Pony. "I've been practicing that flying dismount for quite a while. Like it?"

"It was pretty good," she said, her face revealing nothing.

Behind her, Jimmy was leaning in his saddle to see better, his eyes round with awe.

"It's rough going up ahead!" Caleb called back to

the boys. "Everyone climb down. We'll lead our horses up this next stretch. And don't even *think* of trying a backward somersault dismount. That takes years of practice."

He scrambled up beside Billy, took the blessedly patient gelding's rein and led him forward. They stopped to rest where the trail leveled out into a grove of softwood. Sunlight splintered through the conifers, and the wind tugged a sweet, lonesome sound from the branches. "How much farther?" Jimmy asked.

"Another half hour, wouldn't you say, Badger?"

Badger pulled a bandanna out of his hip pocket and blew his nose loudly into it. "More or less," he said. "You boys runnin' out of steam already?"

"No," Jimmy said, patting his horse's neck. "But I think Sparky's getting tired."

"Sparky can take a good long noontime break," Badger said. "We all can."

Martin was rubbing his thighs. "I keep getting these cramps," he said.

"That's 'cause you ain't used to ridin', and it's hard goin'. The ride back down won't be so bad. We can take the Piney Creek trail. It's longer but it ain't so steep. Easier on the horses, too. All right, boys," Badger said. "Let's haul into the saddle. Keep your eyes peeled for grizzly. We're in their territory now."

Caleb couldn't refrain from glancing around at Badger's ominous words. Funny, he hadn't thought about that big grizzly for a long time now, maybe because all winter long it had been denned up somewhere, sleeping through those long bitter blizzards. But Badger was right. Chances were good that the big old bear who had killed Senator George Smith and one of Jessie's horses last fall was up here, grubbing around for its next meal. Maybe it was a sow with cubs. They could be very aggressive and protective, and in short bursts they could run as fast as a race-horse. "Okay, Billy," he said, stabbing his toe into the stirrup and pulling himself back into the saddle. "Another day, another adventure."

He led out and Pony fell in behind. They rode be-yond the grove of trees and into a brilliant sweep of sunshine, and in a few moments Caleb forgot all about the grizzly bear because he was looking at a buffalo cow grazing upwind. She had her back to him, approximately two hundred yards away. He raised his hand, pointing, and drew Billy to a halt. Pony and the boys rode up beside him, until they were eight abreast, facing into the wind and watching that soli-tary buffalo cow. "Can't we get a little closer?" Jimmy said.

"No," Pony replied. "This is close enough."

"Why is she all by herself?" Dan asked.

"I'm not sure," she said. "Maybe she isn't. Maybe the rest of the herd is near."

A white-crowned sparrow lifted its voice in song from a nearby thicket and Martin shifted in his saddle. "I have to pee," he said.

Caleb nodded. "Go ahead."

Martin slid out of the saddle and handed his horse's reins to Badger. He hitched at his belt as he walked, startling the sparrow into flight and causing the buf-falo cow to lift her head and turn. The thicket wasn't far from where they sat their horses. No more than a hundred feet. Martin was nearly there when the buf-falo suddenly wheeled about and sprinted into a dead run, aiming her twelve-hundred-pound massive body directly at the boy.

Martin froze.

Caleb heard a sudden movement beside him, the churning dig of hooves as both Pony and Badger simultaneously spurred their horses toward Martin while Caleb and the boys remained frozen with horror, staring at the big chunks of sod being unearthed by the buffalo's terrifying charge.

Badger was leading Martin's horse, and the boy took the reins but couldn't get his foot in the stirrup. Instantly the old man was down on the ground, boosting the boy as if he weighed nothing, throwing him up over his saddle like a sack of grain and then reaching for his own horse's rein, but by then the cow was close. Too close! Badger's horse shied and bolted.

Caleb drove his heels into Billy's flanks, hoping to divert the angry cow, but the gelding wanted no part of that plan. He flung his head up with a snort and took several rapid steps backward, causing the boys' horses to do the same. He kicked Billy again, and again the gelding backed up at full speed away from the furious buffalo cow.

Caleb saw Pony leap out of her saddle and reach for something under her jacket. She drew forth a pistol, raised it in both hands to eye level and watched the cow gallop toward her as coolly as if she were in a staged Wild West show. Just before reaching her, the cow skidded to a stop, tossing her massive shaggy head with a spray of saliva. Her tail was up, and after a few calculating moments she made three stiff-legged aggressive hops toward the slender young woman.

Pony pulled the trigger, and the report ripped apart the high silence.

The cow stopped abruptly, shook her head and

snorted. Another string of saliva fell from her mouth and nostrils. She made a loud grunt deep in her throat, and an answering sound came from the thicket.

"What'll we do?" Jimmy asked, and hearing his young strident voice, Pony slowly and smoothly reached one arm toward Caleb and the boys, palm out, a silent command for them to keep quiet and stay where they were. The other hand kept the pistol pointed steadily at the cow's head.

"Badger," Pony said, never taking her eyes from the cow. "Get on my horse. Move slowly." Badger did as he was told, and as soon as he had eased himself into the saddle, she said, "Back him up, and I'll back up beside you. If the cow charges again, I'll shoot one more time and then you pull me up behind you."

Caleb watched while Badger backed Dobey up, step by quiet step, while the buffalo cow stood in an attitude of rigid aggression, tail still raised, and each breath an angry snort of defiance. Pony held the pistol in one hand and kept the other on Dobey's shoulder as she stepped back with the horse. Moving slowly so as not to alarm the cow, they made their way back to Caleb and the boys.

"I don't think she'll chase us any farther," Pony said, reaching behind her to tuck the pistol back in the waistband of her jeans. "She has a calf hidden in that thicket. Martin, are you all right? Where are your glasses?"

"I'm fine," Martin replied, having managed to sit up in the saddle and stick his feet into the stirrups. "But my glasses fell off back there. I can't see anything without them.

Pony watched the cow push into the thicket while

making deep guttural noises in her throat, and she heard answering plaintive sounds from the hidden calf. "I'll get them," she said. "Give Badger your horse and ride behind Jimmy until we can catch his."

"I'll get Martin's glasses," Caleb said.

"No. You stay with the boys," Pony said. As soon as Badger was on Martin's horse, Pony mounted Dobey and nudged the gray gelding with her heels. She kept Dobey at a slow walk and when she reached the place where Badger had thrown the boy onto the horse, she reined him in, stepped down, plucked something out of the grass, immediately climbed back onto the horse and walked the gelding away. When she reached the group, she pulled Martin's glasses out of her pocket and examined them, polishing the thick lenses on the tail of her plaid flannel shirt. "They look okay," she said, handing them to the boy.

Caleb watched her, unable to speak. Behind them the cow's anxious grunts and snorts had diminished somewhat, but the bushes still crackled and trembled as she moved about. He glanced at the boys and at Badger. They were all in a similar state of shock, but Badger leaned over the shoulder of his horse and spat.

"Well, boss, we may not have found the herd, but the boys got to see a buff, up close and personal," he said, wiping his mouth with the back of his sleeve.

"That calf is hurt or sick," Pony said, adjusting her hat and behaving as if the incident hadn't been anything to get excited about. "We should check it out."

Caleb stared. "And just how do you propose we do that?"

"The cow's not in very good humor right now," Pony said. "But after a while, she will settle down and move out again to graze. While I drive her away from the calf, you and Roon can take a look, and if the calf is hurt or sick, we'll bring it back with us. Do you think you could carry it in front of you all the way to the ranch?''

''How big is it?''

''Thirty, forty pounds, maybe. Maybe less.''

''Sure,'' Caleb said. ''The calf isn't a problem, but what about that cow? She'll be running us off the side of the mountain.''

''We'll confuse her. Scare her. Hopefully she'll run to where the rest of the herd is and stay with them. She's coming out now. Look.''

Caleb looked. The big cow crashed out of the bush. She looked mad and mean to him. She swung her big head and glared in their direction. ''Maybe her calf is okay, and she's just wanting us to leave so she can feed it.''

''Something's wrong,'' Pony stated. ''For some reason that calf is too weak to nurse or she would not be standing there, looking at us. And the noises the calf is making are not that of a healthy animal. Roon, do you think you can do this?''

Roon didn't hesitate. He nodded and stared at Caleb, his expression a silent challenge. Caleb felt himself bristling. He glanced at Pony. ''That pistol of yours sounds pretty powerful, but the bullet just bounced off her head.''

Pony nodded. ''Yes. My bullets were hand loaded by Pete Two Shirts with about one thimbleful of BB's in each. They are intended to warn buffalo off, not kill them. That shot did nothing more than sting her, and make her reconsider.''

One thimbleful of BB's had been between her and

death, and yet she had stood so calmly, so bravely. Caleb smoothed Billy's mane and studied Pony's face. She was a marvelous creation of untamed beauty and undaunted courage. The words came unbidden to him and they described her perfectly. He shook his head and looked at the cow who watched them with great suspicion. "All right," he said. "But I want you all to know that this isn't required of you. If that buffalo calf is sick or hurt, maybe that's just natural selection at work. Maybe we shouldn't be risking our own safety to save it. I don't want anyone getting hurt, and that cow could easily kill."

"Maybe," Badger said. "But hell, boss, we kilt enough of them, didn't we? We nearly wiped every last buff off the face of the earth. Wouldn't it be a good thing if we could save this little one?"

Roon looked at Badger, but the boy's dark eyes were unreadable. Pony looked at Caleb and her eyes were pleading. Caleb drew a deep breath and let it out slowly. "They can run as fast as racehorses and outmaneuver just about anything on this planet," he said to her.

"I know," she replied. "I'll ride alone against her. Dobey, in case you may not realize, is a true buffalo horse. Not many would stand the way he did in the face of a charging buffalo. I'll chase that cow off, then you and Roon ride in and get the calf. The rest of you boys start back down the trail right now. We'll catch up."

"No!" Jimmy protested. "We want to help."

"Badger, you get those boys moving," she said, reaching for her pistol.

Badger spat over the shoulder of his horse and glared. "Nope," he said. "I may be an old man, and these might be a bunch of greenhorn kids still wet behind the ears, but we can do what needs to be done. Boys,'' he said, addressing Jimmy, Martin, Dan and Joe. ''You think you can ride like hell across this meadow, shoutin' and hollerin' and makin' a helluva racket, to that tall pine at the far side?''

The boys all nodded enthusiastically.

''Now, wouldn't all that noise and commotion create a lot of chaos and confuse that mother cow just a little bit?'' Badger said to Pony.

''Yes,'' she admitted.

''And wouldn't that give Boss and Roon more time to save that little feller?''

She nodded. ''But the boys, except for Roon, don't ride very well.''

''Hell, they've ridden this far without fallin' off,'' Badger said. ''I bet they can ride to that big pine. I'd stake my reputation on it. You boys game?''

''We can do it,'' Jimmy said, and the other boys voiced their agreement.

''Badger,'' Caleb said. ''Did you bring a real gun?''

''I ain't never rode up into these mountains without one, boss,'' Badger said. He reached into his right saddlebag and drew forth a big .45-caliber pistol. ''An inch behind and an inch below the ear, and she'll be one dead buffalo cow, but I'll only do it if we get in over our heads and there ain't no other way out. That little buff needs its mother, and I guess we all remember what that's like.''

Caleb nodded. ''All right. You call the shots,'' he said to Pony. ''No pun intended. And if this all goes to hell—''

''It won't,'' Pony said.

"You say when." They stared at each other, and he felt himself slipping into a dangerous place in that moment before she shifted her eyes and cocked her pistol.

She dug her heels into Dobey's flanks and let out a scream that would have curdled the blood of the staunchest Indian fighters of old. The grey gelding pinned its ears back and flattened into a dead gallop toward the glaring cow. Pony fired off a round when she came up to the cow's side, and the great beast began to run away, snorting and shaking its head.

"Let's ride!" Badger said to the boys, and let out a cowboy holler as old as the trails that traced up from Texas, swinging his rope down against his horse's rump as he did.

Caleb looked at Roon and the boy glared back at him as mad and full of resentment as the cow buffalo. "Ready?" he asked, urging Billy forward. The bay gelding readily obliged, leaving Roon scrambling to catch up. In seconds Billy had reached the thicket, and Caleb was leaping out of the saddle and plunging into the bush. He spied the ball of golden fur in the shade, heard the frightened bleat, felt the painful thump of the calf's hoof thrashing against him as he bent and scooped up the little creature. The calf was pitifully light in his arms. Roon was just reining in his horse when Caleb stepped out of the thicket. "Here. You take it!" he snapped, placing the calf into the boy's outstretched arms.

He snatched up Billy's trailing rein, dug his foot into the stirrup and craned his neck desperately as he pulled himself into the saddle, trying to catch some glimpse of Pony and the buffalo cow. They were already small in the distance, dwarfed by the sheer magnitude of the mountain wilderness. The boys and Badger were making a huge ruckus and running pell-mell toward the big pine. He glanced at Roon. "You okay? You want me to carry the calf?"

Roon's dark eyes flickered briefly to Caleb's. "I can do it."

"I know you can," Caleb replied. "I hope I didn't hurt her when I picked her up."

Roon dropped his eyes back to the calf. "No, you did okay," he said.

Together they reined their horses around and returned to the trailhead, where they watched and waited until Pony stopped chasing after the cow. Soon she, the boys and Badger were heading safely back toward him while the cow continued her run along the shoulder of Montana Mountain, heading in the direction of the cut that led to Piney Creek.

Caleb hoped she would find the rest of the herd there, and in their company find some solace. He looked at the small creature that Roon cradled in his arms. It was so weak it couldn't hold its head up and he felt a surge of pity and a premonition of doom. "Poor little thing," he murmured. "Sometimes life just isn't fair."

IT WAS SUNSET, and Pete Two Shirts paced the porch the way Guthrie would have if his hip wasn't so painful. He leaned against the rail, Blue at his feet, and silently cursed himself. He should've told McCutcheon not to take the boys up on the mountain. Chaperoning a bunch of green kids into country that rough and wild was too much. McCutcheon could barely manage the ride himself, and yet he'd almost welcomed the challenge as if it was his own proving ground; as if by doing this, he could show these kids that he was a man to be reckoned with.

Foolishness, dammit. Pure foolishness! Guthrie dropped a hand to Blue's head and let his fingers slide over the silky crown and play with one of her ears. Blue was pregnant. Doc Cooper worked a cow dog that was half Border collie with some Australian shepherd and blue heeler tossed in, and Jessie had taken a shine to that dog the moment she'd first seen it some six years back. So when she'd come home for her brief visit at spring break, she said, "Guthrie, the next time Blue comes into heat—and it should be sometime this month—take her over to Cooper's place and introduce her to Zorro. Blue's getting old. It's time we got some pups out of her and started training them up."

And so Blue was going to be a first-time mother at close to nine years of age. According to all the charts, that made her over fifty years old in human years. He glanced down at her and in spite of his mounting anxiety about McCutcheon and the others, he felt a twinge of pure and genuine delight that Blue was going to have herself a litter of pups. Somehow that fact gave a brightness to his life that made bearable the long lonesome stretch of days until Jessie came home for good.

Ramalda had been cooking since breakfast. This was a sign that she was out of sorts, anxious and fully expecting some sort of huge disaster. She had waddled onto the porch an hour ago holding a wooden spoon and had scowled out at the mountains, heaved a tumultuous sigh and fixed him with a baleful stare. "Too long," she said, shaking her head. "They gone way too long!"

Yes, dammit, way too long. He glanced to where Pete stood, staring at the woods. "Maybe we should start out after 'em before it gets dark," he said. "Bring a bunch of flashlights and such."

Pete shook his head. "No need. They'll be back inside half an hour."

Guthrie didn't ask how Pete could know such a thing. He must have seen something—a flash of movement, a bird flushing out of the brush and flying off. He waited and watched, and sure enough, twenty minutes later the first rider emerged, followed by seven others. They rode into the corral, all except for McCutcheon, who headed Billy up to the ranch house and drew rein at the foot of the steps. He nodded to Pete and Guthrie, his expression weary, but his smile wide with relief.

"Well, we made it," he said.

"Did you see the buffalo?"

He nodded again. "Matter of fact, we brought one home with us, a little she-calf that's too weak to nurse. Looks like she has a broken leg. Pete, I don't know what act of Providence brought you here today, but we could sure use your expertise. I'm going to give Doc Cooper a call, too, and see if there's anything we can do to save her."

Pete shoved his hat back on his head. "Where's the mother cow?"

"She was upset about us taking her little one, but we had no choice. The calf would've died if we'd left it there. Pony chased her over toward Piney Creek, and I'm hoping she finds the rest of the herd."

The change in Pete's demeanor was so subtle that Guthrie almost didn't catch it, but there was no mistaking his tone of voice. "You let Pony chase a buffalo cow away from her calf?"

McCutcheon met Pete's dark stare with his own calm blue gaze. "You tell me how to keep Pony from doing what Pony wants to do, and I'll listen," he said.

Ramalda broke the tension of the moment when she came out onto the porch, the screen door banging behind her. She held a big carving knife in her hand and she waved it in the air as she blasted McCutcheon in nonstop Spanish for at least one full minute, ending the tirade with a jab of the knife in his general direction and a handful of English words. "Supper ready long ago, but you late again!" She turned and stomped back inside.

"Well, I'll call Doc Cooper," Guthrie said. He glanced at Pete. "I'd appreciate it if you could take a look at that calf, and tell the boys that supper's waitin'."

Pete made no reply. He descended the porch steps, walked past McCutcheon without a glance and headed for the pole barn. McCutcheon sighed and caught Guthrie's eye. "I couldn't have stopped her," he said.

Guthrie nodded. "Jessie's the same way. Once her mind's set, there's no changing it."

"I've never seen anything like what I saw today. First, Pony and Badger saved Martin's life when that buffalo cow was about to run the boy down, and then she risked her own life again to protect Badger." McCutcheon shook his head, still marveling. "I've never seen that kind of courage before. On top of all that, she wouldn't leave the little calf there to die. She chased that mother buffalo away so Roon and I could get the calf, and Roon carried it all the way back. He won't let anyone else near it.'' McCutcheon paused and shook his head. ''I sure hope the little critter lives, because I think taking care of that calf might help Roon a lot.''

Guthrie drew a deep breath. ''Boss, Roon's little brother was killed last week in a car wreck. That's why Pete came out here today.''

McCutcheon sat absolutely still for a long moment, and then he looked back down toward the barn.

''I told Pete that I thought Pony should be the one to tell him,'' Guthrie said.

McCutcheon nodded and rubbed the back of his neck. ''Damn!'' His shoulders slumped, and the look he gave Guthrie was one of despair. ''Tell Dr. Cooper to hurry.''

PONY SAT with the small of her back pressed against a stack of hay bales. She heard a truck door slam as Dr. Cooper departed. It was late. Dark and quiet. The glow of the oil lamp cast a small circle of light upon the deep bed of straw and the boy who sat in it cradling the little calf in his arms. They were alone in the stall, she and Roon and the calf. Caleb had herded the rest of the boys up to the house. Pete and Badger had left with Guthrie to spend the night at his cabin, but Roon had refused leave the pole barn, even to eat supper. Pony had brought him a plate of food but he'd only picked at it.

The boy had held the calf's head while the veterinarian guided the stomach tube down its throat and pumped the mix of electrolytes and nutrients into the listless creature. He'd steadied the calf's broken leg while the vet had applied the plaster cast. During all of this, he had said nothing. Even now, he was silent, his eyes watching the rise and fall of the calf's sunken rib cage.

During supper Pete had explained that sometimes after a cow gives birth, an inexperienced bull can't tell the difference between her calving smell or the scent of her being in heat. He said that sometimes a bull will try to mount the cow, and the calf gets injured in the fracas. Pete thought that was probably what had happened.

"So how do we keep it from happening again?" McCutcheon had asked.

"Get more bulls. Older bulls who know the correct social behavior."

Shortly after, Pete had stood up from the table and given Pony a long, significant look that had hollowed her stomach. She'd followed him onto the porch and he asked her to walk with him along the creek just before the vet had arrived. "I have some bad news about Roon's youngest brother," he'd said as they stood beside the rushing water.

So now Pony sat with the boy in the quiet of the barn, watching the impossibly frail baby buffalo struggle for life and trying to find the right moment to break the terrible news to Roon. She tightened her arms around her knees. "You did a brave thing today," she said. "You gave this little one a chance at life by carrying her down the mountain in your arms."

"We took her away from her mother." Roon raised his eyes to hers. "That wasn't brave. It was wrong."

"If we had left her there, she would have starved."

"It wouldn't have mattered."

"Why do you say that?"

"Because we were too late. She's too weak. She'll

die anyway, afraid and in a strange place, far from her mother.''

"Maybe," Pony acknowledged. "But maybe not. I don't know what will happen, Roon, or if what we did was right or wrong. I only know what my heart tells me, and my heart told me that we had to try."

Roon was silent for a few moments. "That buffalo cow would have killed us to protect her calf. Not all mothers would do that, you know."

Pony studied him. "Are you talking about human mothers? Are you saying that a human mother would not fight that way for her children?"

"A human mother doesn't have to fight that way. All she has to do is care, and sometimes she can't even do that," he burst out in a rare show of emotion.

"Your mother cares about you, Roon. You may not believe that, but it's true. I care very much about you, too, and I would fight for you the same way that mother buffalo did if it were necessary. I would fight for you that same way."

"But you're not my mother."

"No. And you are not that calf's mother, yet you carried her in your arms, and here you are sitting with her in the dark, willing her to live so that we can take her back up on the mountain and return her to her real mother. You do that because you care."

"The only person in my family who cares about me is my brother Ralph," Roon said. "He asked me to write him. He was going to send me their new address but I haven't gotten it yet. Nana would tell you if she got any mail for me, wouldn't she?"

Icy dread chilled Pony's heart. "Roon," she began, but before she could continue there was a rustle of movement behind them and the sound of soft footsteps approaching. Caleb stepped into the stall and crouched down on his heels. He glanced at Pony, and she lowered her eyes with a faint negative movement of her head.

"Dr. Cooper's coming by again first thing in the morning to give the calf another feeding," he said, speaking softly. "Pete said as soon as she gets strong enough to stand, she might be able to nurse off a regular milk cow. You ever heard of anything like that?"

Pony nodded. "We did that for a few orphaned calves and it worked. The milk cows accepted them."

"Cooper said he could find us a good milking cow and I told him to have it delivered here as soon as possible. Five boys and one little buffalo calf... Maybe I should've ordered two milk cows." He grinned faintly. "How's she doing?"

Pony shook her head. "She's still very weak."

"Roon, I'll spend the night with her," Caleb offered. "I'll bring my sleeping bag down and stay right here beside her. Why don't you go up to the house with Pony and get some rest."

Roon looked at Caleb and shook his head. "No," he said. "I'll stay."

"All right. It's your choice." He rose to his full height and glanced at Pony. "Can I talk to you?"

She followed him out of the barn. The night was cool, and as they walked down toward the creek she caught the tang of wood smoke and heard the distant mournful wail of a coyote. Without warning, tears flooded her eyes and spilled down her cheeks. "I'm sorry. I just couldn't tell him," she said, her throat closing around the words.

She felt his hand reach out and take hers in a warm,

firm grip, and not even her anguish over Roon's loss could negate the pleasure of his touch. He said nothing, just walked beside her in silence holding her hand, his strength giving her comfort. They walked along the banks of the creek and listened to the water as it rushed out of the mountains and rippled toward the sea. Finally, they returned to the barn.

"I'll tell him now," she said before they went inside.

He squeezed her hand gently. "No. I'll do it."

Pony watched as Caleb squatted beside Roon, reached a hand to smooth the golden fur of the buffalo calf, then shifted his hand to grip the boy's shoulder. "Roon, I have some very bad news." Roon flinched from the touch and his eyes lifted to McCutcheon's. "Your brother Ralph was killed in a car accident over a week ago up in Canada. Pete came as soon as he heard. I'm so sorry."

Those dark eyes were unblinking as they studied McCutcheon's face for what seemed an eternity. Had he understood? Was he in shock? Pony was searching for something to say when suddenly Roon nodded and dropped his eyes, his shoulders stiff and his face expressionless.

"I knew there had to be a reason why he hadn't written," he said.

CHAPTER SEVEN

"NOW PAY ATTENTION, boys," Badger said, wiping a trickle of tobacco juice from the corner of his mouth and holding up a pair of wire cutters. "These are the tools of your new trade. This here's a pair of wire cutters, and this," he said, lifting another much larger contraption, "is what we call a wire stretcher. Mighty handy damn thing, too, as you're about to find out. These," he said, waving a pair of sturdy leather gloves, "are mandatory when working with barbed wire. Don't ever let me catch you without a pair, and when they wear out, holler. We got plenty on hand, no pun intended."

The boys stood in a line watching him in the early light. Ramalda was in the kitchen washing the breakfast dishes, and Guthrie was down in the barn with Pony, Caleb, Pete, Roon and that tiny buffalo calf. Dr. Cooper had just given it its second feeding, and the way things were going, Badger was afraid this fence project might never get off the ground. He was determined to get things rolling. Summer was short and the job ahead of them was damn long.

The sound of a vehicle approaching the ranch house disrupted Badger's train of thought, and he turned and squinted at the truck towing a horse trailer. "Dang, this place is gettin' to be crazier'n a three-ring circus!" he grumbled as the truck drove past the house and down to the barn. "That's Evan Small. Looks like he's brung us one of his milkers." He turned back to the boys and sighed. "All right, dammit, you guys go see what's happenin'. But remember this. A wild critter don't like to be stared at, so don't you be gawkin' at that poor little thing."

The boys stampeded for the barn, reaching it as Evan Small unloaded the big Holstein heifer from the trailer and led her through the open door. Badger stood for a moment and then spat over the porch railing. "Hell, I mights well go look myself as stand here wondering." He followed the boys down to the barn. He could hear the low murmur of voices as he approached. The boys huddled in a group outside the stall. Guthrie, Pete and McCutcheon leaned over the partition, Pony stood with the boys, Evan Small had hold of the cow's halter, and Roon was helping Doc Cooper steady the calf's head as they propped the little critter up next to the cow's bulging udder.

"She only just calved late last night," Evan said. "She's full of good first milk, and she's a real gentle cow."

Cooper grunted, squeezing one of the cow's teats and directing a stream of warm milk at the calf's mouth. He used his finger to rub the sweet taste of it between the calf's lips while Roon steadied her head. The calf was still so weak she couldn't stand or hold her own head up. Cooper tried several more times to persuade the calf to latch on to the teat and suckle, but she just didn't have the strength. Finally he nodded to Roon, and they eased her back down into the bed of straw.

Doc Cooper stood up and shook his head.

"I'll come by at noon, and we'll tube feed her

again. Meanwhile, milk the cow and keep her handy. Tie her on the far side of the stall so's she can see and smell the calf.'' He looked at Roon. ''You might put some of her milk in a bottle and try that on the calf, too. Let her lie so she's comfortable and just raise her head up. Don't force her. She might inhale the milk and choke.'' He nodded at the boy approvingly. ''You're doing a good job nursing her. I didn't think she'd last the night.''

The old veterinarian gathered his gear into a cordura bag and left the barn, accompanied by everyone but Roon. He walked out to his truck and stashed the bag on the passenger's seat, wiped his hands on a crumpled rag he found there and looked at Guthrie. ''Don't get your hopes up.''

Guthrie nodded. ''Thanks for comin' by, Doc.''

''Like I said, I'll swing by at lunchtime, too.''

''I'll be sure to tell Ramalda to set another place.''

They stood in a silent group and watched him depart, followed shortly after by Evan Small and Pete Two Shirts. It was McCutcheon who finally broke the silence. ''Keep positive thoughts,'' he said to the ring of glum faces. ''Nothing good ever happens without positive thoughts.'' He squared his shoulders and tugged his hat down over his eyes. ''Now, we've got five hours till Ramalda expects us in that kitchen for lunch. Let's go tear down some fence.''

''What about Roon?'' Jimmy asked.

''Roon has a job to do that's just as important as ours,'' Badger pitched in. ''Keepin' that little buffler calf alive ain't easy, but if he can do it, he'll be savin' this ranch three thousand dollars, 'cause that's about what a weaned female buffler calf is runnin' right now. And if she lives forty years and has thirty calves, she'll have earned this ranch…well, you boys figure it out. Thirty times three thousand dollars. We'll figure on the low side for price, just to be safe. Bull calves don't fetch as much as heifers. Who can tell me what that little buffler calf will have earned us forty years from now?"

"Nine thousand dollars," Jimmy said.

"No, *ninety* thousand, stupid," Martin corrected. "All you got to do is add the zero and multiply three times three, just like Pony said."

"Ninety thousand dollars ain't a bad career for a buffler," Badger said. "So I'd say Roon has an important job. But if that little calf dies, it won't be for lack of his tryin' to save her. So all we can do is what Boss says. Keep thinkin' positive thoughts." He shifted the wad of tobacco in his cheek and glanced at Pony, who nodded. "And there's somethin' else you need to know about Roon," he said.

The boys looked questioningly at Pony. "Roon's little brother, Ralph, was killed in a car crash over a week ago," she told them quietly.

The boys stood in silence and stared at the barn.

"Does he know?" Jimmy asked, his young voice cracking with emotion.

Pony nodded, glancing at Caleb. "We told him last night."

"And he spent the night all alone in the barn with that sick calf?"

"Mr. McCutcheon and I stayed with him," Pony said quietly.

Badger watched the boys. They stared down at the ground as if the answer to all life's mysteries lay beneath their feet. "So that's how it stands with Roon," Badger said. "You boys go easy on him. Help him

over this rough stretch, 'cause there ain't nothin'
worse in this whole wide world than losin' someone
who loves you.''

PONY WAS SO TIRED she felt as though the sun's
warmth was lulling her into a kind of senselessness.
She took hold of the loose coil of barbed wire and
wound it around the big unwieldy roll that sprang out
and snagged her clothing and cut her flesh. But she
was grateful for the hard work. And she was tired. So
very tired. That was good, too. She needed to be dis-
tracted. She needed to forget about Roon, about the
newest tragedy in his tragic life, about the dying buffalo calf…and about Caleb McCutcheon.

She needed to forget how she had felt last night
when Caleb McCutcheon had reached out and taken
her hand. She needed to forget how gently he had
told Roon about the death of his little brother and
how, hours later, he'd held the boy in his arms while
Roon had broken down and sobbed. She could not
open her heart to Caleb McCutcheon. Such a thing
could not happen. Would not happen. He was white.
She was Indian. They belonged in two different
worlds, and that would never change.

She needed to remember who she was, and what
she was all about.

The barbed wire was vicious. In just one morning
she had come to see it as an enemy that had to be
overcome and she welcomed the battle. She was so
immersed in the work that she didn't notice Caleb
coming to stand beside her. She startled when she felt
a hand on her shoulder. She turned and looked up
into the eyes of the man she was trying so desperately
not to think about.

"Time for lunch," he said.

She nodded and followed him to the truck, climbing into the back with the boys because she couldn't trust herself to sit beside him on the bench seat. Being near him was dangerous because she knew she would want him to reach out and hold her hand again. So she sat with the boys, who were comparing injuries and barbed-wire war stories. They laughed aloud and talked about how hungry they were and how good Ramalda's cooking would taste. Pony closed her eyes, wondering how Roon and the baby buffalo were doing. Was the little calf still alive?

RAMALDA HAD OUTDONE herself for the boys' first full day at work. She had prepared a meal that would have done the highest king proud, and yet when the truckload of hungry boys arrived at the ranch house, they paid not the slightest attention to the delectable smells wafting from her kitchen. Instead, as one entity, they moved toward the pole barn. Ramalda came out on the porch, put her big fists on her big hips and scowled.

"Oh, now, don't be put out," Badger soothed, easing himself onto the wall bench. "If you put something up for Roon, I'll carry it down to him," he offered. "The boy ain't eaten much in the past few days. He's had a rough time of it and that's a fact." After considerable muttering and fussing about in the kitchen, Ramalda emerged holding a basket and handed it to him.

With a weary moan Badger stood and started down to the barn. Dr. Cooper was there. Badger shifted the heavy basket of food and when he reached the door of the barn he paused and listened, trying to gauge what was happening inside. Tragedy or triumph?

"Hold her just like that," Dr. Cooper said. "Tip the bottle up a little more. That's it."

Badger stepped inside the barn. He could see everyone grouped around a stall, hovering like a host of apprenticing midwives in the midst of a hard delivery. At least the little buff wasn't dead. "That's good," Dr. Cooper said. "That's damn good. She's drinking. Can you see? Watch her close, boys. She's swallowing. Look at that stream of bubbles. See that? By God, that's fine. She's drinking on her own!"

He could see their faces in the dim light. The boys, the young woman who called herself Pony, Guthrie and McCutcheon. Doc Cooper.

"Well, I'll be damned," Dr. Cooper said. "That's the kind of miracle I never expected to see here today."

"Amen," Badger said, his voice hoarse with emotion.

BY EARLY JULY, the summer had settled into a kind of rhythm that gave Caleb a feeling of immense satisfaction. The boys were doing well. As Badger had predicted, they weren't breaking any speed records when it came to pulling down fences and, in fact, he wasn't sure they actually accomplished much at all in the course of a day, but they weren't misbehaving, either. They showed up for breakfast, listened to Guthrie and Badger hash out the day's schedule, spent the morning on the fence line with Pony riding herd on them and doing the bulk of the work herself, came back for lunch riding in the back of Pony's pickup, then went back and worked until suppertime.

Steven Young Bear had come by each Saturday, timing his arrival to take advantage of one of Ramalda's delicious suppers and bringing a big cardboard box of snack food that he knew a bunch of boys without access to a corner store would appreciate. He always included a few items for Ramalda, Badger and Caleb.

"Aiy!" Ramalda had beamed, holding up the long strings of dried red chilis and garlic.

"Well, I guess I could chew it," Badger allowed, hefting the foil container of Red Man and eyeing Steven with moderating suspicion.

Caleb had hefted the bat, put on the glove, and then tossed the baseball in one hand, eyebrows raised at Pony's brother. "Thanks, but what am I supposed to do with this? My big league days are over."

Steven had nodded in his somber way. "True. But I figured the boys might want a lesson or two from you, being as you were nominated three times for the baseball hall of fame."

"I didn't make it," Caleb pointed out.

"You would have, if you hadn't been injured in the middle of your best season ever," Steven had said. "You can give a lot to these kids. Teach them how to throw a ball and how to hit one. Start a Little League team and be their famous coach."

"Yeah," Badger agreed, diving into the bag of chewing tobacco. "You could call yourselves the Red Men."

For his sister, Steven brought news from the reservation and Nana, as well as a big stack of books. "Strictly radical reading," he said when he handed them to her, and for the first time ever, Caleb heard her laugh. Such a beautiful sound.

For two weeks Roon had devoted himself exclusively to nursing the little buffalo calf, who showed no interest at all in the Holstein heifer and instead attached herself to the boy. Once she could stand and walk about on her own, Roon joined the work detail and so did the calf. The boys would hoist her into the back of the truck and hold her while Pony drove out to the work area. The little creature would hobble along after Roon, whose job was to saw off the fence posts after the barbed wire had been removed. This kept the calf away from the dangerous coils. The boys had argued that they should each be allowed a turn at baby-sitting the calf, but the little buffalo wanted only Roon.

"She thinks he's her mother," Pony told them, and so now the boys called him Mother Roon. Roon didn't seem to mind the teasing. He took his job very seriously, and the little calf grew stronger by the day. When it became obvious that she would live, Caleb posed the question to Roon one evening at the supper table. "What are you going to call her? She needs a name."

Roon thought about it for a while, his dark eyes somber. "Absa," he said.

Pony nodded her approval. "That's a good name." She looked at Caleb. "It is the name for the Crow Indians," she said. "Absaroka. Absa. Children of the raven."

In her spare time, Pony drew up plans for corrals of solid seven-foot high fencing and an alley of sheet metal welded to heavy iron pipe down which the buffalo would be herded into the chute itself. From the chute—also of steel tubing—there were several gates opening into separate corrals for sorting and isolating the animals. She showed Caleb the plans and explained how the structure would work. Then she, Caleb and Guthrie met with a contractor. The corrals would be finished just in time for Pony to inspect them before returning to her teaching job on the reservation in September.

It was only July, and already Caleb was dreading her departure. He had come to enjoy her company far more than he deemed wise, and had tried to squelch the feelings that stirred in him whenever she was near, but to no avail.

"Well, boss," Badger said, interrupting Caleb's evening meditation as he joined him on the cabin porch. "You look like you're trying to solve all the world's problems. Gettin' anywhere?"

Caleb grinned. "Nope."

"Look at 'em," the old man said, nodding his head toward the boys sprawled on the grass near the edge of the creek. The calf was curled up beside Roon, a golden ball of fur with a white cast on one leg. Pony was on her feet, open book in one hand and long stick in the other, pacing slowly back and forth, reading aloud from some lesson plan and using the long stick to emphasize certain points. He couldn't hear her voice over the sound of the creek but it resonated in his mind with all its soft feminine modulations—the gentleness and the strength and the beauty of it.

"Ramalda sent me down to fetch all of you for supper."

"The Livingston Roundup starts tomorrow."

Badger nodded. "They're having a parade in the afternoon. The rodeo starts at eight, and I expect there'll be fireworks, too."

Caleb rubbed his chin, watching Pony pace back

and forth, wondering what she was reading to them and wishing he was close enough to hear. "Think the boys might like to go?"

"Yepper." Badger turned and started back to the ranch house, but he paused for a moment at the corner of the cabin. "If I were you," he said, "I'd invite that pretty little schoolmarm, too."

July 4
Dear Jessie,
I'm sitting here in the living room at the ranch. It's hotter than Hades outside and the horses are standing in the shade of the trees along the creek. Ramalda is napping. Her snores are apt to blast the shingles off the roof. McCutcheon has taken Pony and the boys to Livingston to see the parade, and later, the rodeo and fireworks. They won't be home till late. Roon has charged me with taking care of Absa. She's behaving pretty well and she's eating for me, but I'm not Roon and she sure knows it. Doc Cooper says the cast can come off her leg next week, and then I don't know what will happen. The best thing would be to see if we can find her mother, but a lot of time has passed and she might not take the calf back. Anyway, her milk will have dried up, more than likely. So we'll probably have to keep Absa here at the ranch until she's weaned on to grass, and even then, nobody knows if she'll be able to return to the herd. Right now she's sleeping at my feet just like a big dog. Ramalda would skin me alive if she caught her in here but I hope we'll be gone before she wakes up.

Guthrie paused from his painstaking hunt-and-peck typing and glanced out the window again. Storm clouds were building over the mountains. They needed rain, but he hoped the fireworks wouldn't get rained out.

Speaking of dogs, Blue's lying right at my feet. She's like a second mother to Absa, but Absa doesn't like it much when Blue tries to herd her around. Blue's definitely pregnant. Mc-Cutcheon says he wants a girl pup. Doc Cooper wants a male. I know you said you wanted to keep two, so now I guess it's up to Blue to make sure we can fill all them orders.

Guthrie glanced down at Blue, who lay curled up against Absa. She twitched a little in her sleep and he reached down and trailed his fingers over her head.

I think McCutcheon is happy with how things are going. The buffalo are doing real well, we had seven calves born this spring, and we're planning to buy more cows and bulls at auction this fall, maybe in South Dakota. Pony is helping a lot with the groundwork, showing us how to turn this place into a working buffalo ranch. I already told you how she feels about making the ranch pay for itself and we feel the same way. So that's what we're going to try to do. This will help the boys to learn something useful. They aren't really interested in tearing down fences, that's for sure, but Badger's been teaching them about the horses and they really like that, and anything to do with the buffalo they think is okay.

They also like anything to do with baseball, ever since McCutcheon started teaching them what that game's all about. The way they're going at it, the next Babe Ruth'll be a full-blood.

Speaking of McCutcheon, he's gone and bought himself a Chevy Suburban. It's huge. Wait till you see it, Jess. Dark hunter green, same color as Steven's Jeep. Picture this. On the doors, in gilt lettering, "Bow and Arrow, Katy Junction, Montana." And between the ranch name and the address is the symbol of the Bow and Arrow brand. The doors look really sharp, but like I told him, it's still just a Chevy. He says Ford doesn't make an SUV that can carry so many people. I guess he's forgetting that in a couple months he's gonna be losing all his summer help…or maybe he knows something I don't?

Guthrie paused to flex his fingers and gaze out at the sultry afternoon. He wondered how McCutcheon was making out. Chaperoning five teenage boys was no picnic. There was no telling what kind of trouble they could get into.…

PONY COULDN'T REMEMBER ever experiencing a day as fine as this one. From the moment she had awakened, there had been a kind of magic about it. The dawn had been pink and gold with promise, the air buoyant with the sweet spicy smell of the wild roses blooming along the creek, and the boys had been buzzing with the anticipation of an afternoon and evening at a rodeo. Caleb opened his wallet before they left the ranch and gave each boy a crisp one-hundred-dollar bill, a gesture of such unexpected generosity that they all stared at him, speechless.

"You boys've earned it. Just don't spend it all in one place. Now climb aboard."

But when they headed for his pickup and began climbing into the back, he gave a short, sharp whistle and held up his hands in a time-out gesture. Then he pointed down toward his cabin. "Got a surprise for you," he said. "We're going to town in style today, and every single one of you will be wearing a seat belt."

While they set out to discover what the surprise was, Pony thanked him. "Giving them the money wasn't necessary," she added. "They've probably eaten ten times that amount already, and the summer is young. Besides, the fence work is going pretty slowly."

He slipped his wallet back into his hip pocket and then reached out and took her hands, turning them over in his own and studying the calluses and cuts. "The fence work is hard on you. I don't like to see that."

"My hands are fine," she said, pulling them away and hiding them behind her while her heart raced at his touch.

"We're going to rent one of those fence rollers for the barbed wire, and Guthrie can oversee those boys. I'd rather put you to work at the computer. Can you keyboard?"

She nodded. "Of course, but..."

"Good. There's a ton of information to input and Guthrie's hopeless. He's worse than I am when it comes to that kind of stuff."

"But…"

He shook his head. "No arguments. Today we aren't even going to discuss ranch work. Today is strictly pleasure. Come on. I want you to see this rig I just bought. I traded my useless Mercedes for it and I made a good trade, if I do say so myself."

Pony was as dazzled as the boys were by the fancy new Suburban. She ran her hands over the soft leather seats and admired the high-tech gadgets. It was the first time in her life she'd ever ridden in a brand-new vehicle.

By midafternoon they arrived in town, just in time to find a parking space and see the parade. The boys watched the parade politely, which Pony recognized as extraordinary behavior for a bunch of kids trying to act tough. They kept their hands shoved in their pockets, wore dark shades and cowboy hats, and she knew that those crisp hundred-dollar bills were tightly clutched in sweaty palms and that they were itching to go spend them on carnival rides and games and junk food.

"Okay, boys," Caleb said after the parade had passed. "Martin, you have a watch. So does Joe. Let's pick a place and a time to meet."

Pony felt a lurch of apprehension but she kept quiet. "What time does the rodeo start?" Jimmy said.

"It said eight o'clock in the newspaper." Caleb tapped the face of his wristwatch. "That gives us nearly four hours to kill, but in two hours we'll meet at the Ferris wheel. I want to take you someplace for supper. Someplace that serves buffalo steaks and burgers." He glanced among them. "So stick together, stay out of trouble, have a bunch of fun and we'll meet at 6:00 p.m."

They didn't hesitate more than a fraction of a heart-beat before vanishing into the crowd, and Pony looked up at him with a troubled frown. "That may have been a mistake," she said.

He grinned and took her hand as if he'd been wanting to do so for hours. "Maybe, and Lord knows I've made my share of them. But those boys need to kick up their heels, and how else could I get you all to myself for a few hours?"

She lowered her eyes, breathless and disoriented by both his words and his touch. She could think of no response and he waited for none. He tucked her hand beneath his arm and they began to walk. Three steps—just three—and Pony knew this was right where she wanted to be, walking beside this tall, quiet, good-hearted man. All of her strictly traditional convictions paled in his presence, and she became increasingly aware of an emotion she rarely felt. Happiness.

"So what do you think?" he said after they had been walking for a while, neither of them noticing or caring where they had been or where they were going.

"About what?"

"About how it's been so far. The summer. The boys. The buffalo."

"Good," she said. "It's been good." She wanted to tell him so much more, but she couldn't find the words to express what was in her heart.

"What about Roon?" he said.

"He's doing okay." She glanced up at him and then quickly away, startled by the intensity of his blue eyes. "He's lucky to have the job he has. It has helped him to deal with his brother's death."

"Roon's good with the animals. He saved that little buffalo calf. He didn't give her the option of dying."

"Absa will die," she said, feeling him check his stride at her words. "But in her own time. Roon somehow knows this, the way the young rarely do. Perhaps it is because he has come so close to death himself."

Caleb stopped. He took both her hands in his and his expression was so solemn that she felt an ominous pressure build beneath her lungs. "I lost a brother, too," he said. "In a car crash, the same way Roon did. My only sibling." Caleb's warm, strong hands tightened on hers. "He was in a car full of drunk teenagers. The passenger window was down and he was sitting on the edge of the door, half out of the car, banging on the roof and howling a challenge to the moon. The car ran up onto the sidewalk and flipped, and he was pinned underneath it. My uncle was a cop, one of the first at the scene. He held my brother while he died. So if you think Roon is okay, I can only tell you that it took me thirty years to be okay again, and I still lie awake some nights thinking about how different my life might have been if my brother had lived."

Pony stared up at him. "You think Roon is still in danger."

"I think Roon's worth saving, and I'm trying to figure out how to do it."

She nodded. "Me, too."

"One summer isn't enough."

She stared. "It is a beginning," she said.

"And a beginning is good, but there has to be a middle, too, and it should lead to a good ending."

"Roon's doing okay," she said quietly.

"Roon shouldn't have to deal with the kind of issues he's dealing with!" Caleb burst out. "If there's just one time in a person's life that ought to be smooth sailing, it's the teenage years, because even when everything's perfect, being an adolescent in this day and age is pretty damn tough."

She gazed up at him, marveling at his compassion. "All we can do is be there for him."

"But what about a year from now? Ten years from now? Where will you and I be then? Where will Roon be? How can you help someone when they aren't even around?"

She squeezed his hands. "You'll be around, and as long as you stay where you are, he will know where to find you. He can come to you if he needs to, and you won't turn him away. You're that kind of person."

Caleb shook his head in frustration. "It isn't enough. Roon needs more than that. So do the other boys. It isn't enough to show them a world that maybe they might like to try living in, and then send them back to a world where they still haven't found their place. A world that offers them an heroic past, but an uncertain future."

"So what would you do, Mr. McCutcheon?" Pony asked. "Keep them prisoners on your ranch? They have a history, a culture you can't begin to understand."

"I know that," he said quietly. "And I'm not trying to change it or take it away from them." He tore his eyes away from hers and stared into the distance for a long moment. His intense gaze took her breath away when it latched back on to her. "Hell, I don't know what I'm trying to say. I want to help, but I don't want you to think I'm patronizing you, because I'm not. I envy you your history and your culture. I didn't have anything like that. But I had a wonderful mother, and sometimes I think a wonderful mother can make up for just about anything.''

''Steven told me you grew up poor.''

''My mother raised the two of us by herself. She waitressed at a greasy spoon, worked at a laundry, took in mending. She made sure we had everything we needed. She came to all my baseball games when I was a kid. Never missed one. When the baseball scholarship offers started coming in from the colleges, she somehow managed to scrape together the funds needed to get me to the interviews.''

''She wounds wonderful.''

Caleb nodded. ''She was. She told me I could do anything I wanted to do, be anything I wanted to be. She told me that so often that I eventually began to believe it. I signed a contract with the White Sox before I graduated college. My mother invested every penny I gave her. I didn't realize that until she died. She made me a rich man.''

Pony smiled. ''She made you much more than rich. You have a good and honest heart, Caleb McCutcheon, and a good and honest heart is worth more than all the money in the world.''

He shook his head. ''It's money that makes things happen. It was money that bought me the Bow and Arrow, not my good heart. It was money that let me buy those buffalo, and that allowed me to hire you to advise me. Not my good and honest heart.''

She regarded him thoughtfully. ''I believe you have it backward, Mr. McCutcheon. Without a good and honest heart, all the money you have made would have been for nothing, squandered on foolish things. It would have made no difference at all to anyone except to you. But now…''

Now, she thought, looking up at him, now her own life was changed. Now her path was changed. As the thought took hold, Pony was no longer sure about what made the sun rise in the east or why the sky was blue. She felt like a child full of fear and wonder, gazing upon this man who was opening the door to a room that she had previously believed to be forbidden, but one that she wanted desperately to enter.

''Now?'' he prompted, his grip tightening.

''But now…'' she began again, and at that very moment she heard someone call her name. She turned her head, instantly alert. One of the boys in trouble? She heard the voice again and felt her body tense. Could it be…? Materializing out of the Fourth of July crowd came an all-too-familiar figure. He walked toward them, lean and graceful, that big silver rodeo buckle sparkling in the afternoon sunlight.

Pete Two Shirts.

''Pony,'' he said as he spotted her, and she felt the very best part of the day slipping through her fingers as McCutcheon's hands released hers.

''Pete,'' McCutcheon said with a nod of greeting, accepting the offered handshake. ''You must be here for the rodeo.''

Pete returned the nod. ''Wouldn't miss it. I won my first big chunk of money at this rodeo, and that was a few years back.'' He looked at Pony. ''How's Roon doing?''

''He's doing all right. He's here with the other boys.''

''What about that buffalo calf?''

"She's fine. Roon named her Absa. He takes care of her."

Pete nodded again. His dark eyes glanced between Caleb and Pony. "Are you staying for the rodeo?"

"Sure," Caleb said. "I've never seen one before. What are you competing in?"

"Bronc and bull riding tonight. Already drew my horse. A real snuffy mustang colt out of Colorado called Twister. First season on the circuit and no one's ever ridden him to the mark."

"Maybe you'll be the first," Caleb said.

"I'm sure going to try," Pete said. "You should check out the team-penning demonstration," he said. "It's not an official event this year but they're thinking of making it one. They're holding it at 7:00 p.m., just before the start of the rodeo. The boys would like it. It's fun to watch." He nodded to them both and then moved on in that catlike saunter of his.

"What's team penning?" Caleb said.

"It's…" She glanced up at him gratefully. "It's something relatively new on the rodeo circuit. Popular. There are three riders on each team, and out of a herd of about thirty numbered cows, the riders have to cut three cows wearing three particular numbers and herd them into a pen before their time runs out. The team with the best time wins. It's wild and fast, and Pete's right. The boys would like it very much."

Caleb's eyes held hers. "We can stay and watch Pete ride that colt, too."

She felt herself tense. "He's the best Indian cowboy to ride on the national circuit. He has a good reputation."

"He's a good man. I like Pete."

The intensity of his gaze made her turn away. She

began to walk down the side street just to escape the unasked questions that she read in his eyes. She heard him following her, falling into step beside her. "I'm sorry," he said. "It's none of my business."

She stopped abruptly and faced him, feeling the blood drain from her head. She wanted to tell him the truth. She wanted to sit with him and talk until everything had been said. She wanted him to know how it had been with her, and what part Pete had played in the darkest period of her past, and how every time she saw him those bitter memories came flooding back, but she didn't know where to begin. Worse, she was afraid of how he might feel about her afterward. Perhaps he would never want to hold her hand again. Perhaps he would ask her to take the boys and leave the ranch if he knew....

He watched her with a concerned expression as she struggled with her emotions and then he took her gently by the arm and led her into the shade of a tree and sat her down on a bench. "We won't speak about this anymore," he said. "You sit right here. I'm going to go get you something cool to drink."

"I'm fine."

"You don't look fine. I know you don't like iced tea or coffee. How about lemonade?"

She nodded and watched him walk down the sidewalk toward the long line of vendors' carts. She felt a twist of anguish at the look she had seen in his eyes. He had sensed the dark secret between her and Pete and the knowledge had hurt him, but rather than turn away from her he was trying to help. She did not deserve such kindness. She was not worthy of it, yet she needed it so desperately that she kept her eyes fixed on the place where he'd vanished into the crowd and waited with bated breath until he reappeared.

"Here," he said, handing her a tall paper cup and sitting beside her. "Sip it slowly."

She took an obedient sip. It was ice-cold, tart and good. "My grandmother liked lemonade," she said, studying him the way he studied her. "She said it was one of the few good things the white man invented."

Caleb thought about this for a moment and then grinned. "Well, obviously she'd never watched team penning."

CHAPTER EIGHT

AT TEN MINUTES past six Caleb was ready to call in the National Guard. The boys were missing. It was like Pony had said. Giving them such absolute freedom in an atmosphere teaming with temptation and one-hundred-dollar bills burning holes in their pockets had been sheer folly on his part. Who knew where they might be, or what trouble they might have gotten themselves into. At eleven minutes past six, he was pacing back and forth, silently cursing his stupidity while Pony stood, watching him with eyes that gave nothing away.

He had no idea what she thought about him. She wouldn't be far off the mark if she called him a fool, yet when he paused his pacing to look at her there wasn't the slightest hint of reproach in her manner or her eyes. She simply was there, the way the Ferris wheel was there, the way the bright lights were there, and the milling crowds. She was frightening in that respect. He could never fathom what she was thinking or feeling…except when Pete Two Shirts was near.

He stopped and looked at his watch. Twelve minutes past the hour. He lifted his eyes to hers. ''They're in some kind of trouble.''

She shook her head so faintly that the movement was almost invisible. ''They'll come,'' she said.

''They're late.''

"They're Indians."

"What's that supposed to mean?" He closed the distance between them and stood before her, baffled.

"They live on Indian time. It's different from your time."

"But they have wristwatches, the same as I do. Why should their time be any different? I told them to meet us here at six and now it's..." He glanced down at his wrist. "It's fifteen minutes past the hour."

Pony's eyes were calm. "That is nothing," she said. "Be patient."

Five long minutes later he spotted them walking through the crowd. They were swaggering along, hands in pockets, wearing expressions that came the closest to being happy that he had ever seen. The relief that swept through Caleb effectively squelched the earlier irritation. "You boys look like you've been having way too much fun."

"We did all the rides except the stupid ones," Jimmy said.

"There's a band, a live band," Martin added, pushing his glasses up. "It's down at the park by the river. And there's a place there, a saloon called the Kickin' Mule. It serves buffalo steaks and burgers. The menu was posted outside the door. People are dancing out front, right in the grass."

Caleb glanced at Pony. "The Kickin' Mule. Sounds like my kind of place. We can eat a burger and do the Texas two-step at the same time."

"The Texas two-step?" Pony said.

"It's easy. I'll teach you." To the boys he said, "Lead the way," and with Pony walking beside him in a companionable way that he was beginning to like very much, he followed.

STEVEN YOUNG BEAR was sitting with his back against the rough bark of a big cottonwood growing near the river. It was nice here in the shade, and he could see the band playing on the banner-draped bandstand, the people below dancing, whooping and yipping and clapping their hands when they turned and stomped their feet. It was good music. A good band. He raised his plastic cup for a sip of soda and glanced at his friend, Pete Two Shirts.

"Less than two hours until the rodeo."

Pete looked at him and grinned. "I'm ready."

"You're crazy," Steven corrected with an answering grin of his own.

An hour ago, when Pete and Steven had first arrived at the fairgrounds, they had stopped to look at the horse Pete had drawn. The mustangs were kept in a common corral and driven out as they were needed. Twister had kept to himself, a young four-year-old, fresh off the range with the ways of a wild horse still deeply embedded in him. Pete pointed out how the colt missed nothing. He did not plunge his nose into the water bucket like a domestic horse would do. He lowered it carefully and only as far as he needed in order to keep his eyes clear to watch for danger. He lifted his dripping muzzle and stared right at Pete, and Steven had looked at his friend in mild surprise.

"I think he knows you're riding him tonight," he said.

Pete had rounded his shoulders, turned away from the colt and glanced at his friend. "A Crow's wealth used to be measured in the number of horses he had.

Hell, Steven, it wasn't all that long ago. Twister's past is all tangled up with our own history, and each of us came to the brink of extinction. It makes me feel kind of strange, looking at him that way. It makes me want to throw open that damn gate and give him back his freedom and his old ways."

The two men stood side by side and gazed at mustang over corral fence.

"He's pretty good-looking, huh?" Steven said.

"Pretty mean," Pete amended. "The Bureau of Land Management adoption program rejected him as untrainable, so he was sold off to a rodeo outfit. He's only been on the circuit for a few short months, but he already has a killer reputation. Hates people. No one's been able to ride him, and some have been attacked if the chase riders couldn't intervene quick enough. One man got bitten by him last week. Damn horse broke the guy's arm."

Steven shifted his gaze to his friend's face. "And tonight it's your turn to ride him, or be killed or maimed."

"The crowds love that stuff." Pete shrugged. "It's dangerous as hell to use a horse that mean, but they use three chase ponies with him now, two to drive the crazy bastard away from the fallen rider, and the third to get the fallen rider to safety."

Steven knew that Pete, in spite of all the injuries he'd gotten over the years, was not afraid to ride the mustang. He'd never been afraid to ride a horse. Any horse. Steven shook his head.

"Like I said, you really are crazy," he concluded somberly. "And on that note, let me buy you your last supper." He had taken Pete to a place down on the river that served up good burgers and had a live

dance band playing out front. It was enjoyable just to
sit in the shade and watch the people dancing. He
raised his plastic cup for another sip of soda and froze
as his eyes caught sight of his sister stepping onto the
green with Caleb McCutcheon and the five boys.
"Hey," he said. "There's Pony. Let's go say hello."
He set his cup down and was getting to his feet when
Pete grabbed his arm.

"You go visit with her. I said hello earlier, and I
need to keep focused." While Steven watched, Pete
poured the rest of his soda onto the ground, stood up
in one lithe movement and tossed his cup in the nearest trash container. "I'll go back to the fairgrounds,
hang with the cowboys. Maybe I'll see you later."

Steven lingered for a moment after Pete left, watching as Caleb McCutcheon guided his sister and the
boys to an outside table. He watched the tall rancher
pull out a chair for Pony and saw the upward glance
she flashed him as she sat. He observed the expression
on McCutcheon's face and instantly changed his mind
about paying them a visit. Five boys were enough of
a deterrent to the kind of chemistry he saw working
at that table. The last thing Pony needed right now
was her big brother joining the crowd.

He'd catch up with her later to ask how things were
going out at the Bow and Arrow, though from the
looks of things they were going pretty well. It was
high time that things went well for his sister. She
deserved better than the deprived life she had meted
out to herself. She deserved to have a wealthy rancher
like Caleb McCutcheon pull out a chair for her and...

Steven's train of thought hit a wall and came to a
crashing halt. Caleb McCutcheon and his sister?
Could Pony be falling for a *white* man? *Pony?* One

of the most traditional and stubborn-minded young women on the reservation?

With a shake of his head and a faint smile, Steven Young Bear turned and followed after his crazy old friend, Pete.

THEY ORDERED BUFFALO BURGERS and fries and sat outside at one of the tables, listening to the band and watching the dancers as the afternoon waned and the air cooled. "Is that the Texas two-step?" Pony asked, a little frown creasing the smooth skin between her eyebrows.

"Yes." Caleb had ordered a beer, and he took a swallow. "It's pretty simple."

"Is that all there is to it?"

"Well, you can add whatever you want, but that's the basic step. Think you can manage it?"

"She can do that dance easy," Jimmy scoffed. "She has lots of trophies for dancing."

Caleb leaned back in his chair and gave Pony an appraising glance, but she dropped her eyes to her plate and picked up her burger. "What kind of dancing?"

"She won top honors at the Crow Fair for five years in a row as best woman straight dancer," Jimmy said, proprietary pride warming his young voice. "The Crow Fair is the biggest in the nation."

"She won the ladies' buckskin dance, too," Martin added. "She'd win everything hands down, but she wears her grandmother's dresses, and they're real plain. So the judges don't want to look at her, but they have to because she's the best dancer even though she doesn't wear the best clothes."

"Yeah, the things she wears are way too old and

drab,'' Jimmy said. ''She needs to get some new ones.''

''I do not,'' Pony said. ''Those dresses are my *great*-grandmother's,'' she corrected. ''And they are beautiful. They don't need all those bright colors because they are real and they are beautiful. They are made of elk skin,'' she said in an aside to Caleb. ''My great-grandmother dyed porcupine quills and worked them into traditional designs. The trade beads she used are old glass from the 1800s. Both the dress and the moccasins are very valuable.''

''But the judges like the bright colors,'' Jimmy said stubbornly.

''They like the flashy stuff,'' Roon said, ''but that doesn't mean flashy is better.''

''It's better if you want to win,'' Martin insisted. ''My cousin dances. He does the fancy dance. That's really fast and flashy.''

''Yeah, but he never wins anything. It isn't enough to be fast and flashy,'' Joe said.

''Well, maybe not, but it helps.'' Martin pushed his glasses up and inhaled another fistful of French fries. ''Anyhow, Pony can do that Texas two-step, no sweat, even if she isn't wearing her great-grandmother's dull old dress.''

Caleb watched Pony with a faint smile. ''Want to give it a try?'' he said.

Her eyes widened, as dark and beautiful as those of a startled doe. ''Right now?'' she said.

He rose out of his chair and extended his hand to her. ''There's no time like the present.''

She took his hand reluctantly and allowed herself to be led to the outskirts of the dancing, where they faced each other, and before he could lose his nerve, he drew her close, one hand around her waist, the other clasping her hand and holding it shoulder high. Her free hand rested lightly on his shoulder. "Just listen to the music and follow my lead," he murmured, but his words were unnecessary because the rhythm of the dance seemed to move within her, and she followed him with a natural grace that he envied, doing the two-step as if she'd done it all her life.

Too soon the song was over, and his hand tightened on hers. "One more?" he said. And please, he added a silent plea to the band, make it a long one....

Being this close to her was intoxicating. He bent his head over hers and breathed the sweetness of her hair and skin. Eyes half-closed, he let the music and the lyrics release feelings that had been building within him ever since he first met this extraordinary woman.

As the song ended he released her slowly. She dropped her eyes and turned away. They were walking back to their table when a man blocked their way. He was young, heavyset, and he'd had too much to drink. His face was flushed and his eyes were bright. He reached out for Pony's arm and said to Caleb with a leer, "You don't mind, do ya, big fella, if I steal a dance with your pretty little squaw?"

For a moment Caleb just stood there, digesting with disbelief the words he'd just heard, and then a surge of anger propelled him forward. He knocked the man's arm away and would have flattened him in the next moment if Pony hadn't stepped between them and laid her hand as light as a feather upon his arm. "Caleb," she said in a cautioning voice.

"Hey, mister, all I wanted was a dance," the man

said in a wounded voice, backing up a few unsteady steps before diving into the crowd.

"Come on." Pony's fingers tightened on his arm, and at length he turned and escorted her to the table. He could feel the bitter anger coursing through him as he pulled out her chair and seated her. "I'm sorry about that," he said.

"It wasn't your fault."

"He shouldn't have said that."

"It doesn't matter," Pony said, shaking her head.

"Yes, it does." He glared out at the crowd but there was no sign of the drunk. "It matters a great deal." The boys followed this exchange without comment. Perhaps they'd seen this kind of thing before. "You boys done eating?" he said. They nodded. "Good. Let's blow this joint." He picked up his beer and finished it, reached for his wallet and caught the waitress's eye as she passed. Moments later they were leaving the Kickin' Mule and walking back toward the fairgrounds, to where the rodeo was about to begin.

"BULL RIDING," Jimmy said, sitting on the very edge of the bleacher overlooking the arena. "That's the toughest event of them all. Those critters are mean and they have big horns."

"Nah! Bareback bronc riding," Dan said. "Remember the time that guy was killed by that bronc at Crow Fair? Horse tossed him off and kicked him in the head right in front of the judges. Boom! Dead. Just like that."

"Boys," Pony said. "The team-penning demonstration is about to begin. Watch closely, because we'll be doing this sort of thing with the buffalo before too long.''

That got their attention. They looked down at the arena where a group of cattle milled warily about, being held at one end by two horsemen. At the other end of the arena a small pen had been erected. The gate was open and a chalk line had been drawn across the arena three-quarters of the way to the pen. ''That's the foul line,'' Pony said, reading from the rodeo pamphlet she held. ''No more than one cow can cross that line unless it's one of the three that are being penned. The three riders have to pick out the three cows the judges tell them to. See the numbers painted on the cows? There are three cows with zeros, three with one's, et cetera, and so if the judge says, 'Seven,' the riders have to find the three cows wearing the number seven, cut them out of the herd and drive them into the pen.''

Martin heaved an exaggerated sigh. ''What's so difficult about that?'' he said just as the third rider jogged her horse into the arena and the faceless announcer blared, ''Three!'' over the loudspeaker.

''Yeeeehaaaawww!'' The riders let out whoops that rocked the summer evening and there was instant pandemonium. The riders kicked their horses, the horses sprinted and spun, the cattle dashed and dodged, the riders' voices screamed shrilly over it all, ''Hey cow! Hey cow! Hey cow!'' or ''Chaw! Chaw! Chaw!'' Dust rose, cattle bawled in panic, and then, miraculously, one cow with a big number three painted on its side was in the holding pen. Another was being cut out of the herd and hazed down the arena as the first rider kept the milling cattle away from the foul line and kept the first cow from rejoining the herd. The second number-three cow was penned, and finally, the third rider herded the third cow into the pen and the gate slammed shut.

"Time!" the loudspeaker blared. "Sixty-two seconds! Not a bad ride!" The crowd burst into enthusiastic applause as the dust settled.

"They have to get all three cattle in the pen in under ninety seconds," Pony explained when the noise had abated. The boys were still staring.

"Wow," Jimmy breathed. "You think we'll ever be able to ride like that?"

The cattle were being herded out of the arena and the temporary corral was being taken down in preparation for the next event. "Sure," Caleb said. "Maybe next season you can even compete in team penning."

"*Next* season?" Martin said. All the boys studied Caleb intently while Pony pretended to read the rodeo pamphlet.

"Well, I'd say this season would be a little too soon. That sort of riding and teamwork requires a lot of practice."

"Bareback bronc riding is next," Pony said, changing the subject.

"Does Pete ride in that?" Martin said.

"Yeah, stupid," Jimmy said. "That's how he broke his leg that time at Crow Fair, the same year the other guy got his head kicked in."

The loudspeaker blared again, giving the lineup of riders and horses. Pete was riding fifth on Twister. Pony clutched the pamphlet in her hands. Twister. The name was ominous, but bucking horses often had bad-sounding names. It was part of their image.

From where Pony and the group sat, they could see

the first rider perched on the edge of the chute while the crew struggled with the horse, tightening the leather strap behind its withers. The cowboy snugged down his hat, pulled his gloves tight and then dropped onto the horse's back and curled his gloved fingers beneath the leather strap. There was a lot of fussing and fidgeting before the rider gave a nod and the gate burst open. He only stayed aboard five seconds before being tossed into the dirt of the arena. He jumped up, grabbed his hat, dusted off his britches and trotted over to the fence. That was the end for rider number one. Number two fared worse. Number three rode it out to the buzzer, but his horse was predictable. "They call that kind of horse a dead-easy ride," Pony said, quoting something she'd heard Pete say long ago.

"What about Pete's horse, Twister?" Jimmy asked.

"That kind of horse is like a bolt of lightning wrapped in barbed wire and blown up with dynamite," she said, watching as number four came out of the chute on a horse called Gunshot. It was a good ride on a good horse and it put the rider in the lead.

"Pete's next," Martin said, leaning forward and pushing his glasses back up his nose and craning to see. "What's he doing? How does he look?"

"He looks like all the others except he's an Indian," Jimmy said.

"I'd say that makes him look a whole lot better than all the others," Roon said. "Pete's the best horseman here," he said. "He's going to ride that mustang. You wait and see."

Pony was unaware that she had crumpled her rodeo

program until Caleb reached over and squeezed her hand reassuringly. "He'll be all right," he said.

She could see Pete perched on the edge of the chute, black hat pulled down, studying the bay mustang he was about to ride. He glanced up as if he felt her looking at him, and for a moment their eyes locked. She stood as he lowered himself astride Twister.

Caleb rose to his feet to stand beside her. Pete gave the nod, the chute opened and suddenly the whole crowd stood, too, because they knew the reputation of this wild and dangerous mustang who had never been ridden to the bell. People shouted and screamed and much as Pony didn't want to watch, she couldn't tear her eyes away. Four seconds, five…

It was impossible that Pete could still be aboard. Six seconds. Seven… The mustang gave no pattern to his desperate attempts to dislodge the man from his back.

No man could possibly ride that horse, yet one man was. The screams of the crowd and the deafening blare of the announcer dulled Pony's senses. She felt light-headed. "Nine! Ten!" The crowd went insane. Then, as if the little mustang had begun to realize that he couldn't rid himself of the man on his back, he flung himself at the fence.

Twister climbed halfway up the fence and fell backward in a writhing tangle of panic and fear with Pete trying to fling himself clear. They went down together in a crashing heap. The mustang scrambled up with a desperate lunge, spinning on his hind legs and parrying at the chase ponies who tried to drive him off. He flung himself at the fence again, trying to scale it, and caught one foreleg between the stout

boards. For a moment it seemed as if he was hopelessly entangled, but then he wrenched free and fell
backward once again. Pete had gained his feet and
made it to the fence. He began to pull himself up,
climbing painfully, and was helped by reaching hands
from above who seized onto him and lifted him over
the fence to safety. The cheers and applause of the
crowd drowned out the loudspeaker proclaiming Pete
the new leader of the bareback bronc riding.

Pony sat down abruptly as her muscles turned to
water. She listened to the screams and applause of the
crowd and the enthusiastic blare of the announcer's
voice and felt suddenly very ill. She felt a hand on
her arm, lifting her back to her feet. An arm around
her shoulders, protectively supporting her. Caleb.

She let herself be led from the stadium, relieved to
get away from the noise and brutality of it all. She
leaned against him, grateful for his calm strength as
they moved from the arena. The boys were anxious
to find Pete. "He got a perfect score!" she heard
Jimmy saying. "Has anyone ever gotten a perfect
score before?"

"Has any *Indian* ever gotten a perfect score," Martin corrected.

"No, stupid," Jimmy said. "I mean, this is really
something. Pete got a perfect score. That makes him
famous!"

"Boys," Pony said, stopping abruptly. "Pete is
hurt, and that beautiful wild horse is hurt. What are
you talking about?"

"Money," Roon said, his voice mirroring his
scowl. "They're talking about money."

"Yeah, that's right, Mother Roon. Pete could make

a lot of money from this," Jimmy said defensively. "What's wrong with that?"

"Why don't we go check on him and make sure he's okay," Caleb said, his low, firm voice ending the conversation. "Maybe we can give him a lift to the hospital. After what just happened, I'm sure he'll need it."

Pony was surprised to find her brother Steven with Pete in the corrals. Pete's shirt was off and the rodeo's veterinarian was taping his ribs and grumbling about how damn foolish rodeo riders were. "If just half the world's population had your mentality," he muttered as he wrapped the wide adhesive tape around and around, "there'd be no world population at all."

"I could argue that point," Pete said, lowering his arms when the procedure was finished and reaching for his shirt, "but I have a bull to ride."

"You have some busted ribs. Ride at your own risk."

"I always do, Doc. You know that." He nodded at Pony. "Hello."

"You're crazy," she said.

Pete grinned. "I know. Your brother just told me the same thing."

"How's Twister?" McCutcheon asked the veterinarian.

"I don't think the leg is broken but he's got bad tendon damage, that's plain enough. He's through with the rodeo and it's just as well. The poor thing hated it, but he gave Pete, here, the ride of his life. He'll never draw another horse like that."

Pete buttoned his shirt while the veterinarian packed up his gear and departed. Steven shook each of the boys' hands in greeting and then shook Mc-

Cutcheon's as well. "Things going well at the ranch?" he asked, and Caleb nodded.

"Couldn't be better. Your sister's great. She really knows the buffalo."

"She had a good teacher," Pete said, tucking his shirttail into his jeans and giving her a faint grin.

Pony felt her cheeks warm under her brother's keen scrutiny, and in the awkward silence that followed, the boys stared at Pete as if he were a god.

"You got a perfect score!" Jimmy suddenly burst out. "That makes you perfect."

Pete reached for his hat and pulled it over his long black hair. "No, Jimmy. I'm not perfect. Did you see the horse I rode?" Jimmy nodded. "Everything about that mustang was perfect, from the way he was built right down to his attitude. He didn't want to be civilized. He didn't want to be tamed. He didn't want to be domesticated. He wanted to be free. That horse I rode was perfect, and by riding him tonight, I killed him. So how perfect does that make me?"

Jimmy stared and then dropped his eyes.

"He's not dead," Caleb said.

Pete shrugged. "He will be. They'll ship him out in the morning and process him into dog food cans."

"Where is he now?"

"They hazed him into that chute over there, thinking the vet might be able to fix him up. But there's the hell of it. He's so wild he won't let anyone touch him, especially his lower legs."

"Wild horses don't like to have their legs touched," Roon said. "Their legs are all they have to carry them away from danger."

Pete nodded. "True, Roon. So the way things stand, we can't help him."

"Maybe all he needs is a good long rest," Caleb said.

"Maybe," Pete said. "But there's no guarantee he'll ever be sound again. The rodeo boss already handed down the verdict and he's a practical man."

"What's the going price for eight hundred pounds of horse meat?" Caleb said.

Pete looked at Caleb for a long appraising moment. "Not much," he said.

"Who do I talk to about buying him?"

"The rodeo boss. He owns all these broncs. I'll find him for you." Pete shot Caleb a quizzical glance. "You sure you want to do this?"

Caleb didn't hesitate. "I think that horse deserves a chance."

"He'll want more money from you than he will from me or the knacker."

Caleb withdrew a blank check from his wallet, signed it and handed the piece of paper to Pete, who took it with a nod. "All right. I'll catch up with him tonight and strike the best bargain I can. I'll trailer the colt over to your place in the morning." He paused, hitched a painful breath and then looked at Roon. "My guess is you'll be the one to get through to that mustang, if anyone can," he said, and when Roon didn't reply, he said, "You know the language and you have a way, but be careful around him. He has a lot of anger inside, and you'll need a lot of patience."

He shook Caleb's hand and slapped Steven's shoulder. "And now if you'll excuse me, I have a bull to ride," he said. He glanced at Pony, nodded to the boys and walked back toward the arena in a tucked-over limp.

"Maybe we should go watch him," Jimmy said after a long moment.

But suddenly there was a deep bass thump and a bright spangle of light across the dark sky, and Martin said, "Fireworks! Down at the park!"

"But what if he gets hurt again?" Jimmy said.

"I'll stick with him," Steven said. "Don't worry. He'll be okay."

"I'm for the fireworks, boys," Caleb said, and it seemed that the boys were of the same opinion, because as a group they immediately began walking toward the river. Pony hesitated. She looked over at the corral that held the injured mustang, then walked quietly there. In the darkness, lit by sporadic bursts of dazzling light, she gazed between the fence board at the trembling hide of the frightened colt. She felt Caleb's presence beside her and wished she had the courage to reach out for his hand. Instead, she made a gentle, soothing noise and the colt's head lifted and turned. She saw the dark shine of that wild eye as he sought her out. She spoke to the mustang in her native tongue and it was as if the animal understood she was a sympathetic spirit who wanted to help.

Caleb reached for her hand and she was grateful for the strong warmth of his grasp. She whispered, "I'll see you tomorrow," to the injured horse and then allowed Caleb to lead her toward the river. After several minutes of silence, she said, "Thank you."

"For what?"

"For trying to save Twister."

"It's not practical, but I guess I'm not a very practical man."

She smiled at him as the dark sky was illuminated in another burst of bright fireworks. "I think that you're a wonderful man, Caleb McCutcheon,'' she said. ''Thank you for being so impractical. And thank you for being so kind to the boys. And thank you...'' Her hand tightened on his as she struggled for the words to tell him how she felt. For a moment they regarded each other in the fading light. Suddenly he stepped closer and his other hand slipped to the curve of her waist as if it belonged there.

''Pony,'' he said, in a voice rough with emotion. She closed her eyes in anticipation of a kiss....

''Hey! Hurry up!'' Jimmy's strident tone reached them from somewhere up ahead. ''We're going to miss the fireworks.''

THE SMALL SOUND that woke him came from the floor; a soft scurrying that stopped when he opened his eyes and tried to focus. He was lying on his stomach, one arm dangling over the edge of the mattress and the bedsheet tangled around his hips. He blinked and saw a pair of bright eyes staring up at him. A mouse sat within an easy jump of his hand.

Morning already. Late morning, he amended, noticing the patches of sunlight on the ground.

''She told me she thought I was wonderful,'' he mumbled to the mouse, ''and she told Pete she thought he was crazy. I guess that puts me ahead a little, but I have a long way to go, because I'm pretty sure she's still in love with Pete.'' The mouse stared as if waiting for more. ''You see, this is what I think,'' Caleb continued. ''I think they were in love once, but something bad happened between them and they broke up. They still care about each other, but for some reason they can't get beyond that bad thing that happened.''

The mouse's whiskers twitched.

"I know I'm being foolish to think she might fall in love with me even a little bit. I mean, we've only known each other a few weeks. But that doesn't matter, does it? How long you know someone isn't as important as how strongly you feel about them, right? And last night we *both* felt something strong."

The mouse dropped to all four feet and disappeared. Caleb rolled onto his back with a moan. He ached all over. Maybe that was because all night long in his troubled dreams he'd been beating up the drunk who'd insulted Pony. If Caleb felt this bad after beating up an imaginary foe, he could only imagine how Pete must be feeling this morning.

He sat up with a surge of adrenaline. Pete was probably already on the road, hauling that wild mustang out to the ranch. And here he was, lying in bed like a lazy gentleman rancher, the one thing in the world he didn't want to be perceived as by Pony. He climbed out of bed and was showered, dressed and pulling on his boots when he heard the thump of footsteps on the porch. He pushed open the screen door and saw Guthrie standing there holding a pot of coffee.

"Ramalda sent me down to make sure you were alive," he said, giving Caleb a brief up and down. "Those boys must've wrung you out."

Caleb carried two mugs onto the porch, and Guthrie filled them both. They sat side by side watching the creek run by and enjoying Ramalda's hot strong brew. "We got home late," Caleb said.

"Yessir. The boys told me all about it. They told me about the mustang, too. I moved the horses around and freed up the small corral. We can hold him there until we figure out what our next move will be.''

''I know that buying an injured wild horse isn't the smartest thing I've ever done,'' Caleb said. ''But dammit, it just happened.''

''I've heard of that mustang. He's all the buzz in the bronc-riding world.''

''Not anymore. Nor do I have the foggiest idea what a person does with a crippled horse that hates people.'' Caleb drank some more of his coffee. ''How's Absa?''

''She behaved pretty well yesterday. Blue helped me baby-sit. And I milked that damn cow. Twice. I don't like milk cows. They kick.''

''She kicked you?''

''Yessir. Twice.''

''I'm pulling Pony off the fence detail. You, Badger and I can handle the boys. She'll be more useful overseeing the construction of the holding corrals and entering data into the computer than cutting up her hands with that damn barbed wire. She'll probably be better at milking the cow, too.''

Guthrie gave him a hopeful look. ''She agreed to that?''

''Not really. She didn't like the insinuation that I thought she was too delicate for fence work.''

The younger man grinned. ''Jessie would've called me a few choice names if I'd done the same. She might even have kicked me in the shin.'' He paused and listened. ''I hear somethin' comin'.''

Leaning over the porch rail, they caught a glimpse of Pete's old truck hauling an equally decrepit trailer across the bridge toward the ranch house. Caleb finished his coffee and set the cup on the porch rail. ''I wonder if maybe Pete would want to keep that horse,'' he said hopefully.

Guthrie was already starting down the steps and he looked back. ''What for?''

''If that hurt leg gets better, he could sell Twister back to the rodeo and make a killing.''

Guthrie grinned. ''Pete would've bought the horse himself if he thought it had a snowball's chance in hell of recoverin'.''

CHAPTER NINE

PONY WAS IN THE BARN with Roon and Absa when Pete drove into the yard. It was just past 10:00 a.m. and Caleb had not come up to the house for breakfast. She wondered if she had said or done something the night before that might have made him want to keep to himself or if maybe he needed a break from her and the boys. She walked out of the barn and into the hot sunlight and stood beside the corral while Roon indicated where Pete needed to park the trailer. Pete waved, then backed the old trailer right up to the open gate of the small holding corral. He cut the engine, popped the rusted door open and sat there looking at her.

"How are you feeling?" she said.

He gave her a weary but triumphant grin. "Rich," he said, and patted his jacket pocket. "I won the bareback riding and it was a good purse. Got dumped by the bull, but what the hell. You need to borrow some money? I'll give you a good interest rate."

The other boys had heard the truck, too, and appeared as Caleb and Guthrie walked into sight from the path leading to the cabin. Pete eased himself out of the cab, pulled down his black hat and fished a piece of paper out of his jacket pocket, handing it to Caleb when he drew near. "It's the bill of sale," he said. "And a receipt for the check."

Caleb glanced at it, nodded, and put the paper in his own pocket. "Roon," he said, "maybe Absa shouldn't be near when we unload this horse. We don't want her getting kicked. And you boys keep back. I don't want anyone getting hurt." They all nodded. Caleb glanced at Pony. "Good morning," he said.

"Good morning." She dropped her eyes and hoped he didn't notice the flush of color that warmed her face. Pete walked behind the trailer and undid the latches, lowering the ramp to the ground. He climbed into the empty stall beside the bay mustang. Speaking quietly, he untied the halter rope. Still on the other side of the stall partition, he slowly backed the mustang out.

They watched the tortuous process—Twister was unable to put weight on his left foreleg. Finally the colt was standing three-legged on the packed dirt of the ranch yard. The little mustang had lost all of his wild spirit. Nothing remained but a shrunken ghost of his former self, a shell filled with pain and fear. His knee was grossly swollen, and below the knee the edema was so severe that no definition of a fetlock remained. The colt tried to keep the limb off the ground, but without being able to bend the knee, the hoof scraped in the dirt as he hobbled. Pony lowered her eyes, unable to watch. She heard Guthrie swear softly.

"It's bad, isn't it?" Caleb said to Guthrie.

"Yessir. But I'm not swearin' about the knee."

"What then?"

"I don't know as I've ever seen a more classic face," Guthrie said. "Look at that chest, those withers, the set of his tail. But how come he's not gelded?

I thought the BLM made that mandatory on wild horses when they were sold off or adopted out.''

''They do,'' Pete said. ''But the rodeo boss was dragging his heels. Figured he'd get around to it when they served him with legal papers, and in the meantime he'd take full advantage of that extra shot of energy and pure stallion meanness.''

''And the vet said the leg ain't broke?''

''That's what he told us last night,'' Caleb said. ''But it looks pretty bad to me. A lot worse than it did yesterday.''

Guthrie nodded. ''Injuries often look worse the day after. Pete, have you tried hosing the leg down?''

Pete shook his head. ''Hell, I tried to get someone to hose *me* down this morning, but no takers.''

''Roon, why don't you go in the barn and get the hose hanging on the wall by door. We'll connect it to the drain faucet of that stock tank in the corral and try some cold water on that knee. See if he stands still for it.''

Roon went to get the hose while Pete led the colt into the corral and up to the stock tank, but the moment Roon reappeared carrying the hose the mustang threw its head back with a snort of alarm. Roon immediately backed away.

''Okay,'' Guthrie said. ''It looks like that plan's a no-go.''

''Might've been hit with a hose once,'' Pete said. ''Some wranglers will use sections of a hose to move horses through chutes, load them into stock trailers. Whatever.''

''Yeah,'' Guthrie said, rubbing the back of his neck with a look of disgust. ''Whatever.''

''Well, what can we try next?'' Caleb asked.

They all stared at Twister. "What do you think, Roon?" Guthrie asked. "If we can't bring water to the horse, maybe we can bring the horse to water. I never met a mustang yet that didn't like to splash around in the water."

"Yeah," Pete said. "Good idea. I could trailer him back down to the creek."

"There's a deep sandy pool just below the cabin," Guthrie said. He glanced at Roon. "Put a hackamore on old Sparky. You can ride him and lead the mustang into the swimming hole."

Roon nodded and turned toward the barn with the hose. By the time Pete had reloaded the injured horse into the trailer, Roon was already riding Sparky down to the creek with Absa hobbling alongside. Pony couldn't help but smile at the sight. Roon was in his element. It was as if he'd found a calling in tending to these animals. The little buffalo calf and the injured mustang had given his life a purpose, and he took that purpose very seriously.

Pony saw Caleb and Guthrie turn away from the corral and start down the path toward the cabin, followed by the boys. Caleb's expression was solemn. She wanted to reassure him that he had done the right thing but she remained where she was, following him only with her eyes. Pete climbed back into his truck. "Roon's doing okay," he said. "And that little buffalo calf is looking real good."

She nodded and turned down the path the others had taken.

"You look good, too, Pony. Happier than you have in a long time." She stopped, and his next words caused a surge of dread. "We need to talk later, about some things."

She nodded slowly. Then continued toward the creek.

She walked so quickly that she stumbled on a root and fell to her knees, skinning her hands and knocking the breath from her. She knelt on the ground and felt tears fill her eyes. When she stood, she heard Pete's truck driving slowly. She hesitated for a moment before turning back toward the barn, walking at first, then breaking into a run.

"TORTILLAS," Caleb mused aloud as he watched the mustang being unloaded for the second time from the trailer that was now parked beside the creek.

Guthrie eyed him from beneath his hat brim. "You got something up your sleeve, boss?"

"Ramalda's fresh corn tortillas. There isn't a horse on the face of this planet that could resist one. I'm going to beg a handful from her. Maybe Roon can start making friends with that wild demon while it's standing in the creek soaking its leg."

"Maybe," Guthrie said. "Just don't expect too much too quick."

Caleb walked back up the path feeling more optimistic. Guthrie and Pete were both good horsemen. They weren't giving up on Twister, and neither was Roon. Maybe a few of Ramalda's corn tortillas would help.

He reached the barn and skidded to a stop when he spotted Pony leading the gray mustang, Dobey, out of the corral, all saddled and bridled and ready to ride.

"Hey?" he said, and she wheeled, startled, and stood looking like a child caught doing something naughty. "What's up?" he said as he approached.

"I thought I'd better check on the contractors and

see how the corrals are coming...and the pens, and the chute...and..."

He put his hand on Dobey's neck to smooth the thick tangle of mane but his eyes never left hers. "Did Pete say something to upset you?" he asked.

Her dark eyes were stricken. She shook her head and her voice was a fierce denial. "No!"

"But you're running away from him, aren't you?" She didn't answer, or couldn't. He let his hand drop from Dobey's neck and then raised it in a futile gesture. "I'm sorry. You can do anything you want to do, Pony, you know that. I just want you to be happy. Do you need some food to take with you? I can get Ramalda to fix you something."

She shook her head again, and this time her voice was a whisper. "No."

He nodded. "All right. Can we expect you back for the noon meal?" Long silence. He narrowed his eyes and nodded again. "You be back in time for supper, or I swear I'll have half of Park County out looking for you. And Pony? If there's anything at all that I can do to help..."

She turned away from him and stepped into the saddle with smooth grace, looked down at him briefly then reined Dobey around and lifted him in to a lope, heading for the trail that led up toward the pass.

Heading for the high country, and the place where the buffalo roamed.

Caleb walked to the ranch house, but his heart followed the slender girl on the gray mustang. He asked Ramalda for the tortillas, and the old Mexican woman, guessing his intent, gave him her heated opinion in Spanish about feeding her good cooking to the likes of a useless mustang. Then she stopped abruptly and gave Caleb a searching stare. She reached out and grasped his arm.

"Tu cabeza y tu corazon son dos vocas que hablan como una!" She paused and then translated haltingly. "Your head and your heart are two voices that need to speak as one."

He felt his shoulders slump and nodded dejectedly. "I'm in love with her, Ramalda," he said. "I know it's wrong. It's wrong in so many ways, but it feels so right."

Ramalda sighed. She gave him a big stack of fresh, soft corn tortillas. She squeezed his arm again, and he walked back to the creek.

"He's liking it," Guthrie said as Caleb reached the bank. "The cold water feels good to him."

Pete looked around questioningly. "Where's Pony? She started down here a while ago."

"She went up to check on the contractors who are building the buffalo pens," he said, keeping his eyes fixed on the bay mustang to avoid having to look at Pete.

Pete said nothing, but his silence was disconcerting. It was as if he knew why Pony hadn't come.

"Ramalda's expecting you up at the house," Guthrie said. "I told her you'd been trampled by a horse and gored by a Brahman bull, and that you're hungry and hurting."

Pete struggled to his feet and nodded. "Thanks," he said. "I haven't had breakfast yet. Got anything stronger than aspirin up there?"

"Badger might. He's due back any moment. He made an early-mornin' grocery run for Ramalda and must've stopped at the Longhorn to visit with Charlie and Bernie. C'mon. I'll walk up with you." Guthrie glanced over his shoulder. "Hey, you boys watch that calf! She might try to swim out to Roon but that's not a good idea with her cast.''

"Okay," Martin said. He got up and ambled over to where Absa stood on the creek bank, looking as if she might jump in at any moment. He laced his arms around the little calf's neck and sat down, effectively anchoring her.

"How long should they stay in the water?" Caleb asked as Pete and Guthrie started off.

"As long as the colt can stand it," Guthrie said. "Then we'll load him back in the trailer and haul him back up to the corral."

Caleb nodded and sat down between Jimmy and Dan, balancing the stack of Ramalda's soft tortillas on his knee. "We'll give these to Roon when he brings the colt ashore. He can use them to make friends with Twister."

"You think he's going to make it?" Jimmy asked him.

They looked out into the middle of the shade dappled pool. The mustang stood quietly, all vestiges of aggression, pain and fear being drawn from him by the cool soothing creek water. His eyes were half closed in a state of semicomatose relaxation despite the nearness of Roon and Sparky.

"I don't know," Caleb said bluntly. "Hell, boys, I don't know if any of us is going to make it. All I know is we have to try the best we can."

PONY RODE as if pursued. She let Dobey have his head and he flattened out and ran, his hooves making the sound of sharp, rapid-fire thunder on the ground. The wind blew through her. It was July, and it was hot, yet up here in the high country, the wind was wonderfully cool.

As the trail steepened, they slowed to a walk. Pony paused to look down over the rugged country they had traveled in the past two hours. The land that spread out below them was wild and beautiful and empty. She and Dobey were alone.

Alone.

The word might have a sweet and welcome ring to it, except for the memory of Caleb McCutcheon and the way he had looked at her before she'd left. Pony dropped her head and drew a shaky breath. She felt Dobey's flanks heaving and was overcome by a rush of remorse. She swung out of the saddle and loosened the girth. She rubbed the horse's sweaty neck and led him slowly along the trail, wishing she had the courage to confront her past, because she knew that until she did, it would always block her path to happiness.

AFTER LUNCH, Pete Two Shirts departed the ranch, and Guthrie and Badger rounded up the boys to "work on the fence and earn our supper." Caleb watched them pile into Guthrie's truck, Absa riding in back amidst the kids. He declined the offer to join them.

"I'll saddle Billy and catch up with you," he said. The fence wasn't more than a mile from the ranch buildings, and it had been a few days since he'd last ridden the gelding. The screen door banged behind him, and he heard the heavy shuffling steps of Ramalda as she came up behind him. She was holding an old flour sack, the top of it goosenecked and tied with a stout piece of twine. He raised an eyebrow when she thrust it toward him.

"Food," she said.

"Ramalda, I'm only riding out to the first cross fence, and you just fed me."

"Not for you, for *her*."

Caleb lifted the sack out of Ramalda's hand. It was heavy. "For Pony?"

"Ella tiene muchas problemas," Ramalda said. "Her heart is troubled."

Caleb was taken aback. "She said she wanted to be alone."

Ramalda shook her head. "Sometimes it is not good to be alone."

"But…" Caleb looked down at the sack. Confusion mired his thoughts. Ramalda firmly believed that her food would solve all the problems of the world. "How can I be sure that this is a bad time for her to be alone?"

"Because I says so!"

Caleb wasn't going to argue. He nodded, then turned and descended the porch steps, pausing at the bottom to look back at her. She pointed toward the corrals and he obediently set off. Ramalda obviously expected him to ride up into the high country after Pony, find her in the midst of a five-thousand-acre wilderness, feed her and comfort her with his company. It was pointless to argue that his chances of finding her were poor, and that the last person she probably wanted to see right now was her meddling boss. He saddled Billy with a level of anxiety that the gelding picked up on, and by the time Caleb pulled himself into the saddle, the horse was bunched up beneath him like a bronc about to explode out of the chute. Caleb ran a calming hand down the animal's neck as he headed Billy up the valley, but it did no good.

It may have been a hot afternoon, but a little heat never stopped a good horse from scorching the trail, and for the first mile it was all Caleb could do to stay in the saddle. "Easy, easy," he soothed into Billy's flattened ears, but the words seemed to have the opposite effect, and pulling on the reins proved equally futile.

By the time Billy had run the edge off, Caleb was exhausted. The gelding dropped into a brisk single-foot, tossing his head and snorting with exuberance, sweat lathering his powerful shoulders. "Damn you, Billy," Caleb muttered as he fumbled with the sack of food, trying to tighten the lashing that held it to the saddle horn. "And damn that old Mexican woman! I know this isn't right. Pony wants to be alone. Why else would she have ridden off by herself if she didn't want to be alone."

What had Pete done to her, to make her act this way? What awful thing had happened between them? She had denied that Pete had physically hurt her, but she could be covering up for him. Maybe she was afraid of him. Maybe he drank and got mean. Caleb shook his head, puzzled. He didn't read Pete that way at all. No, it was something else, and it was none of Caleb's business…except that he cared about her.

Maybe Pony would never feel toward him the way he felt about her, but that didn't change the fact that she mattered a great deal to him, and that if anyone ever tried to hurt her, or lay a hand on her like that drunk did last night…

Was it only last night that they had been together, and life had been so good?

Caleb touched his heels to Billy's flanks. "Okay, old boy. I'm rested. Let's burn some more trail. I'd like to deliver Pony's lunch before suppertime."

SHE FOUND THE BUFFALO grazing in a high mountain park threaded by a clear swift shallow stream. The wind was in her face as Dobey came out of the woods at the edge of the vast, sun-swept meadow. She saw his ears twitch at some distant movement and followed the swing of his head. And there they were, maybe half a mile away. The cows, their spring calves and the big bull, too. They hadn't spotted Dobey, and she held him still, transfixed by the sight of the buffalo. She swung out of the saddle and tied Dobey in the shade at the edge of the meadow, loosening the girth and giving his damp shoulder an appreciative rub.

It was hot, but the strong breeze and deep shade made it comfortable. She sat at the foot of a tree and rested against it, drawing a deep breath. The rigor of the ride had tired her but left her feeling better. She watched the buffalo, small at this distance, yet close enough that she could observe the antics of the calves as they played amongst themselves for short periods before returning to their mothers. One calf returned to its mother at a full gallop and butted her in the side, but the mother paid no attention whatsoever and continued her placid grazing.

She drew her knees up to her chest and felt a sharp pang of hunger. Breakfast had been served at dawn. Now it was midafternoon and she wondered what Ramalda had prepared for the noon meal. She wondered how the injured mustang was doing, wondered if Pete had left the ranch yet, and if Caleb would really organize a search party if she wasn't back in time for supper. Probably. He had seemed quite determined.

Being up high like this made the ranch seem remote. Looking down on the herd of bison, grazing in such a setting, made her feel as if she had entered another time, and that when she rode back down the mountain she might find a village of tepees where the ranch house stood.

Who might she find in that village, and would anyone know her name?

The buffalo calf who had butted its mother was making another charge. Once again it bounced off its mother's massive side, and again the cow calmly ignored it. Pony smiled and then quite unexpectedly her eyes flooded with tears. She wiped them away impatiently but something buried deep inside had been brought to the surface by the antics of the little buffalo calf and the response of its patient mother. More tears ran down her cheeks, and she wiped them on her shirtsleeve.

"Don't be foolish," she berated herself, and to her complete mortification her words ended in a strangled sob. She buried her face in her hands, unable to stop the hot flood of tears and the horrible gasping noises of pain and grief. She had no idea how long she huddled there, releasing all the emotions she'd kept bottled inside for years. Finally, the low rumble of thunder roused her, and she lifted her head.

Black clouds towered over the mountain peaks to the west. The sky above her was still a sun-washed blue, but Pony knew the speed of these mountain storms. She heard Dobey give a snort of alarm and turned her head. He was looking at something standing on the edge of the woods not fifty feet away. Her heart rate jumped as she struggled to her feet. A man moved out of the shadows. She stared in disbelief as she recognized her boss. He was holding a bulging cloth sack in one hand and looking as if he'd just robbed a bank.

"What are you doing here?" she said, perfectly aware that her face was ravaged.

"Ramalda was worried about you," he said, holding both hands at shoulder height as if he was afraid she would pull a pistol out and shoot him. He gave the heavy sack a shake. "She sent food."

"How did you find me?"

He lifted his shoulders apologetically. "It wasn't as hard as I thought it would be. I followed your tracks."

"You shouldn't have come."

"I know. I'm sorry."

She wiped her cheeks with the palms of her hands. "I never cry."

"I know."

"I needed to be alone."

"I know. I'm sorry," he repeated.

"Please put your hands down, Mr. McCutcheon. I'm not going to shoot you, though maybe I should."

He nodded and lowered his arms. Another rumble of thunder made them both look. "That storm's coming fast," he said, glancing at the towering wall of thunderheads. "If we ride like hell we might make it to the line camp."

"What line camp?"

"That creek down there is Piney Creek. See that big grove of trees midway across the meadow? There's a cabin there, on the other side of the creek. It's about a mile from here. Get your horse."

He didn't wait to see if she did, but turned to retrieve his own. She wondered how long he'd been
there. Obviously he'd spotted her, gotten off his horse
and come ahead on foot. He might have been standing
there for several minutes, but no, Dobey would have
warned her. Caleb McCutcheon obviously knew that
she'd been crying, but he hadn't been spying. Moments later, McCutcheon reappeared astride Billy.
The wind had picked up, and a sharp crack of thunder
made Billy jump sideways and snort in alarm.

"Come on, hurry up," Caleb said. She tightened
Dobey's girth, untied him from the tree and swung
into the saddle. "All set?" he said, and she nodded.
"Okay, then. Let's ride."

And ride they did, down the gentle slope at a dead
gallop and out onto the flat meadow, sending the buffalo stampeding. They leaned over their horses' withers and charged at the wall of black sky skewered
with bright flashes of lightning that swept toward
them, raced toward the thick grove of evergreens that
sheltered the little cabin. Caleb reached the creek first
and Billy hit the water at a lope that threw up a ream
of spray. Four big lunges and they were across.

Pony checked her horse and followed Caleb's lead,
but midway across, Dobey stumbled on the loose
river rocks and nearly went down, neatly pitching her
over his shoulder. As she scrambled to her feet,
Dobey dashed off without her, disappearing into the
trees. A bolt of lightning split the sky and the explo-
sive burst of thunder shook the ground. Pony lurched
out of the water as the rain began to fall. She felt the
drops drumming hard on her head, realized that she'd
lost her hat, and turned to look for it. There was a
simultaneous brilliant blue streak of lightning and

boom of thunder, and a lone tree not more than one hundred yards out in the meadow burst apart. She stared, transfixed.

"Pony!"

She heard her name over the savagery of the storm and turned again. Caleb was running toward her, and before she could move he had scooped her into his arms. He didn't have very far to go before reaching the cabin. The door was open and he carried her inside, kicking it shut against the wall of wind and water. He set her down and held her at arm's length. She stared at him in the dimness, dazed and a little out of breath.

"Are you all right?" he asked, his gaze intent and his hands shifting to touch the sides of her face.

"I lost my hat," she said.

"The hell with your hat. We can get you a new one. You sure you're all right? No broken bones?"

"No broken bones."

Rainwater still streamed from his Stetson as he scrutinized her with those clear blue eyes. His thumbs gently brushed the rainwater from her cheeks, and for one heart-stopping moment she thought he was going to pull her close and kiss her, but she was wrong. "Thank God," he said. His eyes and hands released her as he turned away, removing his hat and tossing it onto the table.

"Thank God," he repeated, a little out of breath himself. "You're soaking wet."

"So are you," she said over the drumming of raindrops on the roof. "Where are the horses?"

"In the lean-to out back. They're both okay." He glanced around the dim interior of the cabin. "Looks like we might be stuck here for a little while."

She nodded and listened to the fury of the storm. "Good," she said softly, thinking that being carried to this little log cabin in the arms of Caleb McCutcheon was probably one of the best things that had ever happened to her, but her voice was drowned out by the thunder.

"What's that?"

Oh, for the courage to tell him how she felt! "I said, that's good. It will give us time to eat all that food you brought."

CALEB UNPACKED Ramalda's sack. He hoped his hands weren't shaking. Damn, he'd come so close to kissing her. So close! He pulled out package after package, neatly wrapped for travel. There were the corn tortillas, of course, and a container of spiced lamb stew; several rolled enchiladas and something tightly wrapped in corn husks. There was a flask of hot coffee, which seemed an odd beverage for a hot July day, but he was grateful for it now, because as he unloaded the sack he could hear the sharp rattle of hail on the cabin roof. Ramalda had packed two fat oranges, as well. There was easily enough food to hold them for a couple of days.

Not a bad idea. Two days with Pony in this remote cabin...and two nights.

"Pull up a chair," he said, looking around for the oil lamp. He found the lamp, lit it and set it on the table. "I think I'll fire up the woodstove, too. We need to dry ourselves out."

Lighting the fire was simple. Everything was laid and ready to go, and the matches were in a glass jar on the table. Pretty soon wood was snapping and crackling and the tang of pine smoke flavored the air. He sat down and poured two cups of coffee.

"That was quite a ride," Pony said. "I wasn't sure I could keep up with you."

"Hell, I was completely out of control," he said with a faint grin that ended in an unabashed laugh. "Just hanging on for dear life."

"But when you crossed the creek…"

He laughed again. "I closed my eyes and prayed. Shortly after that, when I realized Billy wasn't going to stop at the cabin, I jumped."

She stared. "You mean, you actually jumped?"

"Yes. Once he felt me leave the saddle, he stopped dead in his tracks, and I put him in the lean-to. Your horse ran up and joined him. That thunderstorm kind of spooked Billy, but he's been wired all day," Caleb said. "My fault, I guess. I was worried about you, and he picked up on it."

Pony cupped her hands around the mug of hot coffee. "I just needed some time alone."

"Pete's coming to the ranch obviously upset you."

"This has nothing to do with Pete." She dropped her eyes away from his.

"What, then?" Caleb said, leaning closer. "You were crying. Are you that unhappy here?"

Pony shook her head but she couldn't meet his eyes. "I like it here very much. I was crying because I felt sad, that's all. Sometimes I just feel that way."

Caleb straightened and shook his head, baffled.

She changed the subject. "So you jumped off Billy because you couldn't stop him?"

"Well, now you know the truth of it. I can't ride, I can't throw a rope, either, and Lord knows it'll be a long time before I'm comfortable at a rodeo." He took a sip of coffee and sighed. "Hell, I buy horses that walk on three legs. I guess I'm not much of a cowboy."

She lifted her mug and met his eyes over the rim of it. "That's all right. I'm not much of an Indian."

"I'll be the first to admit that I don't know many Indians, but I can't see how you could possibly be a better person than you are."

"If my grandmother could see the world I live in now, she would shake her head," Pony said. " I am a *kaalisbaapite*," she explained quietly. "A grandmother's grandchild. That is different from a mother's daughter, because a mother's daughter is raised to live in the modern times, and a grandmother's granddaughter is taught all the old ways. I was raised by my grandmother, Eliza Shane. I learned all the old traditions and customs and songs and all the plants to make medicines and all the ways of the animals. She taught me all that she knew."

"And yet you went on to graduate from one of the best colleges in the nation."

"My brother, Steven, used to tease me when I was young. He said, 'You will grow up and be like the buffalo. You will go back into the mountain to hide from the modern world, and we will never see Pony again.'"

"Pony. Your nickname. Where did that come from?"

She lowered her eyes and set her mug back on the table with a faint smile.

"I followed Steven everywhere when I was little, and when I got too tired to keep up, he would stop and say, 'Pony up!' and swing me onto his shoulder.

His friends started calling me Pony and pretty soon everyone did. The name stayed with me."

"The two of you must have been close."

"Yes. There were six of us, but Steven and I were always the closest. My baby sister and my oldest brother both died before our parents did. Our father was a steelworker. When he was killed on a job in New York City, Steven tried to hold everything together, but our mother went to pieces. She couldn't cope. Eventually she was put in an institution where she stayed until she died, and I was sent to live with my grandmother. My old aunt, Nana, took Steven and my two younger brothers. I think it was then that Steven decided he wanted to get off the reservation. He left as soon as he could, but the other two still live there with their families. He thought that after my grandmother died it was time I moved out of her world. He pushed me through the reservation school system, and then he pushed me harder and harder. He tried so hard to make me see that life could be good in the world he had chosen."

"But you didn't want that."

"I am an Indian," she said. "I want to be able to live like an Indian, and I want *that* life to be good." He was riveted by the conviction he saw in her eyes. "But Steven showed me something important. He showed me that white people will listen to an Indian who has succeeded in their world and who can talk to them in their language."

"So you went to college."

Pony nodded. "I did well. I studied hard. Steven paid for everything. He wanted me to learn useful things so I could invoke changes for our people."

"After accomplishing all that, how could you possibly say that you're not much of an Indian?'' Caleb asked.

This time she leaned toward him. ''Because after all that, Mr. McCutcheon, when I tried to use everything I had learned to make good changes for the People, no one listened.'' Pony gripped her mug, her dark eyes intense. ''Because after accomplishing all those important things, I am and will always be just a woman.''

Caleb sat back in his chair and studied her, his eyes memorizing the proud beauty of her face, and the lips that he had very nearly kissed. ''I think you're accomplishing great things,'' he said. ''What you're doing for the boys is priceless. You may think you haven't made a difference, but you've made a tremendous one. And I for one am damn glad that you're a woman.''

Some of the bitterness left her eyes as he spoke, and she lowered them, her thick dark lashes brushing her smooth cheeks. ''Thank you,'' she murmured. ''But what I do really doesn't matter much. I try to teach the children the old ways, teach them about their history and their heritage, but each year I look at the young faces in my classroom and I see that the People are fading away. Each year there are fewer traditional full-bloods on the reservation because there are more marriages between other tribes and to the whites. The true Crow Indian will one day be found only in history books.''

Caleb felt a sudden chill that had nothing to do with his wet clothing. ''That may be, but you can't prevent people from marrying outside their own race. Love has rarely recognized or respected racial boundaries.''

''True,'' she conceded, flashing him a brief look

that he couldn't fathom. "In the end, all of the babies born on this planet will be of mixed race."

"Is that necessarily a bad thing?"

"It's a sad thing, Mr. McCutcheon, because we will gradually lose our old ways and traditions. The language will be lost. Our connection to the earth will be weakened. Our spirits will be torn in two."

Caleb pushed out of his chair and walked to the cabin door. He opened it and stared out at the turbulent world. His head spun and his heart was heavy. Pony could never feel for him the way he felt for her. He walked in the wrong world, and the wrong blood ran in his veins. She would want any children she bore to be full-blooded Crow, who would carry on the legacy and the culture and traditions of this very special grandmother's granddaughter for at least another generation.

He felt the rain and sleet hitting him and welcomed the honest violence of nature. He embraced the fierce mountain storm and the lightning that ripped apart the black sky. He stood in the doorway of the cabin and wished that one of those savage bolts of lightning would strike him and end his torment. But nothing happened, and so he shut the door again, turned to her and said, "Go ahead and eat. Ramalda will be insulted if we carry all that food back with us."

They returned to the ranch by dusk, riding quietly off the mountain in the fiery glory of a rain-washed sunset. He took Dobey's rein from her when she dismounted. She untied the sack of Ramalda's food from her saddle horn and turned to him. "We hardly touched the food."

"Give it to me," he said, taking it from her. "I'll stash it somewhere. If Ramalda sees we didn't eat, she'll think we're sick, and if she thinks we're sick, we're doomed.''

Pony nodded, smiled briefly, and then looked away. "I'll help Ramalda with supper."

"I'll take care of the horses," he said. He stood cemented to the ground, a thousand unspoken words playing havoc with his outward calm. He cursed himself for standing in dumb silence while the woman he loved turned slowly away from him. Most of all, he cursed himself for not kissing her at Piney Creek. Maybe if he had, things would have turned out differently.

CHAPTER TEN

GUTHRIE SHOVED the pair of pliers into his hip pocket and squinted down the fence line to where the boys struggled with the ball of barbed wire, two of them trying to roll the loose wire onto the ball, the other two watching and giving lots of snide advice. Roon was down in the swale, cutting off fence posts and keeping an eye on Absa. It was close to quitting time, and Guthrie felt a sudden sharp longing for an ice-cold beer and a cool dip in the swimming hole. He heard the approach of a truck crawling at a snail's pace up the rough track. Badger, no doubt, coming to take the day's tangle of old fencing down to the stash they'd made below the pole barn.

"Okay, let's wrap it up!" he called, and the boys immediately abandoned their struggle. "One of you go get Roon. We still have time for a swim before supper."

They always showed the most enthusiasm when they were piling into the back of the truck at the end of the day, but Guthrie couldn't complain. All in all, things had gone pretty smoothly. Pony had a great deal to do with that. She rousted them out of bed in the morning, made sure they were washed and seated at the table when Ramalda dished up breakfast, and got them loaded into the truck at the start of the work-day. He didn't notice that she nagged or cajoled; the boys just seemed to do her bidding without too much fuss. They obviously liked and respected her.

They weren't the only ones. Guthrie had noticed how quiet Caleb McCutcheon had become in the past week, ever since the afternoon he'd ridden up the mountain to find her. Guthrie sensed a melancholy in his boss that could only come from an aching heart. He recognized the symptoms because he'd suffered them himself not too long ago. There was really nothing anyone could do to help him over that rocky road. McCutcheon hadn't asked for advice and wasn't willing to discuss his feelings.

But Guthrie wondered how long Caleb would try to pretend nothing was wrong and how long Pony would try to act untroubled by McCutcheon's presence. Sooner or later, something had to give.

In the meantime, he'd corral the boys and take them for a swim. He'd float on his back in the cool waters of that deep pool and count the weeks, the days, the hours and the minutes until Jessie came home again for good.

The approaching vehicle lumbered into view over the rise. It wasn't Badger. It was McCutcheon's pickup, but McCutcheon wasn't driving. Pony? Guthrie reached up and touched his hat brim, keening his eyes and studying the slow approach.

No, not Pony.

His heart skipped a beat. Could it possibly be…?

"Jess!" he shouted, breaking into a run. He reached the truck just as it pulled to a stop and he wrenched the door open, feasting his eyes on the woman he loved.

"Hey, cowboy," she said, smiling up at him. "I've been waiting a long time for you to kiss me. I had hoped to surprise you, but paralyzing you wasn't my intention. I guess I should've called ahead.''

He didn't speak. Couldn't. He pulled her into his arms and felt hers wrap tightly around him. He buried his face in the sweetness of her hair, kissed the tender, ticklish spot on the side of her neck, kissed her forehead, the crest of her high cheekbone, the corner of her mouth. He kissed her lips with the desperation of a soul starved for love, and he might have devoured her completely if he hadn't become aware of five pairs of eyes watching.

Six, really. Absa was also staring at them.

''Why, hello,'' Jessie said, breathless and flustered, her face flushed and her eyes alight as she looked around. ''You must be the new ranch hands.''

''I CAME TO SEE the mustang, of course,'' Jessie said at supper, helping herself to a fresh biscuit and casting a teasing glance in Guthrie's direction. ''After getting Guthrie's letter, I was overcome with curiosity.''

Badger snorted. ''You were overcome by something else entirely,'' he said, passing the platter of ribs. ''And I believe *that* mustang's name is Guthrie Sloane.''

Pony listened to the friendly banter and cast shy glances at the young woman who sat next to Guthrie. *The* Jessie Weaver. She was beautiful and full of life, and she filled the room with her happy energy. The boys were enchanted by her stories of veterinary studies and her summer internship with the famous horse vet Dr. Rainey. Roon, especially. Halfway through her meal, Jessie jumped out of her chair and threw her arms around the cook. ''*Muchas gracias*, Ramalda!'' she said. ''I haven't had such good food since my last visit home.'' The old woman's face glowed with pleasure.

After the meal, Jessie and Pony helped with the dishes in spite of Ramalda's protests. As they tidied up, Jessie asked about the buffalo.

''They are doing well,'' Pony responded, feeling awkward.

''What about you? How's the summer going for you and the boys? Do you like it here?''

''We like it here very much.'' Pony took a plate from Jessie's hand and met the young woman's eyes. ''It's a very nice place to be.''

''Perhaps tomorrow the two of us can ride up to see the buffalo,'' Jessie suggested. ''Ramalda can pack us a lunch.''

Pony's eyes flew to Jessie's face. She tried to think of some reason why she couldn't go, but her mind was a blank. Jessie read her expression and gave her a reassuring smile. ''It'll be fun. We can get to know each other.''

GUTHRIE COULD HARDLY WAIT to say good-night and whisk Jessie back to his cabin on Bear Creek. ''I thought you'd never stop talking,'' he grumbled as he opened the truck door for her and helped her in. He climbed behind the wheel and began the five-mile drive. ''It must be near to midnight.''

''It's only 9:00 p.m.,'' Jessie said. ''Tell me what's wrong with Mr. McCutcheon. He hardly said a word during supper. He rarely even smiled. That's not like him.''

''Maybe the boys are wearin' him out,'' Guthrie said, trying to avoid the subject.

''No,'' Jessie mused aloud. ''What's ailing him has

nothing to do with those five boys." She trailed one of her hands out the truck window and sighed. "He and Pony seem to have the same symptoms."

Guthrie hunched his shoulders. "I wouldn't know about that."

He felt her sharp gaze. "Is that a fact? You forget that you and I were suffering similar pains not that long ago."

Guthrie shook his head in feigned ignorance. "Truth is, I haven't been around them much lately. Me and Badger have been riding herd on the boys and working on ripping up the fence. I thought them boys would be a lot more trouble than they are, but they're doing all right."

"Good workers?"

"Hell, no. Badger swears he's going to have a stroke just watching how slow they work. You never did see such a sluggish bunch. At the rate they're going, we figure this job'll take another ten or fifteen years. But at least they're behaving themselves, and come evening, Pony gives them their school lessons."

"She's in love with Mr. McCutcheon."

"You think so?" he asked. "Pete's been hanging around pretty regular."

"Pete might be hanging around, but I seriously doubt he's in the running. I can read heart signs, Guthrie. It's McCutcheon she loves, and he's smitten with her, too."

Guthrie downshifted as the truck dipped into a dry wash. "Maybe, or maybe he's just working through some things. You know. His baseball career ended so abruptly, and now he's struggling with the logistics of ranching..."

Jessie shook her head. "No way. This is about

Pony. For some reason things aren't going well at all between them.'' Jessie sighed. ''He's such a good man, and she seems like such a nice person. I'm only here for a few days, but maybe there's something I can do to help....''

PONY COULD SEE McCutcheon from the living-room window. Seated at the computer desk, her chin resting in her palm, she watched him walk up from the barn in the late-morning sunlight. He looked very somber. He had looked that way for some time now, and she wondered if the misery she felt was reflected in his countenance. She was in love with him and she'd believed he'd felt the same way about her. Yet something in his behavior toward her had changed. She'd thought at first that she had done something wrong, but when she asked him about it he looked at her with a puzzled expression and shook his head.

''Wrong? Not at all. Don't mind me, I'm just a man of moods.''

But she knew that this was something more than mere moodiness. She had worked hard, hoping that her accomplishments might cheer him. She had entered nearly all the data into the computer, she'd overseen the construction of the holding corrals and chutes, and was negotiating a price for the same contractor to dig the holes for the corner posts of the reinforced boundary fences. In her spare time she worked on the fence line with the boys and Badger and Guthrie, and helped with the haying when the timothy was ripe for cutting. The days were long and busy, and after supper she schooled the boys for about an hour.

The afternoon they spent together on Piney

Creek…that day had marked the beginning of Mc-
Cutcheon's dark mood. They had spoken of many
things in that cabin while the lightning flashed and
the rain and hail drummed on the roof. She must have
said something, done something that had turned him
away. He had not looked at her in the same way since,
and the ride they had shared together back to the
ranch had been ominously quiet.

McCutcheon paused before climbing the porch
steps and glanced behind. Pony shifted her gaze and
spotted Jessie and Guthrie walking hand in hand from
the creek. Guthrie was carrying a bunch of wild flowers. They looked so happy, so in love. Pony felt a
painful twist and pushed away from the desk, standing abruptly and walking into the kitchen. Ramalda
was busy preparing the noontime meal. She had already fixed a bag lunch for Jessie and Pony.

"There is plenty for you both," Ramalda said as
Pony came into the room. "You girls both too thin.
You get sick if you don't eat."

Pony hefted the heavy sack. "Thank you, Ramalda.
Gracias."

When she stepped out onto the porch, McCutcheon
glanced up at her. "I've saddled your horses," he
said. "Dobey and Billy are ready to roll. Have a good
time."

She wanted to thank him, to ask him to come, but
couldn't form the words. Instead she nodded, feeling
perilously close to tears. She descended the steps and
started for the barn, answering Jessie's wave and feeling worse than she had any right to.

Guthrie walked Jessie to the corral and watched as
they readied themselves for the ride.

"You sure you pretty ladies don't want an escort?" he asked hopefully, but Jessie shook her head.

"No, thanks. Girls only this trip," she said, casting Pony a conspiratorial smile as she heeled Billy through the gate.

She bent to retrieve the bouquet from Guthrie's hand and glanced over her shoulder as she straightened. "I hope you don't mind a short side trip, Pony," she said. "I'd like to put these flowers on my father's grave."

"I like to come to these burial grounds," Pony said several minutes later as Jessie laid the flowers at the foot of her father's headstone and knelt for a moment. "It's so peaceful here."

"Yes," Jessie said, looking around. "I wonder who planted the forget-me-nots."

"I transplanted some seedlings I found along the creek."

Jessie glanced at her and smiled. "Thank you. That is a sacred place to me."

"Mr. McCutcheon brought me up here shortly after I began working at the ranch. He told me all he knew about the people buried here. It became a sacred place for me, also."

Several moments passed before the two women returned to their horses. Jessie reined Billy down the path. Pony followed on Dobey, and within minutes, traveling at an easy lope, they were climbing into the high country. The ride would have been exhilarating had Pony been in a better frame of mind.

"You look tired," Jessie said when they stopped to rest their horses. "I'm sorry for going so quickly. I've missed this place. It feels like I've been gone forever."

They rode to the line camp. Jessie dropped out of the saddle and let Billy's rein trail on the ground. She pushed open the cabin door and let the sunshine stream in. "I've always loved this old cabin. It's the perfect place for our honeymoon. Guthrie promised he'd run up the supplies we'll need for the week we'll be hiding out here. It'll be even more beautiful in September, when all the aspen will be turning color and..." She glanced back at Pony. Her words trailed into silence and her happy expression was replaced by a frown. She walked up to Dobey's shoulder and laid her hand on Pony's knee. "Are you all right?"

Pony nodded, embarrassed that she'd let her misery show. "I'm fine."

Jessie studied her skeptically. "Climb down. We'll eat our lunch here. I'll see to the horses, you sit and have a rest."

"I'm all right." Pony tended Dobey herself and then joined Jessie on the bench, leaning her back against the sun-warmed logs. She took the sandwich and the container of juice that Jessie handed her and cradled them in her lap. "The buffalo are probably nearby. It shouldn't be difficult to find them."

"Never mind about finding the buffalo," Jessie said, startling her. "Let's just sit here and soak up the sun. Enjoy the afternoon. It's so good to be back."

Pony glanced sidelong at her. "Does it feel different to you, now that you no longer own the ranch?"

Jessie smiled. "Yes and no. At first it was hard. Hard to let go, hard to think that I'd failed to keep the ranch afloat. But now I feel good about what I did. I owe your brother so much for finding a buyer for the place before the bank took it. Mr. McCutcheon is a wonderful man. He may be rich and famous, but he's the most unassuming man I've ever met. When he was contemplating bringing the buffalo back to this valley, he called me at school to ask what I thought about the idea. He told me he wouldn't do it unless I gave the project my blessing. Can you believe that?''

Pony looked down at her sandwich. ''Yes,'' she said. ''Mr. McCutcheon thinks a great deal of you.''

''He's one in a million.''

''He's one of a kind,'' Pony amended.

''One of a kind,'' Jessie agreed. ''And it's plain he thinks a great deal of you, too,'' Jessie said.

Pony felt her heart leap and she gave Jessie a hopeful look. ''Do you think so?''

''Of course,'' Jessie replied. ''Pony, I'm worried about you. Something's definitely wrong.''

''I'm all right.''

''No, you're not, and neither is Mr. McCutcheon. Both of you are so miserable that even Badger mentioned it, and Badger never talks about stuff like that.''

Pony was completely taken aback by Jessie's blunt words. As the two women regarded each other for a long, searching moment, Pony felt her reserve beginning to crumble. ''I'm afraid that Mr. McCutcheon is unhappy with me,'' she admitted.

It was Jessie's turn to be surprised. ''Why?''

''I'm not sure. Maybe I'm not doing all the things he expects me to do. When I ask him, he puts me off and says that nothing is wrong, but something definitely is.'' She lifted her shoulders in a fatalistic shrug. ''I've been thinking that maybe the boys and I should go back to the reservation.''

''No way!'' Jessie reached out and gave Pony's

hand a comforting squeeze. "Were things always this awkward between the two of you?"

"No. Before this past week, everything was fine, but ever since the afternoon we got caught in the thunderstorm, he's been acting…" Pony swallowed painfully. "It's as if he doesn't want to be around me anymore. We took shelter here, in this very cabin, to wait out the storm. We talked about a lot of things."

"Romantic things?" Jessie said.

Pony flushed. "No. We talked about him wanting to be a real cowboy and about me trying to honor my Indian heritage."

Jessie leaned back against the cabin wall. "Ah," she said wryly. "Cowboys and Indians. The old story."

"He's acted like a stranger toward me ever since."

"That must have been quite a conversation. You must have said something that scared him off."

Pony stared down at the sandwich in her lap, not feeling the least bit hungry. "I told him that soon there would be no more Crow Indians because so many of us were marrying outside of our blood, and I told him that I thought it was important for the Crow to survive as a people."

Jessie sat up. "Lordy," she said. "You told him *that?*"

"It's the truth. There are fewer and fewer full-bloods." Pony looked at Jessie. "I'm sorry. I know you are part Indian. I didn't mean—"

"No offense taken," Jessie said. "It's no secret that I'm about as mixed-up as they come. Crow, Blackfoot and white. I live in three worlds. I understand your feelings, but I don't begrudge a single drop of my ancestral blood. Maybe it's not so much our breeding that counts, but our spiritual beliefs, and preserving our native culture and traditions. The things that are important to us.''

"Maybe," Pony conceded.

"The Bow and Arrow was founded by cowboys *and* Indians, and it was a *good* partnership." Jessie leaned toward Pony. "Don't you see? Caleb McCutcheon thinks you've drawn a line between the two worlds that neither one of you can cross without causing the extinction of a proud and noble people."

Pony felt her stomach twist. "I didn't mean for him to think that."

"Well, what *did* you mean?"

"I meant it as a general statement, that's all. I didn't mean…I didn't want…" She met Jessie's gaze and felt her fingers tighten around the sandwich. "I was just telling him the way things were. Why would that drive him away?"

Jessie shook her head with an exasperated laugh. "Pony, for heaven's sake, are you blind? The man is crazy about you. *That's* why he's been acting so strange. You broke his heart with your idealistic passion to preserve the Crow people." She studied Pony a moment more and then said, "I guess the real question is, how do you feel about him?"

Pony blinked back the sting of tears. "I've never felt this way about anyone," she whispered.

"Then tell him," Jessie said. "For the love of all creation, *tell* him before it's too late. It was almost too late for Guthrie and me because I was so stubborn and foolish. Don't make the same mistake I did. Tell that good man how you feel!"

Pony shook her head. "I can't."

"Why not?" Jessie's dark eyes were earnest. "Do

you *really* believe your mission in life is to bear a Crow child?''

The pain knifed through her and she bent over herself. ''No,'' she whispered.

''Well, *what* then?''

''I can bear no children.'' The words were a tight whisper, raw with pain. Pony closed her eyes and drew an anguished breath. ''So you see how it is. A man like Caleb will want to father children of his own, and I can't give him that.'' Pony lifted her face and gazed at Jessie through the blur of tears. ''I can give him nothing!''

Jessie's voice softened with compassion. ''Perhaps you should let Mr. McCutcheon decide what he wants, and what you can offer him. Isn't happiness the greatest gift of all?''

Pony dropped her face into her hands and sat for a moment in rigid silence, then she shook her head. ''Happiness is nothing but a dream. He wouldn't want me if he knew of my past,'' she whispered, trembling.

There was a corresponding silence from Jessie, and then Pony felt Jessie's fingers gently stroking her hair, brushing it from the side of her face in the tender way a mother would touch a child. ''Your brother Steven holds you in very high regard, and I hold your brother up there among the holy saints and the spirit of the wind. Whatever happened in your past can't be that bad.''

''He doesn't know. *Steven doesn't know!*'' Pony lifted her face out of her trembling hands. ''What I did was terrible, and Steven must never, *ever* know. I can never forgive myself for what happened. How can I possibly expect anyone else to?''

Jessie regarded her somberly, her fingers continuing to gently stroke her hair. "Does this have something to do with Pete?"

Pony brushed away her tears and sat up straight. She stared for a moment across the high, windswept valley to where the mountains drew a bold line against the sky. She drew strength from the grandeur of the lofty peaks, and when she spoke, her voice had lost its wavering tremble.

"I've known Pete all my life. He was Steven's best friend. When he got out of school, Pete managed the tribal bison herd, and I was one of four other students who earned some college money working for him one summer." She drew a sharp breath and turned her eyes away from Jessie's face. "Near the end of the summer one of the other students invited all of us to a party in a town north of the reservation. Pete didn't want to go, but I did, so he drove me. There were a lot of college kids there. I drank too much. Pete wanted to leave but I didn't. Another girl said she'd give me a ride, so Pete finally left after I told him that I didn't need a baby-sitter. But after a while the other girl disappeared, so when some guy who was going my way offered me a ride, I took it. He seemed nice, and I...I wanted to get home."

Pony paused to gather her thoughts. She had never spoken aloud of this to anyone before. She felt Jessie reach out and take her hands in her own. "It's all right," Jessie said. Pony turned her head to look at her. Jessie was so strong. She had been through some fires herself and had emerged all the stronger.

"He didn't take me home," Pony said. Her voice was flat, devoid of emotion. "He..." She swallowed and drew a shallow breath. "I finally got away from him. I had some change in my pocket. I walked through the night until I found a gas station with a pay phone, and I called Pete. He came and got me. He wanted to take me to the hospital, but I told him to bring me home. I only wanted to go home. I didn't want anyone to know what had happened.''

Jessie's hands tightened on hers. ''You were raped.''

Pony nodded. ''I wasn't strong enough. I tried to fight him off but...'' She bent her head and stared at the earth beneath her feet. ''And then I missed my period. One of the other students said she knew of a doctor.... She gave me a phone number and I...I went and...'' She paused. The words sounded so unreal to her, and yet she had lived all of it over and over, a thousand, a million times, and kept the dark secret and terrible guilt hidden within herself for all these years. ''Afterward, I drove myself home. When I didn't show up at work the following Monday, Pete came looking for me. He found me bleeding on the kitchen floor and he took me to the real hospital. I made him promise not to tell anyone.'' She looked at Jessie. ''It was the doctors at the real hospital who told me I wouldn't be able to have any more children.''

''Oh, Pony.'' Jessie's eyes shimmered with tears. ''I'm so sorry. You've kept this inside of you all this time.''

''It should never have happened. I shouldn't have gone to the party. I shouldn't have had those drinks. I should have listened to Pete when he told me it was time to go. I should have gone home with him. But I didn't. It's my fault.''

Jessie shook her head. ''Of course it isn't. Oh God, I can't imagine what I would have done in your shoes.

Maybe the very same thing. It *wasn't* your fault. Do you hear me? It wasn't your fault!'' Jessie released her hands and sprang to her feet, pacing a few steps before swinging around. "Pony, if you could have children, would you still feel the same way toward Mr. McCutcheon? Would you want to have his children?''

The lump in her throat prevented her from speaking. She could only nod.

"Listen, there are people, professionals, who can counsel you, get you beyond this destructive guilt you're feeling. You need to get help.''

Pony shook her head. "Seven years is a lot of time. I'm already well beyond it.''

"No, you're not. You're letting it block your way to happiness. You're letting it prevent you from realizing the life you could have, the life you deserve!''

"I deserve nothing. Mr. McCutcheon deserves much more than I can ever give him. And Pete's a good man, but I can't be around him without remembering, and so…'' Pony drew a shaky breath and let it out slowly. She looked at Jessie. "So now you understand why I must take the boys and leave this place.''

"I understand nothing of the kind. What I do understand is that what you're doing with the boys is a wonderful thing. There are so many children out there who need a loving home, and you've found a way to give five boys a promising future. Pony, I think you're a very special person. Your belief that not being able to have children exempts you from being a loving mother is wrong. It's *wrong!* I think you should tell Mr. McCutcheon everything, the way you just told me. I think you deserve the happiness you could find here with him.''

''I *can't* tell him.'' Pony stated this simply, guilelessly. ''And please, Jessie, you must promise me that you won't.''

CALEB WAS SITTING on his cabin porch after supper, watching the last of the daylight fade from the sky, a book in his lap, when he heard a light step on the path and Jessie's voice calling his name.

''Mr. McCutcheon?'' She climbed the porch steps and shoved her hands deep in her jeans pockets. ''I was hoping we could have a private talk.''

''The name's Caleb, in case you forgot all the important stuff while you were off at school learning to be a veterinarian,'' he said, laying the unread book aside. ''And of course you can. Anything I can do to help with your wedding plans, all you have to do is ask. If you'd rather have the wedding here instead of at Guthrie's place, I'm all for it. I've offered you that option before, if you'll recall.''

''Actually, this isn't about my wedding,'' Jessie said. ''And I do recall. Thank you.''

Caleb gazed up at her quizzically. ''You don't like how things are going at the ranch. You don't like the buffalo.''

''I love how things are here and I think the buffalo are wonderful. Mr. McCutcheon…''

''Caleb.''

''Pony thinks that you're angry with her,'' Jessie said.

Caleb felt an anxious kick in the pit of his stomach. He stood and paced to the rail, quarter turned and faced the dark wall of mountains. "That's ridiculous," he said. "Why would I be angry with her?"

"She thinks you're not satisfied with the job she's doing."

He spun around. "She's doing a great job. A fantastic job!"

"Maybe you should tell her that."

"I will." He paced down the length of the porch and back. "Tonight. I'll tell her tonight." He leaned over the porch rail, watching the river rushing past. "The truth is, even though she only hired on for the summer, I wish she'd stay here permanently. She and the boys."

"Maybe you should tell her that, too."

He shook his head in despair. "It wouldn't matter. She can't stay because she…she needs to be with her own kind. What I mean is, she wants to have babies that are not of mixed blood. She wants to keep the Crow blood pure. The thing is, you see… Oh, hell!" he exclaimed, smacking the palm of his hand on the rail and then whirling to face Jessie. "I'm not mad at Pony, I'm in love with her. And it's killing me!"

"Mr. McCutcheon, that truth is patently evident to everyone here. Why don't you tell her exactly how you feel. Lay your cards on the table. I have a strong hunch that she's just as crazy about you as you are about her."

He shook his head again. "I'm afraid if I do what you suggest, she'll take the boys and leave. And if she leaves here, I don't know what I'll do."

"Mr. McCutcheon," Jessie began.

"Caleb!"

"At the end of the summer, she's planning to leave here anyway. Tell her how you feel! What do you have to lose?"

PONY SAT at the computer and stared at the screen, mentally composing the resignation she intended to give Mr. McCutcheon in the morning. She would make it brief and honest. She would tell him that she was taking the boys and returning to the reservation. She would tell him what she had intended to tell him on their very first night here. She would tell him that she and the boys did not belong here, and the only way to remedy that was to leave.

Jessie had been kind to try and help, but the situation was clearly hopeless and there was little point in prolonging it. She had made the huge mistake of falling in love with a man who deserved so much better than what she had to offer. Caleb was not to blame, nor should he be made to suffer needlessly for her failings.

Pony heard someone climbing the ranch-house steps and glanced out the window, startled to see that it was Caleb himself. She smoothed her hair from her face and straightened her shoulders. She drew a deep breath and let it out slowly. This had been a long, hard day, and she would not be sorry to see it end. She heard the screen door bang shut and started toward the kitchen. Her steps were swift and purposeful, propelling her into the room before she could lose courage and change her mind. "Mr. McCutcheon, I need to speak with you, please," she blurted out as she entered the kitchen.

He stopped just inside the door and removed his

hat. His sandy hair was tousled and his expression was grave. "Yes," he said. "I think we need to talk."

At that moment the wall phone rang. He picked it up, and when it became evident that the call was not going to be a brief one, Pony fled the kitchen and returned to the sanctuary of the living room. She sat back down at the computer and printed out the graphs she had made, as well as all the bookkeeping entries for the past four months. She collated the work swiftly and was putting the sheets into a three-ring binder when she heard his footsteps behind her. Closing the binder, she rose from the desk, holding the logbook in her hands. It was painful to be in the same room with him. But she had to tell him before she lost the courage to do so.

Tell him goodbye.

He paused just inside the doorway. "That call was from a man down in Wyoming," he said. "He's selling his ranch outside of Jeffords, and the new buyer doesn't want the herd of buffalo he's running on it. Four bulls, ten cows, six calves. Healthy and certified brucellosis free. He wanted to know if we were interested. He's also selling his buffalo hauler, a fancy beefed-up aluminum stock trailer."

Pony gripped the three-ring binder to her. "What did you tell him?"

"I said we'd be down to have a look. I figured if we left here at 4:00 a.m. tomorrow morning we'd be in Jeffords by dark. It's about forty miles south of the park boundary."

"Tomorrow?"

"Do you have other plans? I could call him back."

Pony's heart rate trebled. "No, it's just that…"

"If you don't want to go, I understand. But I'd

appreciate your input. You're the expert, and you said we needed more bulls. That's four more.''

She nodded and hesitated. ''How much is he asking?''

''The trailer's a big Featherlite thirty-footer, practically new. For the trailer and the buffalo, sixty grand.''

''That seems a fair price.''

Caleb nodded. ''I say we go down there tomorrow, and if the buffalo aren't all infested with mange and riddled with disease, we bring them back and introduce them to the prettiest mountain valley on this planet. We can take the boys with us and do the scenic tour of the park on the way down. That's the beauty of the Suburban. What do you say?''

''I've never been to Wyoming.''

''We'd be driving right through Yellowstone, coming and going. We could stop at Old Faithful and some of the other geysers and let the boys have a look.''

''How long would we be gone?''

''Two days.'' His eyes held hers. ''I told him we'd come. At that price, those buffalo won't last long.''

She nodded and her heart gave a painful thump. ''All right.''

His relief was visible. ''Good. And just in case I haven't said it lately, I think you're doing a great job. I want to be sure you know how much you're appreciated. Now, what was it you wanted to speak with me about?''

She drew a shallow breath. ''I...'' Her eyes focused on the binder. She lifted it and held it out toward him. ''I've finished the bookkeeping project,'' she said. ''I thought you might want to look it over.''

He reached the report out of her hands. ''Thanks.''

He turned to go and paused at the door. "Four a.m.,"
he said.

She nodded. "We'll be ready."

"HOW DO YOU FEEL about having kids?" Jessie murmured on the edge of sleep, wrapping herself around
him like a warm, living blanket.

"What's that?" Guthrie roused himself and drew
her closer.

"I said, how do you feel about babies?"

"Babies." Guthrie reached a hand to rub his face
in the darkness. "Well, babies are something I don't
have much experience with. I mean, I have plenty of
experience with baby cows and baby horses...."

"I'm talking children. Human ones."

On his guard now. Wide-awake. "How many?"

"How many do you think you might want?"

"I hadn't given it much thought. Just us gettin'
married...well, I guess that's grabbed most of my attention. First things first, and all that." He heard her
give an impatient sigh and hastened to add, "But I
guess however many you decide you want to have is
okay with me. I mean, you're the one who has to do
all the work, carryin' 'em and birthin' 'em and all. I
mean, I can help once they're on the ground, if you
know what I mean. I could learn to change diapers
and stuff like that."

There followed a silence so long that he thought
she'd drifted off to sleep, but all of a sudden she said,
"Guthrie, what if I couldn't have kids? What if I told
you I couldn't bear you a son or a daughter?"

"I dunno. I guess I never thought about *not* having
kids, either."

He felt the sharp prod of her elbow. "Well, think about it now!"

"Okay. I'm thinking." He fidgeted and rubbed his foot against hers beneath the covers. "Well, I guess I'd have to throw you over for some fertile, wide-hipped, big-breasted wench who could pump out a dozen brats in ten years' time."

"Guthrie. I'm serious about this."

His hands had already discovered the truth of her words. She was as tensed as a fiddle string. "Okay, then. Seriously. It wouldn't matter to me. I mean, what's a baby? It's this little red-faced, wrinkled thing that squalls and squirms and eats and poops pretty near constant until it gets bigger, and then it gets into everything pretty constant until it gets even bigger, and then it gets into trouble pretty constant until finally it cuts loose and leaves home. So what's to like about babies, anyhow?"

"Guthrie!"

He sighed tolerantly. "Jess, the bottom line is, raising a bunch of kids with you would be the very best part of my life, but if for some reason it turns out you can't have a baby, we'll find another way. We'll adopt a whole passel of 'em."

"But it wouldn't be the same, would it?"

"What do you mean? Those lucky babies would have you and me both. What more could any baby want?"

"But what about your genes and mine?"

Guthrie pulled her close, kissed her hard and said, "Levi's, baby. They're the only way to go."

CHAPTER ELEVEN

AT 4:00 A.M. the stars were blazing in the velvety sky. The boys were quiet, climbing into the Suburban and buckling their seat belts without being reminded. Roon was the only one absent, opting to stay behind to tend the buffalo calf and the injured mustang. Pony rode in the passenger seat, Caleb climbed behind the wheel, and Guthrie limped up to Pony's side carrying a two big paper sacks. "Trail snacks," he said, handing them to her. "Ramalda didn't want you gettin' hungry on the road." Guthrie glanced at the boys in the back seat. "When you get back, you might want to come over to my place. Blue had her pups last night."

"No kidding?" Caleb said. "Did she have a little female for me?"

"She had three females and three males, so I guess everyone's going to be happy, with two to spare."

Caleb started the Suburban and grinned. "That's good news," he said. He felt better this morning than he'd felt in a long while, and hearing about the pups was an added boost. "Hold the fort while we're gone. We'll be back tomorrow, and if things go well, we'll be hauling a fancy aluminum trailer full of buffalo."

Within two hours they were crossing the northern boundary of Yellowstone National Park. Sunrise found them at Mammoth Hot Springs, where they hiked as a group to view the massive thermal spring. Elk grazed nearby among clumps of sage, calmly wary of their presence. They watched the steam rise from the spring into the cool air while Caleb read the various informative plaques aloud, then walked back to the Suburban, where Pony brought out a flask of coffee for Caleb and poured paper cups of juice for herself and the boys. As Caleb drove farther into the park, they drank, ate oranges and admired the scenery and wildlife. A pleasurable and meandering six hours later found them at Old Faithful, sitting on one of the many benches that ringed the hot spring and eating thick beef sandwiches that Ramalda had packed. Already they had seen countless elk and bison, a black bear and the most exciting sighting of all, a mother grizzly with two cubs rooting in the sod beside a small stream.

Caleb ate his sandwich with the first real hunger he had felt in days. It was good being with Pony and the boys. He tried not to think about anything but this hour, this moment. He concentrated on enjoying the present and not worrying about a future he couldn't possibly share with the woman he'd fallen in love with.

ALTHOUGH HE'D SEEN pictures and videos of Old Faithful erupting, when it did Caleb leaped to his feet, amazed, along with all the other spectators, and when it was over he grinned at Pony and the boys. "That was a real treat," he said. "Even if we don't buy those buffalo, just seeing all we've seen today has made the trip worthwhile."

Six p.m., and they were cooling off in Jenny Lake. Caleb wished they'd brought camping gear. Pony didn't swim, but she rolled her jeans up and waded along the shore while the boys swam and played in the cool clear lake water.

Eight p.m., and they were in Jeffords, registering for three rooms at a local motel. The clerk directed them to a nearby eatery. "It's a wild-and-woolly place after ten o'clock, but the food's real good, and if you like to dance, there's a live band."

Nine p.m., and the six of them were sharing a table at the restaurant. The band was playing a nonstop barrage of country-western tunes, the dance floor was full, the air was blue with cigarette smoke, the food was great, and Caleb was working on his second beer when he made a decision. Jessie was right. What did he have to lose? "Let's dance," he said to Pony.

She rose from her chair without hesitating and took his hand. He led her onto the cramped space and forgot all about his vow to keep his distance. He touched her and forgot everything but the smooth, firm warmth of her hand in his, the curve of her slender waist, the way her other hand rested lightly on his shoulder, the graceful way she moved and the liquid darkness of her eyes when she raised them to his. He felt himself falling into something so deep that he couldn't save himself even if he wanted to, and he didn't. He drew her closer and she came into his arms as if she belonged there.

One song followed another, and three songs later the band took a break. Caleb reluctantly led her back to the table and ordered another beer. The boys were playing video games against the far wall, returning to the table for more coins or another soda. He leaned his elbows on the table, drew his beer close and said, "I'm glad you came."

She was drinking a ginger ale, and a faint smile curved her lips. "Me, too."

"I guess we should be getting back to the motel pretty soon. We have to be out at that ranch early. We'll probably get home pretty late tomorrow night. We'll have to drive straight through, no scenic stops, and hopefully no flat tires or mechanical problems." He lifted his beer for a swallow and set it down. They gazed at each other. Caleb's fingers tightened on his glass.

"What is it?" she said.

"I look at you and I can't help but wonder why you aren't already married and mothering a bunch of your own children."

Her smile instantly faded and her eyes revealed shock at his words. The band was returning to the stage at the back of the room, picking up their instruments. "I'll go get the boys," she said, rising from her chair and heading for the far wall. Caleb moaned aloud as he reached for his wallet. Three beers and he was throwing all caution to the wind, asking the question that had tormented him since that day up on the mountain. Why *wasn't* she married, with a passel of full-blooded Crow children? *Why?*

She loved Pete. She *must* love him, that's why she got so upset every time he showed up at the ranch. She wanted to marry Pete, but maybe he didn't want children. Or maybe he didn't love her. No. Such a thought was ludicrous. Of *course* he loved her and wanted to marry her. Any man would. How could they not?

Caleb lifted his beer and finished it. The band jumped into another lively two-step and he glanced around for Pony, wondering if she'd ever dance with him again. Hell, wondering if she'd ever *speak* to him again. It seemed that every time he tried to tell her how he felt, he said the wrong thing. Perhaps he needed to rethink his strategy. Maybe he should just demonstrate how he felt. Maybe he should just march across the room and ask her to dance one last dance, and while they were close he would kiss her. Maybe then she'd know that he loved her and wanted to spend the rest of his life with her.

His eyes swept the room, caught sight of her and froze. She was standing near the video games, surrounded by three men. The boys stood in an uneasy huddle to one side, watching, as one of the men reached for her. He saw her shake her head and move protectively toward the boys, but another man blocked her retreat even as the first man's hand closed around her arm.

A flash of white-hot anger exploded through Caleb and he jumped up, knocking his chair back. The band played on, people kept dancing as he approached the three men. All of the feelings that had been simmering in him since that incident with the drunk in Livingston had boiled to the surface by the time he reached the three yahoos. He pulled the man's hand off Pony's arm and stepped between them.

"Pony, take the boys and go to the truck," he said, turning to the man.

"Mind your own business," the man snarled, stepping closer. "This is my joint, and I decide who gets served. We don't cater to Indians here."

Caleb punched the man square on the nose, feeling the shock of the blow travel all the way to his shoulder. A second man raised his arm to hit Caleb, but Caleb caught the arm and slammed his attacker head-first into a video machine. Instantly he rounded on the man who had blocked her, grabbing him by the shirt-front, picking him up bodily as if he were weightless and hurling him backward, knocking over a table and sending chairs and people flying.

A woman screamed.

The band was still playing, but people had stopped dancing to watch.

Caleb's rage was so intense that when the third man tried to defend his friends, Caleb turned and knocked him down with a tight, vicious jab. Then, as he reached down and seized the first man who was struggling to his feet, a blinding pain exploded in his head. Bright lights flashed and his vision faded. His knees buckled as hands grabbed him, pulled him up and held him fast. A fist snapped his head back. Another to his stomach doubled him over and left him struggling to breathe. He rocked back under a seemingly endless barrage of blows and then, suddenly, the hands that were pinning his arms let go and he staggered back against the wall, sliding down into a sitting position and fighting his way back to consciousness.

"All right," an authoritative voice said. "I guess that's enough. You boys are having way too much of a good time here. Lucky thing I happened along, huh, Roy? You start this fracas?"

"No, Sheriff, he did. All I did was ask the little lady for a dance and he went berserk and punched me. Look at all this blood. I think my nose is broken!"

"That's not true," Caleb heard Jimmy shout, his young voice strident. "He said we had to leave right away. He said Indians weren't welcome here, then he grabbed her by the arm.''

"Yeah," Martin said. "He said bad things happen to Indians in this town.''

"Sheriff, on my honor, I didn't do anything. I swear that's the truth. If it weren't for Len and Boyd, that man probably would've torn me to pieces. Look at my face! What's my father going to say about this?''

"Roy," the sheriff said, "quit your whining. You and your friends get on out of here. Go jump in the river and cool off.''

Caleb's breath returned, and his eyes came into blurry focus in time to see a heavily jowled man wearing a tan-colored Stetson and a matching tan uniform reach down to haul him to his feet. "You, my unfamiliar and unfortunate friend, are hereby under arrest for disturbing the peace, disorderly conduct, and being stupid enough to give the mayor's son a bloody nose," the sheriff said, snapping a pair of handcuffs around Caleb's wrists. "Come with me real peaceful-like and let's get this ugly episode over with.''

Caleb looked around for Pony and spotted her pressed against the wall with the boys flanking her protectively. "I'm sorry," he said, wiping blood from his mouth and wondering if his eye was going to swell completely shut. "You boys take Pony back to the motel and stay put." He pulled the keys to the Suburban out of his jeans pocket and handed them to Pony. "I'll call you to come pick me up.''

"Come on, come on," the sheriff said, taking him by the upper arm. "I ain't got all night!''

PONY WATCHED THE SHERIFF lead Caleb McCutcheon out the door and closed her trembling fingers tightly around the keys he had handed her. Her heart was racing and she was dry-mouthed with fear. She had no intention of waiting at the motel room for him to call. "Come on, boys. Let's go." They exited the eatery in time to see Caleb being pushed none too gently into the back seat of the cruiser. "Officer, please," she pleaded. "This man did nothing wrong. He was only trying to protect us."

"Maybe so," the sheriff said. "But it wouldn't look right if I let the man who messed up Roy's pretty face walk off without so much as a reprimand. Lady, do what your friend said and take those boys back to the motel. Better yet, for your sake and theirs, get 'em the hell out of town." The sheriff opened his door and climbed into the cruiser. He started the vehicle, pulled away from the curb with a loud chirp of tires and within moments had sped from view.

Pony's fists clenched and the keys bit into her palm. She watched as the car disappeared and tried to quell the panic that flooded through her. "Okay," she said. "I'm going to find the police station and wait right there until Mr. McCutcheon's released."

"We're coming, too," Martin said.

"Yeah," Jimmy said. "We're not going to wait at the motel."

"Oh, yes, you are, with the door locked," she said.

"You heard what that sheriff said," Jimmy protested. "Mr. McCutcheon beat up the mayor's son. Who knows what they might do to him?"

"They won't do anything," Pony said, turning to walk briskly back toward the motel. "He did nothing wrong."

"Really?" Dan said, falling in beside her. "Then why was he arrested? He wasn't drunk. All he did was try to rescue you from those jerks, and he got coldcocked with a beer bottle. The mayor's son and his two friends should have been the ones who got busted, not Mr. McCutcheon."

"He beat up the wrong people in the wrong town," Pony replied grimly.

The boys followed in silence, and when they reached the motel she pointed at their room. "Inside, lock the door, and wait for me."

"No." All four boys squared off and glared at her, and Jimmy said, "He tried to protect you, and now we want to do the same for him. Besides, who knows what might happen to us if you leave us here alone?"

Pony hesitated. "All right. But you're *staying* in the truck. You hear me? You're not coming inside the station. This isn't a safe place for us to be. You keep the doors locked, and if something happens while I'm inside, use the cell phone to call for help."

"Who would we call?" Jimmy said. "The sheriff?"

"Steven," Pony said. She climbed into the driver's seat, reached a piece of paper and a pen from the center console, and scribbled her brother's phone number on it. "You call him if anything goes wrong," she said, handing the scrap of paper to Jimmy.

CALEB SAT on the edge of the stained mattress in the holding cell and cradled his aching head in his hands. He was half-convinced that this was a nightmare and any moment he would wake up in his old log cabin. He would open his eyes and hear the wind blow through the aspen and pine, hear the timeless rush of water over the smooth river stones. Any moment...

"Hey, mister. Mister! Snap out of it. I need you to fill out this form."

The sheriff was thrusting a clipboard through a slot in the bars. He stood up and took it awkwardly, wrists still cuffed together. "Don't you want to fingerprint me?" he asked, feeling angrier by the moment. "Do a strip search?"

"Oh, don't you worry," the sheriff said. "You'll be getting the full treatment. You picked on three of the wrong people, and you're traveling with the very worst kind of people. I'll let you in on a well-known fact. A couple years ago, the mayor's youngest son was killed when the car he was driving was hit head-on by a truckload of drunk Indians. That poor boy was on his way home from a Bible-study meeting. So you see, any time Roy gets around an Indian, a red flag just naturally goes up, and the mayor...well, the mayor's never gotten over losing Jonathan."

Caleb tried to think past the throbbing in his head. "I'm sorry about that, but what happened to the mayor's son has nothing to do with that young woman and those four boys."

"I'm just tellin' you how it is in this town," the sheriff informed him.

"I want to call my lawyer."

"All in due time."

"I want to call my lawyer *now*.That's my right."

"Fill out the form, and I'll see you get to make that call."

Caleb flung the clipboard back at the sheriff. "Bring me a phone and take these damn handcuffs off."

The sheriff sighed and shook his head. "Lordy! I can see you're going to be difficult, and I was kind of hoping for a peaceful night."

PONY PARKED behind the cruiser and cut the engine. She left the key in the ignition and retrieved the cell phone from the center console, making sure it was on. "Do you know how to use this?" she asked, handing the phone to the nearest boy.

"Gee, I don't know," Jimmy said with feigned ignorance. "What is it, anyway?"

She glanced at the other boys. "You stay put and keep the doors locked until you see us come out."

Pony had no idea what she would do when she went into the station. Police procedure was not something she was familiar with. Probably they would want money for bail. Not a large amount, because a fistfight in a redneck bar wasn't a criminal act or even worthy of mention in the local paper. But no doubt they would want something. She pushed open the door and went inside the small station house. It was nothing more than an office with a couple of desks, phones, file cabinets stacked to the ceiling, lots of clutter on the desks and a stale, dirty smell that she didn't like at all. The sheriff was sitting at the biggest desk, and he looked up when she entered. The desk lamp caught the shine of sweat on his jowls. "Oh, my," he said when he recognized her. "I suppose you came to rescue your white knight."

"Is Mr. McCutcheon ready to go?"

"Ready? Little lady, at the rate he's going he'll be here all night. Why don't you just trot back to the motel room and cool your little heels. He'll be in your bed again soon enough."

Pony felt a hot flush of anger. She remembered her grandmother's words and recited them silently in her head as she looked at the sheriff. "I would like to speak to him now," she said.

"Oh, you would, would you? Well now, that's special. That's really special." He heaved up from his chair and reached for the keys hung beside the door that led out back. He opened the door and glanced at her. "Well, come on, little lady, if you want to speak."

Pony crossed the room and followed him into the back hall, which led past a small bathroom—door ajar and toilet seat up—to the holding cell just beyond. Caleb was sitting on the edge of the bunk and when he saw her he rose to his full height and closed his hands around the bars. His lip was split, his face was covered with drying blood, and one of his eyes was nearly swollen shut. "Pony," he said, visibly dismayed to see her. "I told you to wait at the motel."

"I wanted to wait here with you. It shouldn't take long." She glanced at the sheriff. "What's holding things up?"

The sheriff scratched the back of his neck. "He is." He nodded at Caleb. "But it's just as well. The mayor's on his way. He's real anxious to meet the man who beat up his son over dancing rights to a—"

"Good," Caleb interrupted, his voice rough with anger. "I have a few words to say to him about his son's poor manners."

"Please, Mr. McCutcheon," Pony said. "Fill out the paperwork."

"I have the right to call my lawyer first."

She leaned forward and closed her own hands around his, staring intently into his eyes. "Just fill out the paperwork so we can leave this place," she pleaded.

He leaned up against the bars and twined his fingers around hers. "Pony," he said in a voice barely above a whisper. "Go back outside, get into the Suburban, get the boys and drive like hell for Montana. And for the love of God, call your brother for me, would you? We could be in a really bad situation."

"All right, all right, quit your whispering," the sheriff said. "Now come on, little lady. You can see he's just fine, all he needs to do is cooperate."

Pony rounded on the sheriff. "You listen to me," she said in a chilly, venomous voice that left no doubt about the outrage she felt. "This man is rich, and he is famous, and what you are doing with him here tonight will make the front page of newspapers all across the country. You had better be certain that you are following the letter of the law, Sheriff, or you may find yourself in jail, too!"

The sheriff stared at her for a few startled moments and then burst out laughing. "All right, enough's enough. Out. Out! Shoooo, you little Injun! Oh lord, don't you make me laugh! Rich and famous! The letter of the law! Such highfalutin ideas from such a pretty little thing!"

Pony was propelled into the front room and herded toward the door. "I mean it!" she cried out, twisting out of his grasp and whirling to face him. "His name is Caleb McCutcheon. He was a famous baseball player for the Chicago White Sox. He has a lot of money and he owns one of the biggest ranches in Montana. He's a powerful man, and he's here in your town to buy buffalo from—"

"Me," a man's baritone voice spoke from behind

her. She spun around. A thin, tall, acerbic-looking man with snow-white hair, a big handlebar mustache and thick scowling eyebrows glared at her from cold dark eyes. "If his name is Caleb McCutcheon and he's a rancher from Montana, he's here to buy buffalo from me."

"And you are...?" Pony said.

"David DeVier," he said. "I'm the mayor of this town."

"Then perhaps you'll see fit to release Mr. McCutcheon from jail," Pony said. "He did nothing wrong."

DeVier regarded her with the kind of cold contempt that Pony had felt before, but he nodded and shifted his attention to the sheriff. "Turn him loose," he said, then spun and left the station, followed by the three burly men who had accompanied him.

BACK AT THE MOTEL, the boys had finally fallen asleep. Caleb drew water for a hot bath and retrieved a phone number from his wallet. He sat on the edge of the bed and placed the call, hearing a familiar man's voice that brought back memories of another lifetime when his world had revolved around a game called baseball.

"Bob," he said into the receiver. "Sorry to wake you, I know what time it is in New York City. But I need your help. I'm in kind of a bad situation here."

There was a brief pause before the sleep-thickened voice replied. "Caleb McCutcheon. I'll be damned. Man who launched my tumultuous journalistic career.

Where in hell are you, and what in hell are you doing?''

Five minutes later, Caleb hung up the phone. He
crawled into the hot bath, let his sore body relax, and
reflected on the disastrous evening. He was too old to
be fighting like that. Three young men full of whiskey
and testosterone. Once upon a time Caleb had lived
those very same years, but he was too old now. Too
damn old. He tipped his head back and closed his
eyes. The hot water felt good. His head ached and the
lump on his skull was as big as a hen's egg, but he
had washed the blood away and no more had come.
Ice had taken the swelling down in his left eye. He
wasn't on his deathbed yet, though in a few short
hours he was fully aware that he might feel a little
differently.

There was a light tap at his door. He opened his
eyes and sat up in the tub. Had he imagined it? Surely
at this hour the rest of Wyoming was asleep…but no,
there it was again. His room light was on, signaling
to the world beyond the drawn curtains that he was
awake, but who would be tapping on his door at
2:00 a.m.? He could simply ignore the knock. The
door was locked and he was safe. Or…had he remembered to lock it? Had he flipped the dead bolt?
Were those three young men hunting him, still spoil-
ing for a fight? The bathroom door was ajar and he
had a clear shot of the motel-room door. He couldn't
see if the bolt was turned. Maybe he should get out
of the tub and make sure that it was.…

"Mr. McCutcheon?"

He froze. The voice on the other side of the door

was Pony's. What the hell was she still doing up? "Yeah," he said, hastily levering his sore body out of the tub and reaching for a towel. "Hold on, I'm coming."

He answered the door, dripping wet and afraid that something was wrong, that the men had followed them here. He cast a quick glance outside. All clear. He dropped his eyes to hers questioningly and she stared back up at him, clearly taken aback. "I'm sorry. Your light was on and I...I mean, I didn't think you'd be..."

"It's all right. Come in. What's wrong? What's the matter? Are you—"

"You were taking a bath, so maybe I should..."

"I was finished. I was just getting out. Please..." He gestured her inside.

"I'm s-sorry," she stammered, her cheeks flushing with embarrassment. "I didn't mean to—"

"Pony, really, it's all right. Sit down. I'll be back in a moment." He went into the bathroom and dressed hurriedly, wincing at the painful protests from his battered body. In jeans, barefoot and pulling on a T-shirt, he walked back into the room. "Okay," he said. "Tell me what's wrong."

She was still standing by the door holding a small bundle in her hands. "Nothing is wrong," she said. "I brought an ice pack for your eye. Some ointment and bandages for your hand."

He glanced down at his raw knuckles, surprised she'd noticed in all the chaos. "Well, thank you."

"Sit down," she said.

He sat on the edge of the bed and she settled herself

beside him, placing the ice pack gently against his cheek and letting him hold it there while she competently tended his sore hand. "You're pretty good with the bandages," he said, watching her, and he caught a glimpse of wry smile.

"Five boys have taught me a lot about first aid."

"I appreciate it."

"You should take some aspirin."

"Already have."

"There's nothing I can do for your split lip," she said, taping the bandage on his hand and gathering up her supplies.

"You could kiss it," he said, "and make it better."

She lifted startled eyes. "Kissing you now would hurt."

"The pain would be worth it," he replied, lowering the ice pack. Before she had time to react he had lowered his head and kissed her very, very gently. It was sweet, but she was right. It hurt. He drew back and studied her for a moment. "It was definitely worth it," he said.

"Caleb…"

"Worth a second try," he said. "Worth more pain."

"Caleb." She touched a trembling finger to the cut on his lip. "I have to know. Will you go to that man's ranch tomorrow? Will you buy buffalo from the mayor of the town?"

He was taken aback by the question but he didn't hesitate. "Yes," he said.

"How can you even think of doing such a thing?" she cried. "After what happened tonight, and after realizing what *might* have happened, how could you even consider doing business with that man?''

Caleb didn't flinch before her outburst. He regarded her steadily. ''Because of what you said to the sheriff about the newspaper headlines if anything happened to me. I thought about that, and I realized that I was going to drive out there tomorrow and get the best price anyone ever has or ever will on a bunch of buffalo and a fancy aluminum trailer, and that will be the revenge of the Bow and Arrow.'' He took her hands in his and looked her in the eye. ''Do you understand why I have to do that?''

She gazed up at him for a long, searching moment. ''Yes,'' she finally admitted.

''If you don't want me to go, say so now.''

''Would it make a difference what I said?''

''It would make all the difference in the world.''

''Then we will all go. Tomorrow morning, first thing. We will go out to that man's ranch together.''

''I'd rather you and the boys stay here. It would be safer.''

''All of us, or none.'' Her eyes were as black as basalt and as flinty as granite.

''Okay,'' he relented. ''All of us. You, me and the boys.''

She nodded. ''You should keep the ice on that eye.''

''You should get some sleep.''

''Thank you.''

''For what?''

''For what you did tonight. No one has ever fought for me like that before.''

His hands tightened on hers. "Anyone would have done the same."

She slipped her hands quickly from his, and her expression became unreadable. "Good night, Mr. McCutcheon."

She turned and was gone just like that, in one swift graceful movement, in the sharp and final closing of the door. He opened it again and leaned out, watched her walk to her own room and enter. Waited until she had closed her own door and locked it.

"Fool!" he berated himself softly wondering if he would ever say the right thing at the right time. "You damn fool!"

CHAPTER TWELVE

GUTHRIE SLOANE WAS NOT the sort of man given to premonitions, but when McCutcheon had called the ranch at 6:00 a.m. that morning and asked to speak with him, he took the phone from Roon's hand with a feeling of foreboding. And when he finally hung up the phone he stood for a moment, then limped out onto the porch where Badger sat with his cup of coffee.

"They're in trouble," Guthrie said. "They're hundreds of miles away from here in some pissant Wyoming town called Jeffords, and it seems they've gotten themselves in a real deep pile of cow dung."

"Their vehicle broke down?" Badger said.

"McCutcheon got himself arrested and thrown into jail."

"Well now, that's a stretch. He ain't exactly the kind of man who goes looking for trouble."

"Three guys tried to throw Pony and the boys out of some redneck bar, and he mixed it up with them. He got beat up pretty good and arrested."

"I wasn't aware that gettin' beat up while protectin' a pretty lady was a crime."

"The arresting sheriff wouldn't let McCutcheon call his lawyer. Instead, the sheriff called the mayor of the town, who was the father of one of the men who was harassing Pony. I guess McCutcheon broke the mayor's son's nose, and the mayor hates Indians and anyone who hangs out with them because his only other son was killed by a bunch of drunken Indians a few years back.''

Badger sat up straighter. ''Oh, lordamighty, this is startin' to sound real bad. Is Boss still alive?''

''The mayor of that town just happened to be the man Caleb was going to buy the buffalo from. He was released from jail when the mayor realized who he was.''

Badger pondered for a moment. ''So let me get this straight. Boss got out of jail because the mayor wanted to sell him the buffalo?''

Guthrie heard Roon come out onto the porch. ''Yup. He, Pony and the boys spent the night at a motel in Jeffords and this morning they're driving out to the ranch to look at the buffalo. That's why Caleb called. He wanted us to know what had happened and where he'd be in case anything went wrong.'' Guthrie paused. ''He said he'd called somebody else as well. Some big-name reporter in New York. Apparently this guy is connected with a big TV news show.''

Badger snorted. ''Never watch TV.''

''Well, this dude is going to help McCutcheon somehow. At least, that's what's planned.'' Guthrie shoved his hands deep into his pockets. ''Not to say it couldn't still go wrong.''

''Well, shoot a duck!'' Badger stood up with a creaking of joints. ''If somethin' *does* go wrong hundreds of miles away from here, what in the name of Sam Hill are we supposed to do?'' He spat over the porch railing and wiped his chin on his shirtsleeve. ''I sure hope Pony's packin' her buffalo pistol, and she's loaded it with the real thing.''

THE MAYOR OF JEFFORDS lived ten miles outside of town on a ranch called the Rockin' DV. The ranch gate was huge and imposing, and Pony drove the Suburban slowly down the paved driveway, past a large putting green and driving range studded with several man-made ponds, between tall plank fences painted brilliant white, dividing pastures that were obviously mown and manicured on a regular basis. Every tree and bush had been pruned to an exact shape and size. The paved road ended at an enormous custom-built log palace with lots of glass. It stood on the edge of another man-made pond with a little bridge leading to a mown island in the center, complete with a brilliant white gazebo. There was a separate guest house, swimming pool, tennis courts and several luxurious barns.

"Where are the buffalo?" Jimmy said, his head swiveling as Pony parked between a tan Mercedes sedan and a black BMW. "I don't see any buffalo."

"You boys stay in the vehicle and keep the doors locked," Caleb said as he spied the mayor coming out the front entrance of the imposing log mansion. "Pony and I will check out the herd."

He tried not to groan aloud as he opened the door and climbed onto the asphalt. The mayor walked up to him and thrust out his hand. "I'm sorry. We never formally met last night. I'm David DeVier. I wasn't sure you'd come this morning."

"Caleb McCutcheon," he said as they shook. "And I wouldn't miss this for the world. This is my herd manager, Pony Young Bear."

DeVier did not offer to shake Pony's hand. He nodded his white head almost imperceptibly and his chilly eyes rested a moment on the door panel of the hunter-green Suburban with its fancy gilt lettering and the proud symbol of the Bow and Arrow.

"How big is your ranch?" Caleb asked.

"One hundred acres. I keep the buffalo in pastures behind the barns. Follow me."

They fell in behind DeVier and walked to the barns. Seven-foot-tall plank fences formed perfect squares of five acres each. Inside each square several buffalo fed on stacks of hay. "Each group has its own pasture, and they are rotated weekly. I run a bull with each bunch of cows. We feed them hay and cake daily, and as you can see, every pasture has a watering trough."

Caleb peered at the huge animals through the plank fence. Each had a big red ear tag with a black number printed on it. He studied them intently and could find nothing wrong with them, yet somehow these creatures were very different from the buffalo on the Bow and Arrow, or the animals they'd seen driving through Yellowstone the previous day. He looked at them long and hard as he moved along the fence, trying to fathom the difference. Pony said nothing, and her expression was carefully neutral when he glanced at her.

"As you can see, they're in good shape," DeVier said. "These are fine animals and they come from a good registry. They're up to date on their shots and worming. I have all the paperwork on them. You won't find a better group of buffalo at a better price anywhere on this continent."

"I believe that's true," Caleb said, glancing at his watch. "I'll take them. Can you load them into the trailer?"

"My men are standing by. We can have them loaded inside an hour."

Caleb nodded. "Good. I'd like to be on the road before noon. We have a long drive ahead of us. The sooner we can get this wrapped up, the better."

DeVier smiled thinly. "Come inside and we'll draw up the papers."

They followed the mayor into his opulent lodge. He brought them into the great room, with its soaring open ceiling and huge fieldstone fireplace. The furniture was western, upholstered in what looked like the hides of an entire herd of pinto ponies. A huge antler chandelier hung from the ceiling, and over the mantel hung an original Remington. "Please, sit down," DeVier said, gesturing to the hide-covered sofa. "Would you like a drink? No doubt after last night a whiskey would help to ease your discomfiture."

"No, thank you," Caleb said. He wished he could watch DeVier's men load the buffalo into the trailer. How did these buffalo behave? Already he could hear the sounds of four-wheelers revving up, and a man poked his head into the room.

"Sir?" he said to DeVier. "We'd like to hook the trailer up to Mr. McCutcheon's Suburban, but the boys inside the vehicle locked all the doors."

Pony rose. "I'll go out and speak to them." Caleb sensed her eagerness to escape the stifling confines of DeVier's mansion and wished he could follow her. When she'd left the room Caleb waited for DeVier to produce the paperwork for the herd. "If you don't mind," he said, "I think I'll take you up on that offer for a drink."

"Not at all. I'll join you." The mayor poured each

of them a generous shot of whiskey. He raised his glass. "To a satisfactory business transaction," he said.

"Amen." Caleb tossed the drink back and set his glass down on the coffee table. The slow burn of the smooth malt settled in his stomach and he hoped it would ease some of his physical torment, because the handful of aspirin he'd taken earlier hadn't made a dent in the pain.

"Now then, here are the papers on the buffalo. We bought them at auction from a very reputable ranch. The Double A. Perhaps you've heard of it?"

"Yes. They're out of South Dakota."

"That's right. Biggest outfit in the nation raising buffalo right now. Their animals demand top prices."

"I'm sure they do."

"So you understand that I'm giving you a great deal on these buffalo."

"Oh, I understand perfectly, Mayor. I understand that I'm going to be driving out of here with a practically brand-new thirty-foot, twenty-five-thousand-dollar Featherlite stock trailer and twenty head of some of the best buffalo on the northern continent for the price of a black eye, a split lip and some skinned knuckles," Caleb said without missing a beat.

DeVier set his shot glass down carefully. "As you will recall, the price quoted was *sixty* thousand dollars. The price for the buffalo and the trailer is sixty thousand dollars, Mr. McCutcheon. If you aren't willing to pay that, then you're wasting my time and I must ask you to leave."

"And I was more than willing to pay that price until last night. I'll leave when the buffalo are loaded and the bill of sale signed.'' Caleb patted his pockets and frowned. ''Would you have a pen?''

''I don't think you heard me very well.''

''Oh, I heard you just fine.''

''I'm asking you to leave, Mr. McCutcheon. Right now, if you please.''

Caleb sat back on the sofa and studied the mayor's face for a few seconds. ''The sheriff told me what happened to your youngest son, Mayor DeVier. I'm very sorry. But that tragic accident has nothing to do with the people I'm traveling with.''

''You have no right to talk about my son!'' DeVier snapped.

''No right? I was taken into custody and denied the right to call my lawyer, and the sheriff who arrested me didn't read me my Miranda rights. Instead, he called you at home, and you came immediately with three big goons. Don't talk to me about rights, Mayor.''

''I did nothing wrong! You were arrested because you broke up a bar and brutally assaulted several people, including my son!''

''I was arrested because I stopped your son from harassing a woman and four boys who happened to be Indians,'' Caleb countered, his voice hardening. ''It was ten-thirty at night when you came to the police station. Is that normal for you? What awful things might have happened to me, that young woman and those four boys if I hadn't been the wealthy rancher from Montana who had come to town to buy your little herd of buffalo? I may be retired from major league baseball but I still know a lot of big hitting investigative reporters who would love to sink their teeth into a story like this!''

Pony stepped quietly into the living room just as Caleb rose to his feet, his body rigid with anger. She stopped, obviously sensing the tension in the room. Neither man acknowledged her presence. When the phone rang, the shrill noise jarred them all. There were swift footsteps in the hall and a woman in a maid's uniform stepped past Pony.

"That phone call is for you, Mr. Mayor," she said.

"I'm not taking calls at the moment," DeVier snapped.

"Sir, the caller said it was important," the woman apologized. "He produces a TV show in New York City and he wants to speak with you about Caleb McCutcheon."

DeVier stiffened. His icy eyes flickered. "You're bluffing," he said.

Caleb nodded to the desk phone. "Try me."

DeVier hesitated, then picked up the phone. "This is Mayor DeVier," he said. There was a pause while the mayor listened, his eyes fixed on the Remington painting above the mantel. "Yes, that's right," he said, uncertainty edging his voice. And then, "No, that's not true. We don't discriminate against Indians in this town," followed by "No! No, my son was just defending himself against… But he didn't…!" Pause. "Yes. I understand," he said in a voice that had lost all its aggression. DeVier replaced the receiver slowly, his eyes still fixed on the painting. His complexion had taken on a gray pallor.

"Okay," Caleb said. "This is the deal. As soon as you sign that bill of sale, I'll call my friend in New York and tell him to forget all about Mayor DeVier and his legacy of hate and discrimination in a small Wyoming town, which would probably be a very good thing for you if you intend to remain in politics!''

DeVier returned to his chair and sat abruptly, as if all the strength had gone from his legs. He rested trembling hands on the arm rests and his voice shook when he spoke.

''Jonathan was a brilliant boy. He had a great future ahead of him.''

''I'm sure his loss was terrible for you,'' Caleb said. ''But practicing racism is no way to honor his memory.'' He glanced at Pony. ''Are the boys okay?''

''Fine,'' she replied quietly. ''And the buffalo are loaded.''

Caleb nodded. He glanced back at DeVier and studied the man for a moment. ''Thirty thousand,'' he said.

DeVier's eyes raised to his, startled.

''I'll pay you thirty grand for the buffalo and the trailer. And I'll donate the other thirty grand to a scholarship fund on the Crow Indian reservation. In your name, of course. The only reason I'm paying you anything at all after what you did is because my herd manager would want me to, and I respect her opinion very much.''

DeVier's expression revealed weariness and defeat. He nodded his acceptance of the terms. ''I did nothing wrong,'' he said softly.

''Neither did I. Now, if you could please find me a pen?''

The mayor reached into his vest pocket and brought out a gold pen. He laid it on the coffee table. Caleb made several alterations and then pushed the papers toward DeVier. "Just initial the changes and sign the bill of sale," he said. "I'll write the check."

DeVier's hand trembled as he signed. He gave the pen to Caleb. "I'll be sure to send you official verification of your generous donation to the scholarship fund," Caleb said, handing the check to the mayor. "It's tax deductible."

"Please, just leave. Take the damn buffalo and go!"

Caleb stood, reaching up the sheaf of papers and the bill of sale. "I won't say it's been a pleasure doing business with you, Mayor, because it hasn't. But I will tell you that those buffalo will have a good home in Montana."

Ten minutes later they were driving home, towing twenty buffalo in a gleaming silver Featherlite trailer. For a long while they drove in silence. When they entered the boundaries of Yellowstone National Park, it wasn't long before they spotted the first wild buffalo. Caleb slowly pulled the Suburban to the side of the road and stared. "Look at them," he said to Pony. "*Look* at them. Am I crazy, or do they look different from the buffalo we're hauling?"

"They look different," she agreed with a patient nod. "They're free," she explained, as if he were a child who should know such a basic truth. "And a wild creature that is free has its own beauty."

IT WAS DUSK when Guthrie heard the sound of a vehicle climbing the gravel road that led to the ranch. He limped slowly down the porch steps and heard the screen door slam behind him as Jessie, Badger and Roon followed him outside.

"It's them, all right," Badger said. "Get a load of that fancy trailer."

The Suburban's headlights swept across the face of the ranch house, and Caleb pulled to a stop and leaned out. "We'll drive them right up back," he said. "Climb aboard if you want to watch the show."

"The gate's open," Guthrie said as they climbed into the vehicle, headed up the road toward the holding corrals. They passed through the open gate and paused while Jimmy jumped out and closed it behind them. Twenty minutes later they reached the high meadow. Caleb braked to a gentle stop and cut the engine. In the twilight the mountains loomed against the sky like black sentinels. He sat for a few moments absorbing the peace and beauty of the place while the rest waited quietly for his cue.

"It was a long ride," Caleb said at length. "Let's let these buffalo out." He reached for the door handle and paused. "You may think this sounds crazy, but I'd really like to take the tags out of their ears," he said.

Guthrie nodded. "We can do that, but we'll have to unload them into the corral. We can remove the tags in the morning and turn them loose."

"If we hold them in the corral overnight we'll need to bring some hay up for the night feeding," Jessie pointed out.

"We can do that, too, can't we, boys?" Guthrie asked, and they nodded. "Okay then. Let's back the trailer up to the corral. Jimmy, open the gate."

After several minutes, they were dropping the back ramp of the big silver trailer and standing back as the buffalo burst out in one thundering stream. They hit the ground in their strange, stiff-gaited lope and curved around the perimeter of the corral, grunting and snorting and shaking the ground.

"They're good-lookin' buff," Badger said.

"They'll look a whole lot better when they're running free," Caleb replied.

They leaned against the corral, watching until it was nearly dark. "Ramalda's keeping supper for you," Guthrie said. "We figured you'd be home late. Looks like you had quite an adventure."

"Yeah," Caleb said. "We did." He glanced at Roon. "How's Absa and that wild mustang doing?"

"Good."

Caleb looked at Guthrie and Jessie. "How's Blue and her pups?"

"They're doing just fine," Jessie said.

Caleb crossed to where Pony leaned across the corral fence watching the buffalo and draped his arm companionably across her shoulders. "Damn," he said. "It's good to be back home."

WHEN CALEB WALKED into the kitchen, Ramalda turned from the sink and froze. She stared at him for a few horrified moments. *"Dios mio! Que te paso! Parece que estas muerto!"* She lifted her apron over her face and burst into tears.

He had no idea what she'd said, but her actions required no translation. He crossed the room and hugged her awkwardly. "I missed you, too," he said. "We're hungry. I hope you made a lot of food."

Ramalda had outdone herself. She brought dish after dish to the table, hovering with that ever-present scowl and wiping tears from her cheeks repeatedly with her apron. Caleb told the story of what had happened that morning on the Rockin' DV, but after that there wasn't much talk around the table. It had been a long day, and they were all exhausted.

Caleb couldn't eat much. The heat, his fatigue and his aching body all conspired to make Ramalda's tears flow faster and faster as he failed to clean his plate. He got slowly to his feet and reached for his hat on the peg beside the door. He looked at the faces that stared back at him somberly and said, "Long live the Bow and Arrow, and good night to you all."

As he washed up at his cabin he studied his reflection in the old mirror above the sink and grimaced at the stranger that stared back at him, "No wonder that poor old woman cried. You'd scare the soul out of a holy man."

He carried a bottle and a glass onto the porch and sat in the darkness, sipping whiskey and listening to the creek. He thought about the twenty head of buffalo with the red tags in their ears who were milling around up in the holding corral, spending their first night beneath a star-studded Montana sky. He remembered how cold DeVier's eyes had been, and thought about how easy it would be for someone like that to justify any kind of crime in the name of revenge for his murdered son.

And get away with it, over and over again.

"Here's to your generous thirty-thousand-dollar donation, DeVier," he said, taking another sip. "I hope one day you can let go of all that hate before it burns you up inside."

PONY HELPED Ramalda and Jessie tidy up the kitchen and sat at the computer for a little while afterward, thinking that she should enter all the data on the new buffalo. But she didn't turn on the computer. She was

tired and she couldn't stop thinking about Caleb Mc-
Cutcheon and all the things she needed to say to him.
When he'd left the kitchen after supper, she'd wanted
follow him.

She wanted to be near him, but being near him the
way she had been for the past two days wasn't
enough. She wanted more than that. Much more.

She wanted something she could not have, and the
pain was like having the blade of a knife drawn
through her heart. She would have to leave here soon;
being so close to him was a torment she could no
longer endure. Jessie's questioning glance before she
and Guthrie had said their good-nights had only made
Pony feel worse. She was a failure on all fronts.

She stood and lifted her heavy braid off her shoulder. It was so warm. Maybe if she took a swim, it
would help her to sleep.

Maybe. But she doubted it.

IT WAS TOO HOT to sleep. The air was stifling. Caleb
carried the bottle of whiskey with him and walked
down along the edge of the creek to the swimming
hole. The pool was deep, and in the darkness the water sent a liquid murmur along the edges of the bank
that was barely louder than a whisper. He heard the
splash of a trout rising and set the bottle down in the
cradle of a tree root. Moments later he had stripped
out of his clothes and was plunging into the cool water. In just the right spot a person could float in circles
forever, and he found the place and lay on his back,
letting the current spin him slowly around and around
while he caught glimpses of the shining stars through
the interlacing branches of the willow and cottonwood.

He would never survive the rest of the summer. He wanted Pony so badly that he was sure the whole world could see the torment in his eyes. He had no right to feel this way. She had been blunt and honest with him, and he had to respect her for that, but to work alongside her was killing him.

The water was soothing. He could easily spend the entire night like this, floating on his back in this swimming hole and contemplating a future that had Pony in it....

Footsteps. He heard the soft tread of approaching footsteps and back-paddled beneath the overhanging arm of a giant cottonwood on the opposite bank. Who...? He peered through the darkness and saw a shadowy human shape materialize and stand motionless for a moment, not ten feet from the clump of bushes that hid his clothes and the bottle of whiskey. Suddenly the shape began to move, stripping off clothing and laying it piece by piece over a clump of brush.

Well, now, this was a quandary. Should he speak up? He cleared his throat loudly, then, realizing that the resulting noise sounded rather bearlike, he said, "Hello?" When he spoke, the shadow toppled off the edge of the bank and into the pool with a startled and decidedly feminine-sounding cry.

"Pony?" he said when her head came up, sputtering. "It's Caleb."

He heard her gasp. "You might have said something!"

"I just did, and you fell in."

"I mean, before I took most of my clothes off!"

"And spoil all the fun?" When she started scrambling out he said, "Don't go. Please. The water's great, and I promise I'll stay over here. You can have one whole half of the pool. If that doesn't work for you, I'll leave. I've been here long enough.''

She paused in the act of pulling herself onto the bank. ''Your poor body needs the cool water more than I.''

''Well, actually, my heart's in much worse shape than my body.'' He cursed himself silently the moment the words tumbled out. ''I mean, I feel bad for what happened in Wyoming. You and the boys could've gotten hurt, and it was my fault.''

''Your fault? For making that man let go of me? Should you have just let him throw me and the boys out on the street?'' She spoke tersely, her words swift and angry.

''No. That's not what I meant. He shouldn't have touched you, and I'm not sorry I hit him. I'm not sorry I attacked any of them, and as mad as I was, it's a wonder I didn't commit murder.''

''Then why are you sorry?''

He drew a silent breath. ''I'm sorry this world is so screwed up.''

''That's not your fault, Mr. McCutcheon,'' she said, her voice gentling. ''That's just how it is. When we leave the reservation, we know things like that can happen.''

''Things like that should never happen.''

''There are lots of things that shouldn't be. I feel lucky that we're here in this place for the summer. I can notice a big change in the boys. But the summer is more than half over.''

Half over! Caleb felt that familiar surge of anxiety. ''What will happen this fall?''

''We'll go back. I'll teach school, the boys will

learn their lessons and take their GED's and hopefully find paths that will lead them to good places.''

Caleb looped his arm through a protruding cotton-wood root. ''What if there was a school right here, so you didn't have to leave? What if the ranch was a school, a place where kids could work and learn at the same time, sort of a work-study program. They could do their lessons and learn how to successfully manage and market a buffalo herd. How to raise and train and worm and vaccinate and hot-shoe horses. Maybe there could be a special scholarship fund set up for them to go on to an agricultural college, or any other kind of college, for that matter. Roon could go to vet school. Jessie and Doc Cooper would vouch for him if his grades were good enough in college.''

Pony had slipped back into the water and was swimming gently into the current. ''What are you saying, Mr. McCutcheon?'' she said.

Caleb drew a deep breath. ''I'm saying that maybe the end of summer doesn't have to be the end of everything. I want you to stay.''

''I'm a third-grade teacher on the reservation,'' she pointed out.

''Couldn't you teach older students? You're doing it now, and you do it well.''

''Why?'' she said. Her strokes were smooth and graceful and they were bringing her closer and closer. She was straying onto his side of the pool. ''Why do you want to do this?''

He opened his mouth to respond but could not find the words. She was close enough now that he could almost reach out and touch her, and the water began to feel electrically charged.

"Is it pity?" She stopped moving forward. "Is it because you feel sorry for us?"

His heart rate had trebled. "I didn't feel sorry for you when I hired you. I didn't feel sorry for you when you stood off that charging buffalo with a thimbleful of BB's. And I didn't feel sorry for you when you came to the sheriff's office to demand my release. It's not pity. If anything, it's pure selfishness. I want you to stay because I like having you around. You've been a big help with the buffalo. With the fences. And what's the point of owning that big fancy Suburban if I can't squire the whole bunch of you around in it?"

She was within reach now, and he let his free hand drift toward her, surprised and gratified when she gripped it with her own and pulled herself up against the bank beside him. "I think what you are trying to say is nice, but it isn't real," she said. "You don't need us here to ride around in your big vehicle. You don't need us here to help with your fences, or with your buffalo. You don't really need us here at all."

"Yes, I do," he said. "And maybe you think it's not real, but it is." He tightened his grip on her hand and forced up every ounce of his courage. "You see, Pony, I'm—"

"Shh, listen!" she said suddenly. "Someone's coming."

He craned to hear and his heart plummeted. "Sounds like a whole tribe of someones. Must be the boys. Quick! Those bushes, my underwear!"

"You mean you're—"

"Yes, dammit. You would be, too, if I hadn't spoken up when I did!"

She swam to the opposite bank, and he could have

sworn he heard her laugh. Within moments she had reached the bushes where his clothes were hidden. She dived back into the water, hand delivering his cotton boxers as five shadowy forms appeared on the bank.

"Thanks," he muttered to her. Then he raised his voice. "Come on in, boys, the water's great."

There were multiple explosions as they hit the water, reveling in the refreshing cool of it. "Say, Mr. McCutcheon," Jimmy said, splashing his way across the pool. "Where did you learn to fight like that? I've never seen anything like it. If you hadn't got hit with that bottle, you would have wiped all of them out!"

"Let's just pretend that never happened."

"But I want to learn how to fight that way."

"Then you better get born all over again and grow up in the Chicago slums."

"You could teach us."

"Why would I want to teach you how to get hit over the head with a beer bottle and thrown into jail?"

"But—"

"That's what happened, isn't it? It doesn't matter how good you are at anything. If the odds are against you, you're going down, and if you go down fighting, it sure as hell won't be because I taught you how. The only thing I'll teach you is how to throw a baseball. End of conversation."

"But—"

"And now I'll leave you to your swim. But don't forget. Dawn tomorrow. Breakfast. And then we're going to take the red tags out of those buffalo ears and set them free. Dawn comes at what time, Jimmy?"

"Early," Jimmy said, his voice resigned.

"That's right. So don't be late." Caleb swam for the opposite bank, pulled himself out and carried the bundle of clothes and the bottle of whiskey back to his cabin.

CHAPTER THIRTEEN

IT WAS CALEB who was late the following morning. He stood beneath the weak stream of cool water in his gravity-feed shower, willing the muddiness from his head. He took a handful of aspirin, drank a cup of strong coffee, climbed into his pickup and drove to the holding corrals, groaning aloud at every jolting bump. The contractors were there. Pony and the boys were there. Guthrie and Jessie and Badger were there.

And they were all waiting for him.

"Good morning! We decided to give your setup an early test," he said to the foreman of the job, trying not to move like an arthritic old man as he approached the corral fence. He was very much aware of the curious stares as the group of young, vigorous workmen studied his battered face. "I know the corrals aren't quite finished, but I'm hoping they'll be up to the task."

The foreman nodded. "They will be. The only thing that isn't ready is the hydraulic crush. The corrals, the alleyway and the chute are good to go. All you got to do is get the buffalo into them. That oughta be quite a show." He glanced around with a cynical leer. "No horses, huh? How're you planning to do this? On foot?"

Caleb hesitated, but before he could respond, Pony spoke. "Yes," she said. "I'm going to move them down the alleyway and into the chute in groups of five. Badger and the boys will work the sliding doors to separate the animals, Guthrie and Jessie will remove the ear tags from them once they're in the chute. Then we'll open the gate in the far holding corral and send them on their way.''

Caleb stared at her along with the rest of the men. She sounded so sure of herself, this slender woman with the long black braid and the calm dark eyes. Surely she couldn't be serious. She wasn't actually going to go into that corral with those huge grunting, snorting beasts and herd them on foot? The idea was not only dangerous, it was absurd.

Yet even as he tried to think of a more logical way to proceed, Pony was climbing the fence. He stepped forward and grabbed her ankle. ''Wait!'' he said.

She turned her head to look down at him. ''It will be okay, Mr. McCutcheon. I've done this before.''

He released her ankle reluctantly, and she continued up and over the rails, climbing smoothly down the opposite side. ''All right,'' she said, and Caleb realized that Roon had positioned himself on top of the fence by the entrance to the smaller pen. At Pony's words he unlatched the heavy steel gate and swung it open.

The buffalo were grouped closely together on the opposite side of the corral from Pony, watching her. She moved slowly and quietly. Every movement she made had an effect on the buffalo. A shift of her weight, and they moved in one direction. A pause, and they stopped. She moved to the right, they moved to the left; she moved left, they moved right, always keeping the same distance between themselves. It was a beautiful, primitive and sophisticated dance between predator and prey, and Caleb watched in awe, completely overwhelmed by the sight of the one-hundred-pound woman herding over twenty thousand pounds of buffalo with the subtlest of nonthreatening movements.

They began to go through the open gate. First a cow and her calf. Then a young bull. Two cows. Then the rest of them, trotting now, passing through the opening until the last one had entered the small pen. It seemed at first as if Pony had done the impossible, but as she moved to close the gate behind them, the buffalo, sensing the trap, began to charge back toward the opening. The ground shook. Thunder and dust filled the air and the massive creatures stormed toward her, heads lowered. She stood in the face of the onslaught, swinging the gate closed. Caleb lost sight of her in the cloud of dust but he heard the loud crash of steel and a triumphant shout from Roon. When the ruckus died down, there were five buffalo in the smaller pen and fifteen loping around the big corral and Pony was sitting on the top rail of the fence beside Roon.

A moment later she lowered herself into the pen with the five buffalo, and in the same calm, slow, easy way, she herded them into the alleyway, where the boys were working the sliding gates to create individual cubicles for them as they moved toward the chute. Caleb climbed up beside Guthrie and Jessie, leaning over as the first of the cows was trapped directly below. He had never been this close to a buffalo before. He could smell the sweet-grass exhalations of the cow's gusting breaths, and even as Jessie reached to clip the tag from the animal's ear, Caleb sank his fingers into the thick, curly woolliness of her fur, ran his fingers over the smooth curve of her black horn and felt a humbling thrill unlike any he had ever experienced.

Then the sliding door opened and the cow moved out of the chute and into the holding corral at the end. Another buffalo was pushed into the chute. Another ear tag was removed. And so on, smoothly, quickly, until the first five were done. Ten minutes later, the second batch of five was pushed down the alleyway. In two hours the task was completed, and the tagless buffalo were in the far holding pen. Pony walked up beside Caleb and pulled off her leather gloves. "Open the gate, Mr. McCutcheon," she said with a slow smile. "It's time for them to remember what it feels like to be free."

He unlatched the heavy steel gate and swung it wide, standing against the corral fence as the biggest and shaggiest of the cows, calf at her flank, approached the opening. She paused for a moment, staring out with dark, haughty eyes at the tall mountains looming in the distance, and then lifted her tail and jumped into that odd, stiff-gaited lope. The rest of the herd immediately followed her. Dust rose, the earth trembled underfoot, and twenty buffalo reached a speed of thirty miles an hour in a mere hundred feet as they raced across the meadow, throwing up grassy clods of Montana turf. They got to the first ridge and turned almost as one animal—never losing any speed—and raced back down the ridge again. They ran up it, ran back down. Broke into groups and chased each other back and forth.

Caleb and the others stood as a group and silently watched this spectacle, unaware that each of them was grinning. A little bit at first and then ear to ear, watching the buffalo run and play. They looked at each other and laughed, feeling giddy and wonderful inside. "That's something, isn't it?" Caleb said, his lip cracked open and bleeding. "Look at them!"

"You'd never see a bunch of beef cows doin' that," Badger said. "Nossir."

Guthrie was holding twenty red ear tags in his hand. "What do you want me to do with these things?"

"Burn them," Caleb said. "Every single one of those buffalo looks different. We'll give them each a name just like Absa and Goliath, and learn to tell them apart."

The foreman of the contracting crew was the last to turn away from the corrals after the last buffalo had disappeared over the ridge. The big burly man looked at Caleb and shook his head. "I've never seen anything like that," he said, his eyes dazed. "That girl, those buffalo. Never. That was beautiful."

CALEB DECLARED the rest of the day an official holiday. "Buffalo Day," he told the boys. The truth was, Caleb didn't feel capable of doing anything remotely physical, and he felt the boys deserved some free time, too. Guthrie and Jessie drove them all to his place to show them the pups. Blue was accommodatingly patient with all the attention and the eager, grasping hands. She let Caleb pick up one of the little females. The pup's eyes were still closed, she was fat, her nose was all crinkled, and she had puppy breath. She was perfect. Caleb blew a gentle breath back at her and said, "Hello, Tess."

"You can't know that's the one you're keeping," Jimmy said.

"Yes, I can. This is the one. This is Tess." Caleb gently replaced the pup next to her mother, and she immediately burrowed down into the squirming pile, vigorously seeking one of her mother's nipples.

"She looks just like all the rest," Martin said.

"No, she doesn't. She's prettier," Caleb said.

"I think they're all pretty cute. I wish I could have one," Jimmy said.

It took a lot of prying to get the boys back into the Suburban, but the noon meal was a strong draw and eventually they were heading back to the ranch. After another delicious lunch, Caleb took Pony, Jessie and Guthrie aside. "I've been looking over the books," he said. "I think we need to sit down and talk. The figures are pretty grim."

"Where and when?" Guthrie said. "I have to take Jess to the airport soon."

"My porch. Right now."

Ten minutes later Caleb was holding the three-ring binder with the bookkeeping printouts, pacing the length of the cabin porch and scanning the numbers. "According to what I'm reading here, this place will be bankrupt in just under two years. Actually, that's incorrect. It's bankrupt now. We won't even make the property tax payments. So what are we doing wrong? Are my figures off?"

Pony was half sitting on the top porch rail, leaning against a post. "No. If anything, they're optimistic, especially in what you think you can get for a buffalo calf."

"You don't think I'd get at least two thousand for a female calf?"

"If the market was strong, but right now it isn't. The prices are lower for calves. And the perimeter fence is going to cost one dollar per foot. There are sixteen miles of fence, six strand. The figures are all there. Selling ten weaned buffalo calves every fall isn't going to make a dent in the bank loan.''

''But there is no bank loan.''

''This is a real-life projection, Mr. McCutcheon. We want our books to show that the ranch is holding its own, not that you are propping it up. We want the buffalo to support the place. Isn't that what we agreed?''

Both Guthrie and Caleb nodded.

''You need to get at least one hundred head of buffalo on the land as soon as possible. Ten bulls, ninety cows. You need to raise at least fifty calves a year. You need to harvest at least thirty-two year-old bulls every fall, and you need to develop a strong marketing base to sell the meat and the hides and the skulls.''

Caleb stopped pacing and stared at her. ''You mean, *kill* them?''

Pony nodded. ''Yes. And then you need to sell the meat directly to the consumer without paying a middleman. To do that you need two things. A good marketing pitch and a good meat-packing and shipping outfit.''

Caleb shook his head. ''But I don't want to go that route. I want to run a cow-calf operation.''''

''Two days ago we saw an outfit like that. The mayor of Jeffords kept his buffalo that way. He kept his cows and his bulls and sold the calves each year, and he did it for a hobby. He didn't make his living doing it. He probably spent money doing it. But, like you, he could afford to. So you can run the Bow and Arrow as a gentleman's ranch, or you can operate a real working ranch. But you have to choose your path.''

Caleb paced to the edge of the porch and gazed out at the mountains, the peaks slate gray and craggy in the afternoon sunlight. ''Lord,'' he said. ''Why does it all have to be so complicated?'' He looked over his shoulder at Guthrie. ''A hundred buffalo.''

''You have good grass here,'' Guthrie said. ''The land used to support a whole lot more cattle than that, but we employed a rotation system. We pushed the animals from pasture to pasture so they wouldn't overgraze it.''

''The buffalo will regulate themselves that way,'' Pony said. ''They roam. They don't stay in one place and graze an area down to the dirt the way cattle do.''

''But shipping them to the slaughterhouse...'' Caleb paced the length of the porch again and stopped at the opposite end, looking up the creek. ''Herding them into a trailer and hauling them off that way. Fattening them up in crowded feedlot like a bunch of domestic cattle...'' He closed the binder with a thump. ''I don't know. It just seems wrong.''

''We're at least two years away from that,'' Pony said.

''But we need more buffalo. At least five more bulls and seventy more cows,'' Jessie said. ''A big chunk of change.''

''November. That's when some of the auctions are,'' Pony said.

Caleb caught her eye. It was on the tip of his tongue to ask her where she planned to be in November, but instead he said, ''Okay, so we do all these things that you suggest and now it's three years later.

What do you see in your crystal ball for the Bow and
Arrow?''

She gave him that warm, beautiful smile of hers.
''I see the beginning of something good.''

HE WAS READING on the porch two hours later, contemplating the sweet notion of a nap, when he heard
quick, light footsteps and glanced up from the page
to see Pony round the corner of the cabin. ''Come
and see,'' she exclaimed, fairly bursting with excite-
ment. She beckoned impatiently. ''Quickly!''

''What is it?'' He dropped the book as he stood,
walking swiftly to join her.

''Hurry. Follow me, and keep quiet.''

She led him swiftly down the path that bordered
the creek and ended at the swimming hole. When they
neared the pool, she slowed and reached for his hand
to stop him. She advanced in a crouch and then, behind the very bushes where he had stripped naked the
night before, she knelt and pulled him down beside
her. He looked through the branches, totally baffled
by her behavior, then his eyes focused on two horses
standing chest deep in the cool dark water. One of
the horses was Sparky, the old gelding Roon had used
to pony the mustang down to the swimming hole, and
the other was the mustang with the injured leg. Nothing so unusual about that, but...

''Good Lord,'' Caleb breathed. ''Roon's sitting on
Twister.''

''Yes,'' she whispered. ''I was coming down to
pick some watercress for a salad when I spotted them.
Roon didn't see me.''

''But that horse... He's wild. He hates people.
How...?''

"Shh. The horses will hear you. Just watch."

So he held very still and watched as the boy sat on the bay mustang, bare feet dangling in the water, his hands rubbing the colt's withers. Roon stroked with a soothing motion lower onto the mustang's shoulders, then back up, his movements smooth and slow. Then he reached one hand and closed it on Sparky's neck, and very gently slid from the mustang and onto the gelding's broad back. There was no rope attached to Twister's halter. Hell, there wasn't even a *halter* on the killer mustang.

Roon nudged Sparky with his bare heels and the solid old horse waded out of the swimming hole, splashing up onto the sandy bank with the mustang's nose at his hip. Without so much as a backward glance, Roon guided Sparky toward the ranch house and the pole barn. The mustang was putting some weight on the injured leg, and the swelling was almost gone. Absa, who had been lying on the bank like a little golden dog, trotted at Twister's heels. When they were out of earshot Caleb gave an incredulous laugh.

"I wouldn't have believed that unless I saw it," he said, grinning at Pony.

"I know. That's why I came to get you."

"How long has that been going on?"

"I have no idea."

Caleb shook his head. "And he's not going to say anything about it?"

She shrugged. "He will tell us when he wants us to know."

He stood and pulled her to her feet. "That boy has a rare talent. He could be very valuable here at the ranch. It'd be a real shame for him to leave in another short month.''

''Mr. McCutcheon, your ideas about a school are like your ideas about raising buffalo. They aren't real.''

Caleb's spirits sank. ''You'll always think of me as a wealthy buffoon, won't you?''

She shook her head. ''I will never think of you that way. You are a good man with a good heart. But a school for delinquent Indian children? A ranch where no animals ever die?''

''I didn't use the word *delinquent.*''

''No. That's my brother's word. That's what Steven calls them.''

''And I realize that animals die.''

''Everything dies. It's how we live that is important.''

''I think how we die matters, too,'' Caleb said. ''I don't want Bow and Arrow buffalo being shipped to feedlots and slaughterhouses. Is that so wrong?''

Her expression softened. ''No.''

''There has to be a better way.''

''There might be,'' Pony said. ''I have heard of a place in South Dakota that harvests their buffalo right on the land. A meat inspector attends, and then the buffalo are brought immediately to the butcher. The meat is packaged, frozen, taken to a shipping company and mailed out to customers. The buffalo never know the pain and fear and indignity you're worried about.''

Caleb looked at her, brightening. ''Could we do that?''

''If there's a meat-packing plant close enough,'' she said.

"Good. I'll look into it." He paused, his eyes narrowing. "Pony, is it so wrong to want to offer something more than one summer to a bunch of kids I've come to like a great deal?"

"They're Crow. The only place they will ever truly belong is on the reservation."

"That's not so." Caleb reached for her hands. "This land we're standing on right now was Crow territory not that long ago. The Mountain Crow lived in these valleys and hunted in these mountains. Those boys belong here as much as they belong anywhere, and is this such a *bad* place for them to be?"

She hesitated.

"Is it a bad place for *you* to be?" he said.

She shook her head. "I cannot stay."

"Why? Is it because of how you feel about having children?"

Pony recoiled at his words and jerked her hands from his. "Who told you about that?" she said, so instantly and vehemently angry that he took an involuntary step back. "Did Pete tell you? Did Jessie?"

He shook his head, bewildered. "No. You did, up on the mountain. You told me about your people dying off because of all the mixed-blood marriages. *You* told me."

Her eyes became suddenly blank and he felt as if a door had been slammed in his face. "I have to go," she said, turning on her heel and walking swiftly away, following Roon and the horses.

"Pony!" he called after her, but she didn't turn around.

GUTHRIE STARED glumly out the huge plate-glass window at the small silver jet parked in Gate C, the late-afternoon sun glinting off its wing. "That'll be your plane, I guess," he said.

Jessie nodded. "Time to say goodbye, cowboy."

He pulled her close and kissed her like there was no tomorrow. He didn't care who was watching. "I hate saying goodbye to you."

"It's only for a few more weeks," she breathed. "You take care of yourself. Don't overdo it. Mr. Mc-Cutcheon was right. You're pushing yourself too hard."

"I aim to carry you over the threshold on our wedding night."

"I'm not that heavy, Guthrie, and if it comes to that, I'm perfectly capable of walking. Keep me posted on Mr. McCutcheon and Pony," she said as the boarding call came over the loudspeakers.

"You still think there's hope for them?" he said, refusing to release her.

She grinned up at him. "Hope? Guthrie, you're about as romantic as a stone. Of course there's hope. I'm afraid they're going to run off together and get hitched someplace else, and they deserve to have a nice wedding right there on the ranch. Now kiss me one more time and turn me loose, before I miss my flight."

STEVEN YOUNG BEAR CAME to the Bow and Arrow for supper that night. He came because Caleb had invited him, and he brought a package of meat for Ramalda to cook. "Buffalo rib-eye steaks," he said, handing her the bundle wrapped in butcher's paper. "*Tatanka.* Cook them quick and rare or they'll be tough and dry."

She snatched the package from him with one hand

and waved the other toward the door. *"Yo se cocinar la carne! Vete de aqui! Esta es mi cocina!* My kitchen! *My kitchen!* I know how to cook! *Vete!* You go! Go!"

Steven nodded politely and walked out onto the porch where everyone had gathered to watch the sunset. The men drank cold beer while Pony and the boys had juice and soda. "I thought since you're raising them, maybe it might be good to see how they taste," he said, accepting a beer from Badger. He twisted off the cap and scrutinized Caleb's face. "I sure hope Pony didn't do that to you," he said, somber-voiced. "She can be difficult, but I've never known her to beat a man up." Pony ignored her brother's comment, gazing out at the mountains and the pink and violet clouds that shredded themselves against the craggy summits.

"You should have seen Mr. McCutcheon!" Jimmy said, more than willing to tell the tale again. "He took on three big mean rednecks and he knocked them all down, *bam, bam, bam!* just like that."

"Really," Steven said, lifting his beer for a swallow and giving Caleb's battered face another significant look. "And then what happened?"

"They busted a beer bottle over his head, pinned his arms and thrashed him. But he would have won if they hadn't done that."

"Jimmy's obviously seen too many Sylvester Stallone movies at an impressionable age," Caleb said, eyeing the youngest boy. "Me, I grew up on Popeye and cans of spinach."

"Who's Popeye?" Martin said.

"Never mind. I shouldn't have said that. It dates me."

"I remember Popeye," Badger reminisced, smoothing his white mustache.

"Thanks, Badger. That makes me feel a whole lot better." Caleb motioned to a chair. "Have a seat," he said to Steven. "I'm glad you came. I wanted to give you this in person." He reached into his jeans pocket and drew out a crumpled check, smoothing it against his leg. "The man I bought the buffalo from gave me a terrific deal. He sold them to me for half of what he was asking, and wanted me to present the other half of the money to the Crow tribe in his name to be put into a college fund." He handed the check to Steven.

"Thirty thousand dollars." Steven looked up at him quizzically. "He must really like the Crow Indians."

"He hates Indians," Dan said.

"Yeah. That's what started the whole fight in the bar. The mayor's son was trying to throw us out." Jimmy was warming up to the subject again. "Pony told him—"

"All right, Jimmy," Pony said. "We've heard the story enough times."

"So," Steven said to McCutcheon, carefully folding the check, "I guess Pony *did* do that to your face, in a roundabout way."

"I could have taken care of myself!" Pony said, whirling to glare at her brother.

"No way," Jimmy said. "There were *three* of them. They were big and mean and they'd been drinking!"

Pony jumped up and walked into the kitchen. The screen door banged behind her, and Steven took another swallow of cold beer. "She isn't afraid of anything,'' he said mildly. "She was like that growing up. Nothing scared her.''

"She's like that now,'' Caleb said.

"So. The man who hates Indians but mysteriously donates all this money. His name?''

"I'll give you a copy of the bill of sale. All the information you need is on it,'' Caleb said. "I told him he'd receive some sort of written receipt from the tribe so he could use it as a tax write-off.''

"I'll send the letter myself,'' Steven said. "Anything special you want me to say?''

Caleb thought for a moment and then nodded. "Yeah. Tell him I hope he finds peace.''

RAMALDA COOKED the steaks to rare and sizzling perfection and set the big platter in the center of the table along with a cold potato salad garnished with watercress, a platter of deviled eggs and the obligatory kettle of spiced beans and bowl of cold pinole. Caleb opened a bottle of cabernet, Pony poured milk for herself and the boys, and for the next hour everyone dedicated themselves to the excellence of the meal. When every plate was empty Caleb refilled the wineglasses and lounged back in his chair. "Well,'' he said to no one in particular, "what do you think about that buffalo?''

"It was fattened in a feedlot,'' Pony said.

"How can you tell?''

"It was tender, but it had no flavor. It might as well have been a steer because it was fed like a steer, kept in a crowded pen like a steer and shot full of antibiotics like a steer.''

Caleb took a sip of wine and regarded her thoughtfully. "So the buffalo that Pete manages taste different."

Pony nodded. "Free-range buffalo raised on native grasses taste like the real thing. There is no flavor like it."

"So in two years' time, when we sit down at this table to eat a Bow and Arrow buffalo steak, will it taste like a buffalo from Pete's herd?"

Pony reflected for a moment, then shook her head. "Bow and Arrow buffalo will have their own taste because the land here is different, the graze is different. The animals are the same, but where they live becomes a part of what they are."

"Like grapes," Caleb said, studying the dark color of the wine. "There are some people who can taste a cabernet, or any other wine, and tell you exactly where that grape grew."

"Yes." Pony nodded. "Like that."

"Bow and Arrow buffalo will be the finest in the world."

She nodded again. "I think so."

Guthrie raised his glass. "Here's to the Bow and Arrow Buffalo Company!"

Caleb lifted his own glass. "To the Bow and Arrow Buffalo Preserve and School of Native American Studies."

Pony's eyes locked with his. Everyone else raised their glasses. She was the only one who didn't. She reached for her milk, touched it to the rim of his wineglass and said, "To the Bow and Arrow buffalo. Long may they roam."

STEVEN WALKED with his sister after supper. They went down to the creek and followed the trail that paralleled it, and at the swimming hole they paused to watch the trout rising in the twilight. "How's the summer going?" he said.

"Okay. Except for the trip to Wyoming, it's been good."

"You seem quieter than usual."

"I'm a little tired."

Steven picked up an old pinecone and began peeling it apart. "I talked to Pete this morning, after Caleb called me. I wanted to ask him if there were any messages for the boys, but he said no. He wanted me to give you a message, though. He said he'd wanted to talk to you the day he brought the mustang, but he never had the chance."

Pony kept her eyes on the dark waters of the pool. "I had work to do."

"He wanted to tell you that the school board had voted down your proposal to increase the amount of money for counseling troubled kids."

"That's because there is no money," she said with a fatalistic shrug.

"And he wanted to remind you about Crow Fair. People are wondering if you'll dance this year."

"I can't leave here for a whole week."

"The dancing is important. Do you want me to ask McCutcheon if you can attend?"

She gave him a look. "No. I'm able to ask for myself."

"You should dance."

"Maybe. I'll think about it."

Steven tossed the stripped pinecone away and faced his sister squarely. "Pony, maybe it's none of my business, but it seems like there's something wrong.

The last time I visited here you seemed so...so content. Now you seem troubled.''

"I told you, I'm just tired. Don't worry about me!''

"I want you to be happy.''

"I *am* happy.''

"On the outside, maybe, but not where it really counts.'' He picked up another pinecone. "McCutcheon told me about his idea for a school.''

"It's a foolish idea!'' she exclaimed.

"He asked me to look into it. I told him I would.''

"He thinks he can save the world,'' Pony said.

Steven nodded. "I know. I recognize his symptoms because my sister suffers from the same illness.''

Pony reached down, picked up a stone and tossed it into the middle of the pool. "See those ripples, Steven? Watch them closely, because in a few moments they'll be gone. That's all the effect any of us ever has.''

"I told Nana to make sure your dress was ready for Crow Fair,'' Steven said. "If all we ever amount to is a ripple in a stream, then watching you dance is the prettiest ripple a lot of Crow people will ever see.''

She glared at him. "You are such an idiot,'' she said, but before she turned away he saw the bright shine of tears.

STEVEN CAUGHT UP with McCutcheon one more time before heading home. He found him on his cabin porch, trying to read in the fading light. "That'll hurt your eyes,'' Steven said, climbing the steps.

"The days are getting shorter and shorter,'' McCutcheon said, marking the page with a sprig of sage and closing the book. "I keep trying to pretend they aren't, but you're right. I'll go blind at this rate." He nodded to a chair. "Thanks again for coming to supper. And thanks for bringing the buffalo steaks. I know ours will taste better, but they were pretty good." He paused, as if considering his next words. "There's something I want to ask you before you leave."

Steven sat down. "Ask away."

"I know it's none of my business, but Pony and Pete Two Shirts. Were they ever…involved?"

The question startled him, but he shook his head. "Pete was my best friend growing up on the rez, and about seven years ago she worked for him, with the tribal buffalo herd. The summer ended, and she went back to college."

McCutcheon stood up and paced restlessly. "That's it? She worked for him one summer, seven years ago?"

"As far as I know."

"She acts like she's walking on eggs whenever she's around him." McCutcheon walked the length of the porch again and then swung around. "Seven *years* ago?"

Steven nodded. "That's all I know."

"Huh." He dug his hands into his jeans pockets, hunched his shoulders and leaned against a porch post, studying the horizon. "Okay then, there's something else. I need some legal advice."

"All right. But first, are you going to Crow Fair?"

"Crow Fair?" He straightened and turned. "When is it?"

"It starts in three days and lasts a week. It's held outside Crow Agency on the reservation and it's the biggest Indian powwow in the nation. There are over a thousand tepees set up and twenty, thirty thousand Indians attend every year. There are horse races, grand parades, rodeos, and dancing. Lots of dancing. Pony dances at Crow Fair every year, and every year she wins top honors in the women's straight dance and the buckskin dance. She wears her great-grandmother's elk-skin dress, and it's almost as beautiful as Pony is. The elders love to watch her dance. People come from all over the country to watch Pony dance.''

Caleb ran his fingers through his hair. ''The boys told me about it a while ago. But your sister hasn't mentioned it.''

Steven raised his shoulders in a casual shrug. ''Maybe she thought because she was working here, she couldn't go. But even if she can't go, you should. It's something to see.''

''Of course she'll go,'' Caleb said. ''I'll tell her tomorrow morning.'' He turned and lashed out suddenly at the porch post with his booted foot. ''Dammit!'' he said. ''I don't understand that woman.''

Steven watched him and felt the other man's pain as if it were his own. ''Me, neither,'' he admitted, ''and I've known her all my life.''

Caleb slumped back into his chair with an air of dejection. ''All right,'' he said. ''The legal question I need to ask involves my wedding gift to Guthrie and Jessie,'' he said. ''I want to make them full partners in the ranch. They were raised here. They belong to the place, and so should their kids.''

Steven glanced sharply at him and then quickly away. Why couldn't Pony realize that the dreams this man had were not so very different from hers? Surely the two of them could find a way to share the same path.

"Okay," he said. "Ask away."

THAT NIGHT Caleb had a dream that haunted him long after he awakened. Pony was surrounded by dancers, who were moving around her in a circle. She stood at the center, a beautiful woman in a beautiful elk-skin dress, and when Caleb could stay away from her no longer, he broke through the circle. When he was near enough to touch her she looked at him with those dark eyes and said, "I'm sorry, but I cannot dance with you, Mr. McCutcheon. You are not an Indian. I do not dance with anyone unless they are a full-blooded Crow Indian."

He awoke filled with a desperate sense of loss, and when he went up to the ranch house for breakfast the first thing he did was draw her aside. "Crow Fair starts in three days, and you're going."

She bristled. "Did Steven…?"

"I want you to give me a schedule of events so I can bring the boys to watch you dance. There will be no more discussion about this. You'll take my pickup truck. It's safer than yours. You'll get your elk-skin dress from your old aunt and you'll dance at the Crow Fair."

"But—"

"That's my final word," he interrupted curtly. "The boys'll be fine here without you for a week. We'll get by. But I want that schedule. Can you get it for me?"

She nodded, studying her feet while color crept into her cheeks.

"Good. Then it's settled. And there's one other

thing. I want you to think about something while you're away. I want you to consider staying on and teaching at the school your brother is going to set up. I want you to teach here, because…'' Caleb faltered, wishing she would look at him, give him some indication of what she was thinking. ''Because I want you to stay,'' he continued. ''Every time I try to tell you how I feel about you, I mess it up. But the truth is…'' She raised her eyes at that moment and Caleb drew strength from what he read in her expression. ''The truth is—this isn't about the school or the boys or the buffalo, though all these things are important to me. This is about you and me, and the possibility of us sharing a future together.''

She shook her head, a small movement that seized his heart with uncertainty. ''There's something I must tell you before you say anything more,'' she said. ''Something about my past…''

''No,'' Caleb interrupted her again. ''I don't want to discuss your past or mine. I'm asking you to think about our future. I'm in love with you, Pony, and I can't imagine living here without you. Will you think about that?''

For several long moments their eyes held, and then she said, in a voice barely louder than a whisper, ''Yes.''

CHAPTER FOURTEEN

ON THE LAST DAY of Crow Fair, Caleb drove the boys out to Crow Agency. Pony had only been gone for five days yet it felt more like five weeks. Her absence had become an intense and unbearable ache. It didn't help that Caleb knew Pete Two Shirts was at the fair riding in the rodeo. No doubt Pete and Pony had crossed paths.

When Caleb reached the fairground it seemed as if finding one person amongst twenty to thirty thousand other people would be an impossibility. He had never seen anything like the scene that spread itself over the landscape. Hundreds of big tepees, horses being led or ridden. Dogs running around. Thousands of people, young and old, milled about. A helicopter passed overhead, thumping loud and flying low. Two youths riding bareback trotted by, laughing and talking. A young man in dark shades, red bandanna tied around his head, swerved past on a loud Harley. A sound car drove slowly by, announcements blaring continually. The noise was amazing, but over it all Caleb heard the rhythmic pounding of the drum and, flanked by the boys, he found himself being drawn toward it.

The beat grew louder as they approached a large arena surrounded by benches for the dancers, a grandstand for the audience and an area for the emcee and judges where the colorful tribal flags waved in the breeze. In the center of the arena was an arbor made of four upright posts with a roof of interwoven branches. There were eight men seated around the drum, singing and drumming, and the arena itself was crowded with dancing children, some barely old enough to toddle. All were dressed in tribal regalia.

"This is a candy dance," Jimmy said. "Every time the drum stops, the emcee throws candy and the kids pick it up."

As Caleb and the boys approached, the song ended and the brightly attired youngsters dispersed, the littlest being swept into the arms of nearby relatives.

"Okay!" the emcee said. "Good job! Ladies and gentlemen, that was the last of the children's dances for the afternoon. We'll be taking a two-hour break before the evening dancing. I suggest you all get something good to eat and drink, and we'll see you back here then!"

Caleb looked around at the crowd with a growing sense of despair. "How will we ever find her?"

"She said she'd meet us near the arena. She's probably up in the grandstand...." Jimmy scanned the crowded bleachers. "Hey! There she is!"

Caleb's heart leaped as he whirled, looking into the grandstand. He saw Pony waving to them and grinned ear to ear, immediately forgetting that he was chaperoning five boys. He climbed the steps three at a time, oblivious to the curious onlookers as he reached her and came to an abrupt halt, wanting to gather her into his arms but instead reaching out to grasp her hands. "It's good to see you. It's been a long week," he said.

She was smiling, radiant, squeezing his hands as tightly as he held hers. "Have the boys behaved?"

"They've been working hard," Caleb said. "Can you spend some time with us? When do you dance?"

"Not for another two hours. We can get something to eat. Maybe watch some of the rodeo if you want."

Caleb turned to the boys. "Rodeo?" he said.

They all nodded, and he said, "Okay, go ahead. We'll meet back here in two hours."

Within moments they had vanished and Caleb grinned, feasting his eyes. "Was I too obvious?"

She laughed. "I've missed you."

He didn't care who was watching. He drew her into his arms and bent his head over hers. "I thought I'd die of loneliness," he murmured into the sweetness of her hair.

"Me, too."

"Really?" He pulled back to look at her, his heart hammering.

"I wanted to call, to see how things were going. I almost did. But then I thought, what would I say?"

Caleb set her at arm's length and shook his head with exasperation. "Well, you might have started with hello and gone from there. That's how most conversations begin. Let's go for a walk and see if we can't start one in person."

Hand in hand they wandered through the fairgrounds. They bought hot dogs and sodas and ate and drank as they walked past clusters of tepees, always moving away from the noise and the crowd. Finally they found a path that led along the river's edge. "I thought you'd be wearing your grandmother's elkskin dress," he said.

"I have to change into it soon. It's too hot to wear all the time, and it's very heavy."

He stopped abruptly and turned to face her. He took her hand in both of his and before he could lose heart he spoke the words that had been running through his head for the past five days. Hell, for the past summer. "I love you, Pony. I want to marry you. I know I'm not Indian. I didn't grow up in your world, I'll never be a part of your culture, and I can't give you full-blood babies, but Pony, I'll cherish you till the day I die. How we feel about each other has to mean something."

Her voice trembled when she said, "It does. It means a great deal. But Caleb, there's something else you need to know." She led him to the edge of the river and they sat together on the trunk of an old cottonwood tree that the floodwaters had knocked down in past years. "When I told you that our people would one day be no more because of all the mixed marriages, I was not telling you that you and I could never..." She looked at him. "You took that statement out of context."

He gazed at her, puzzled. "I don't understand."

"I am unable to bear children. Full-blooded or mixed-blood. I cannot have a child."

Caleb digested this newest twist with a deepening frown. "Does Pete know that?"

She nodded her head. "Yes."

"Is *that* why he wouldn't marry you?"

"*Marry* me?" Pony stared at him, clearly astonished. "Pete is my friend. The only reason he knows that I cannot have children is because he was my boss that summer, and when I didn't show up to work one morning he came to my place to make sure I was okay. But I wasn't. I was sick—''

Her words choked off, and she looked away, blinking rapidly.

''Pony, you don't have to explain anything to me. What happened in your past doesn't matter.''

''Yes, it does,'' she said. ''It matters very much, and you need to know all of it.'' She composed herself, before continuing slowly. Her voice was taut with emotion, as she repeated what she had told Jessie.

Caleb listened without interrupting as she told of that summer night seven years ago. She spared no details, made no excuses and blamed herself completely for everything that had happened. He felt a white hot sure of anger and outrage when she told him about the rape. He felt his heart twist painfully when she told him about the pregnancy and the botched abortion. He felt that he understood, finally, the terrible burden of guilt she had carried all these years, the dark secret only she and Pete had shared, and the emptiness of knowing she could never bear a child of her own.

As she spoke, he noticed her hands unclench and her body relax. It was as if she was letting go of all the demons that had tormented her for so long.

''So you see,'' she concluded, her voice steady and her gaze direct. ''I'm not the person you think I am. Not the person you fell in love with.''

''Oh, Pony,'' Caleb said, tenderly brushing her hair back from her forehead. ''You're so wrong. The person I'm in love with is sitting right here beside me. You're one of the most beautiful people I've ever known. You did nothing wrong. You were victimized, and I'm sorry for that. But you can't carry that guilt with you any longer. You can't let one awful night ruin the rest of your life. Too many people depend on you. Where would those boys be without you? And what about me?'' Caleb could feel her trembling as she stared at him. He shored up his courage. ''Have you ever been in love with Pete?''

She shook her head. ''No.''

''Do you love me?''

''Yes.'' Her voice was barely above a whisper.

''Then marry me.''

Her dark eyes flooded. ''Don't you understand? I can't give you children!''

''What the hell are you talking about? I'm fathering five of your boys right now!''

''It's not the same. A man wants his own sons.''

Caleb made a noise of frustration deep in his throat. He bent closer, his hands tightening on her shoulders. ''Listen to me, dammit! The only thing I want is you. You're the most important thing in my life. I'm not asking you to give up your teaching career or your identity or your traditions or your culture, and I'm not asking you to bear me a bunch of babies to appease my male ego. I'm asking you to be my partner. Marry me, Pony. We could have a good life together on the ranch. We could start a school there, a good school that would make a big difference in a lot of kids' lives. And if you want babies, little ones, we can adopt as many as you like. I love kids and I think we'd make damn good parents. There are lots of children out there who need good parents.''

She stared at him and her dark eyes flooded with tears again, just before she pulled away from him and stood. ''I have to change for the dancing,'' she said, and, whirling like a frightened deer, she fled back down the path.

He watched her go and wondered bleakly if he could survive a future without her.

THE BOYS FOUND HIM in the grandstand, elbows on his knees, slumped over in misery. They sat down on either side of him without speaking. For a long while nothing was said, and then Martin shifted as if he was trying to find a softer spot on the wooden bleacher. "I think she'll win again this year."

"No, she won't," Jimmy said. "She hasn't danced enough. If you don't dance every dance, the judges don't like it."

"If she only danced once, it would be enough to prove who is best," Roon said.

"Maybe so, but the judges judge," Jimmy said, "not the audience."

The grandstand filled up. Eight Crow men in traditional dress walked out to the drum and sat around it. The emcee tapped the microphone, and the boom of his voice filled the arena.

"Good evening, ladies and gentlemen, and welcome to the ladies' dancing competition. We're starting the evening off with the buckskin dance and here come our contestants. For those of you in the audience who are new to powwows, the ladies' buckskin dance is sometimes referred to as women's traditional dance. It's one of the oldest and most beautiful of the women's dances. This is a very sophisticated dance. You will notice that the dancers' movements are tall, straight and graceful, each step gliding on air, each movement like the wind blowing through a willow.

Watch how their fringe sways when this dance begins....

"And folks, notice how beautifully these ladies are dressed...."

"Can you see her?" Caleb said.

"No. Not yet. Don't worry. Just watch the emcee and the judges," Jimmy said. "They will all be looking at her."

The drum started. The strong singing of the eight men rose over the beat in rippling crescendos, the Head Singer leading in a trebling falsetto, drawing the second singer and chorus in behind him as they beat the drum to a rapid, powerful cadence. Caleb was swept up in the throbbing rhythm, the sound of the song, the energy that moved the dancers. They were beautiful, these women dancing in their brightly colored fringed dresses. Their movements were the epitome of grace. They became the soughing of the wind, the rushing of the waters, the bending of tall grass, the movement of cloud formations over the land.

And then he felt a peculiar thump in his chest and his breath caught.

There she was.

Pony.

Alone in an arena filled with dancers. Alone, moving in a realm apart from the others, gathering the eyes of everyone who watched because of her ethereal beauty and grace. It was not the flash of her dress that caught the eye, for her dress was simple and faded with age, decorated with narrow strips of red trade felt and blue cloth taken from some nameless soldier's uniform. Old glass trade beads and intricate quill work adorned the cape, and its fringe was only half the length of the more modern dresses. The dress that she wore was beautiful, but the spirit that moved within her gave her a kind of grace that transcended that of any mortal being.

Time stood still as Pony danced to the drum.

"Oo-je-en-a-he-ha!" he heard behind him, and turned to look into the face of an elder. The old man was watching her dance, transfixed. "Oo-je-en-a-he-ha!" he said again, and two tears trickled slowly down his wrinkled cheeks.

Caleb faced the arena and she was gone, lost in the swirl of movement below. The drum gave five beats increasing in strength and then the song ended. Applause and cheers filled the air. The emcee's voice droned, "Beautiful, ladies! That was the buckskin dance, folks, and the ladies themselves have requested that the next dance be a two-step. Now, for those of you gents who aren't up to speed out there, if the lady asks you to dance the two-step and you refuse, you owe her ten dollars. Got that? Ten bucks! So, ladies, find your partners and we'll have us a little fun tonight!"

Caleb stood with a rush of alarm. What the hell? No one told him about anything like this!

"Better get down there, quick," Jimmy said. "Before she asks someone else."

He didn't need to be prodded. Within seconds he was threading between the dancers' benches, heading to the arena and searching for Pony. How would he ever find her? There were so many people! The drum began again and he turned in a circle, searching desperately. He felt a hand tug at his sleeve and looked down at a woman bedecked in one of the modern buckskin dresses, the fringe on the brightly beaded cape swinging well below her knees. She smiled shyly and awaited his response.

He froze, not wanting to offend but needing to find the woman he loved. And then over her shoulder he spotted Pony, moving through the crowd toward him. His fingers dug frantically for his wallet, and he peeled off a fifty-dollar bill. "I'm sorry, but I promised this dance to someone else."

Pony stepped into his arms as if she belonged there, but his initial surge of gladness gave over to anxiety as he listened to the rhythm of the drum and watched the other dancers begin to move. "I thought the announcer said this was a two-step," he said, faltering.

"It is," she replied with a soft laugh. "But it's an *Indian* two-step. Don't worry. It's easy. Just keep the rhythm of the drum and watch how the others move. It's the only intertribal dance where we can touch one another."

After a few moments he relaxed and glanced around, overwhelmed by the sight of all the Indian couples in their finest regalia surrounding him, surrounding the drum, dancing. He was the only non-Indian in the arena. The experience was at once intimidating and exhilarating. The rhythm of the drum became the pounding of his heart and he felt lightheaded and young, as if he could dance forever with this beautiful woman in his arms.

"Have you been thinking about us?" he asked.

"Yes," she said.

"Good thoughts?"

Her dark eyes smiled up at him. "I've been thinking about our wedding ceremony. How it should be. White or Indian?"

The Indian two-step wasn't a close dance but Caleb

didn't care. His heart swelled with joy as he pulled
Pony into a passionate embrace and growled, "Hell,
woman, if we're going to be dancing the two-step in
both worlds, then we'd best get married both ways,
just to be safe."

CHAPTER FIFTEEN

STEVEN YOUNG BEAR was just taking his first sip of morning coffee when he heard a knock on his door. He was surprised to find Caleb McCutcheon standing on his step.

"I went to Crow Fair yesterday with the boys to watch Pony dance," Caleb said, following Steven into the kitchen and accepting a cup of coffee. "She won her competition."

Steven nodded calmly. "She always does." He waited, studying the older man's face and feeling a quiet gladness build within.

"She's a beautiful dancer, your sister. A beautiful woman."

"Yes. It's kind of hard to believe we're related."

There was an awkward pause and then Caleb said, "Since your father's dead, I thought it would be best if I asked you."

Steven nodded again. "Okay."

"May I have your sister's hand in marriage?"

Caleb's expression was so painfully earnest that it was all Steven could do to keep a smile from ruining his stony expression. He let a long painful moment slide by and then frowned thoughtfully as he folded his arms across his chest. "How many ponies are you willing to give for her?" he said.

"However many it takes."

"How many do you figure she's worth?"

"A whole lot more than I have. All of the horses at the ranch are Jessie's except for one injured bucking horse. But I have buffalo. A lot of buffalo. And I can get more."

Steven grunted and deepened his frown. "I don't know. Pony can be difficult. She could make life hard for you. She's a traditionalist, borderline radical, really. You'd be marrying into the tribe and all of its politics."

"We talked all night long about that."

"Are you still thinking about creating a school at the ranch?"

"Yes. She'll be the first full-time teacher."

"When were you planning this marriage?"

"We figured we'd wait until a month or so after Guthrie and Jessie's wedding."

Steven grunted again. "Good," he said. "Two weddings in one month is more than I could dress up for." He reached out to shake Caleb's hand and let a broad smile reveal his true feelings. "Does Pony know what you plan to give Guthrie and Jessie for a wedding present?"

"She loved the idea. She said it would make us all like one family."

Steven stood in the open doorway for a long time after Caleb had left, happy for his sister and Caleb McCutcheon, and wondering if he would ever find the same grace that they had. Wondering if he would ever find a woman who would chase the loneliness from his heart and guide him down that shining path to happiness.

BADGER AND CHARLIE were sitting on the porch when Caleb pulled up in the Suburban. It was 10:00 a.m.

and the day was heating up to be a real scorcher. Guthrie and Roon had just finished doctoring a horse with a cut on its flank, and the boys had already decided to hit the swimming hole. Pony was inside working on the books, while Ramalda was making the kitchen hotter than it had any right to be in the month of August.

"Look at him!" Badger said as they watched Caleb get out of the vehicle. "See that? He's strutting!"

Charlie's eyes narrowed, and he nodded. "He's all puffed up like a partridge in springtime, no doubt."

"They got home late last night from Crow Fair. Way past midnight," Badger muttered in an aside, shifting the tobacco in his cheek as Caleb climbed the steps. "Mornin', boss," he said. "We missed you at breakfast."

"Yes, you did," Caleb agreed. "I had to go see someone." He ducked into the kitchen. "Pony? Could you please come out here for minute? Ramalda, you, too." He waited until Guthrie and Roon had gained the porch and then he reached out and drew Pony close. He waited a few moments, unable to suppress the broad grin that lit his face. "We have an announcement to make. Pony and I are getting married."

Roon looked at both of them, still holding the towel he was drying his hands with. "Does this mean we don't have to leave?" Pony smiled and nodded, and the towel dropped from his hands. "I better go tell the rest of them," he said, thundering down the porch steps and sprinting toward the creek.

"Well now, I guess congratulations are in order, but it ain't much of a surprise, leastwise, to me it ain't," Badger said, unfolding his creaking frame from the chair to shake Caleb's hand. "I could'a told you a long time ago the two of you was destined to get hitched."

"I should've just asked you, then." Caleb grinned. "Would have saved me a whole lot of suffering." He shook hands all around and ended with Guthrie. "We're planning a late-October wedding and I'm in the market for a best man."

Guthrie nodded. "I'm not sure I'm the best, but I'd sure be honored." He took Pony's hand in his. "And, ma'am, I'm real happy you're staying put."

"Amen," Badger said, and Ramalda used her apron to wipe the tears that ran down her cheeks while Caleb gently patted her shoulder.

Later that evening, in the gathering hush of blue twilight, Pony sat on the edge of the porch, dangling her feet and bracing elbows on knees, chin in hand, watching the boys field balls that Caleb was tossing up and hitting with a bat. The soft banter of their voices floated up to her, and her heart swelled until she felt as if it would burst with happiness.

"They like it, don't they?" Badger said from where he slumped on the wall bench, trying to roll a smoke. "All of 'em. Boss, too, else they wouldn't be doin' it near about every night."

"Yes," Pony breathed, feeling the beauty of moment and rising to it the way the sun rises to the dawn. "They like it. All of them."

"Well, it's more fun than rippin' down barbed-wire fences, I guess, though I never could find a good reason for the game. Seems to me it don't accomplish much." Badger cussed softly as the tobacco spilled.

His fingers were stiff and swollen with arthritis. He glanced up with surprise when Pony's hands touched his and took the makings from him.

"My old aunt, Nana, taught me to roll these for her when I was a little girl," she said as she settled beside him on the bench and deftly rolled the cigarette.

"But you don't smoke the stuff yourself?" Badger said as she handed it back.

Pony shook her head. "I never could find a good reason for smoking," she said. "Seems to me it doesn't accomplish much."

"You're gettin' to be real sassy," Badger said as she started down the porch steps. She stopped at the bottom and looked up at him as he struck a match and lit the smoke. "Come to think of it, so was Lizzy Kinney, my old flame," he added. Blue smoke curled up around his face and behind she heard the crack of the bat and Jimmy's triumphant yelp as he apparently caught a fly ball that Caleb sent his way. "I guess there ain't nothing a'tall wrong with a good woman being sassy from time to time," Badger concluded as he took another deep draw and leaned back against the weathered boards of the old ranch house.

Pony hid a smile, shoved her hands into her pockets and walked slowly up the old path worn deep behind the ranch buildings that led to the sacred burial place. Behind her the voices of Caleb and the boys faded as she distanced herself from those she loved. At the end of the path she stood in wind-swept silence on the knoll above the ranch house, in the grove of tall, straight lodgepole pine. She read the inscription on the simple granite stone that marked where a woman lay buried.

> Mary Bie Asiitash Weaver, born 1843, died June 2, 1932. Beloved wife of John Weaver and daughter of Little Wolf, Crow medicine man.

Pony let her thoughts wander. One hundred and forty years ago, Mary had come to live in this high mountain valley as the wife of a white man, and she had left a legacy that had endured into the twenty-first century. She'd paved the way for the Crow woman who now stood beside her grave, contemplating both the past and future, and marveling at how they had come full circle.

"Thank you," Pony said quietly, touching the weathered headstone. *"Aho."*

She stood there while the sky turned deep violet, darkening toward the night. The air was a buoyant blending of the high snowy places and golden warmth of the autumn valley, sweet and spicy with the scents of pine and sage. Somewhere in the meadows above the ranch the buffalo roamed, a coyote wailed its mournful lament and the spirit of the wind hissed softly through the trees. Pony was filled with a poignant happiness. *"Ihakaxaaheet, aho. Aho,"* she said. She heard an approaching footstep and a man's familiar and beloved voice answered.

"She speaks, and behold he stands before her."

Caleb approached quietly, and her heart leaped at his unexpected nearness. He drew her gently into his warm strong embrace. "Was I even close?"

"No." She smiled, breathing his masculine scent, a mingling of saddle leather and sweat, pipe tobacco and horses, and relishing the lean, hard strength of his body. "I said, 'The stars are brilliant tonight. Thank you.'"

"The stars *are* brilliant," he murmured, pulling her closer, "but they don't shine the way you do." He kissed her while the tall pines whispered their secrets to each other. He kissed her until her spirit sang and her heart soared and the earth spun beneath her feet.

"I wish we could get married right away," he said breathlessly when they came up for air.

"I know. But Guthrie and Jessie have been planning their wedding...."

"I know." He bent his head to kiss her again and pulled her tightly against him with a low moan. "I know that waiting's the right thing to do. I know they're first in line. I was just thinking that maybe we should elope. Las Vegas isn't all that far away...."

"October does seem very distant, but Las Vegas isn't the place for us." She traced the masculine lines of his face and her fingertips stilled at his chin. "Do you have a good blanket in your cabin?"

"I do. A four-point wool Pendleton. Are you cold?"

"No. I am not cold, but we would need a good blanket."

"For what?"

"For the ceremony," she said.

There was a long pause while he considered her words. "Tonight?" he said, his voice full of hope.

"Tonight."

"What should I do with the blanket?"

"Wrap it around both of us and call me your wife. *Mitawicu.*"

"And then what?"

She smiled as she stepped away from him, taking his hand to lead him to his cabin on the bend of the creek. "Come with me, *mitacante*, and we will let our future together begin."

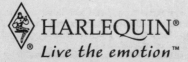

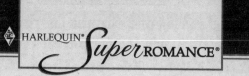

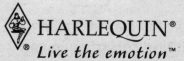

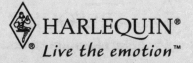

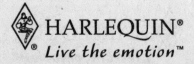